WHEEL OF BLOOD AND MAGIC

BOOK ONE OF THE WHEEL OF BLOOD AND MAGIC SERIES

GRACE PEVEAR

M4L PUBLISHING

To Peggy, thanks for being the best big sister ever. I'm so lucky to have you, and there's no one else I'd rather share my childhood trauma with. To Paige, my most loyal reader, thank you for reading every single thing I send your way. You already know my darkest secrets, so I know there's a home for all my stories with you. To Mary, my chosen family, travel buddy, sender and receiver of endless memes. You keep me grounded and sane. To Gretchen, I wish more than anything I could write you back to life and you were sitting here with me drinking, smoking and talking shit. And to my dog, Scottie, without your relentless need to be up at 5 a.m. every day, this book wouldn't exist.

"Siblings: the only enemy you can't live without."

– Unknown

PART 1

NOW

MARTHA – A TALE OF TWO MEN

CHAPTER 1

Martha sat in her car looking at the little beach house. In all the years she'd been coming here, it hadn't changed. The house itself was the white color of the sand with shutters the pale blue of the afternoon sky. It looked fresher than the last time she saw it. Hints of peeling paint and sagging gutters were gone, as if it had gotten a little facelift.

"Earth to Martha!" Gretchen yelled through the phone.

"Hey, sorry. I just got here. It's so weird to be back by myself. You should have come with me."

"So I could be your third wheel? Complicit in your shenanigans? I know it's shocking, but I'd rather hang out with my parents. And it is winter break."

"I know how you love spending time with your mother." Martha laughed. "Hang on while I grab my stuff and go inside."

"Call me back when you get settled."

"Stay on with me. I feel like when we hang up, I'll be completely alone. Just knowing you're on the other end is my little security blanket."

"Okay, weirdo."

"Thanks." Martha cut the ignition of her little Fiat, fumbled around her purse for her AirPods, and stuck them in her ears. "Okay, I'm back."

She got out of the car and strolled up the sandy path to the house. When she stepped inside, her nose crinkled at the hint of must. She left the door open to air the place out.

"Didn't you and Jake do it for the first time there?"

"Thanks for the reminder. That seems like another lifetime."

"You and your professors. Isn't it going to be weird having sex with Dr. Hottie in the same bed you lost your virginity to your boyfriend?"

"Yes, even for me, that would be too weird. But Jake and I did it in my parents' bed."

"That makes it so much better."

She walked into the living area of the tiny bungalow and gasped. "Oh wow! My dad finally replaced that old TV with the rabbit ears." She picked up the remote and turned it on. "He got a Fire TV, a big one. It takes up the whole wall. Netflix, Apple TV, HBO. I wonder when he did that?"

"Welcome to the twenty-first century!" Gretchen said.

"It's kind of sad, you know? He always made such a big deal about continuing my mom's TV rules."

"Maybe he's got a girlfriend who likes to binge or something."

"Ha! Doubtful, but stranger things... don't you think he'd tell us?"

"Yeah. Your dad's too much of a geek for a girlfriend. And he works too much."

She wandered toward her old room, pausing in the hallway to take in the pictures of her parents that peppered the wall. Dad on a boat with a bunch of guys Martha didn't know. Mom on the same boat reeling in what appeared to be something *Jaws*-like, judging by the arc in the pole she was gripping. Her mother, sitting on the beach in a bikini, raising a beer nestled in an Alabama koozie to the camera. And Martha's favorite: the two of them sitting by a bonfire on the beach kissing, the sun low in the sky behind them.

A hot tear welled and fell down her cheek. She let out a soft sob.

"Are you crying?"

"It makes me sad. I love that I have you to talk to about all my boy problems, but I wish she were here to tell me what to do. I talk to her a lot. Don't know if she hears me or answers me, or if she's even there. I just know if she were here, she'd have all the right things to say."

"Hugs, friend."

"Thanks."

She took a breath, wiped the tears, and opened the door to her room. The white wicker furniture was unraveling in places, paint flaking off. Her wrought-iron daybed looked exactly as it had when she was twelve. Looking at her ancient stuffed animals and white eyelet comforter brought on a longing for her childhood, when life was simple. She picked up Bear and hugged him. His thinning fur was still soft against her cheek. A nauseating nostalgia overwhelmed her. She imagined nights from her childhood hugging Bear as her mother read to her until she fell asleep. Why had she left him here? And why hadn't they made any changes to this place since her mother died? She'd never really thought about this being her childhood furniture before. She hoped Thomas didn't think her childish because of it.

As she placed him back on her bed, she noticed the slightest bit of stuffing peeking out from the seams under his arms. She reached down and ran her finger across the opening and sealed it closed. "Like new." She smiled.

"What?" Gretchen asked curiously.

"My room was showing signs of abandonment. It just needed a little magic."

She continued chatting to Gretchen as she scanned the bookshelves still loaded with her childhood books. Nancy Drew, Walter Farley and Beverly Cleary were her favorites. She ran a finger across the dusty, well-worn spines and again, thoughts of her mother reading to her every night flooded her mind.

"I have this shell collection on my bookshelves," she said. "My mom used to tell me about how the little girl in the moon, I think her name was Selene, left the pretty shells behind as she rode on her magical chariot and dragged the water with her, creating the tides."

"Are you sure this is a good idea? Why didn't you just stay in New Orleans for another night? I think you're way too emotional right now to be hosting your new lover at the bungalow. This is pretty heavy stuff, Martha."

"This might not have been one of my best ideas. I was telling him how much I missed coming here, and he suggested we come together. He wants to see where my childhood memories were made."

"That's sweet. But it seems pretty emotional for you."

"I'm not sure why I'm so emotional. I guess it's showing Thomas a part of my life that's so important to me. You know what I mean? I'm feeling a little vulnerable."

Martha's phone vibrated in her pocket.

I'm here, love. Are you going to invite me in, or do I have to beg?

"Too late. Thomas's here. No regrets, right?" She hung up before Gretchen responded, pulled the AirPods out, and raced back to the front door.

The door was open, and Thomas stood leaning against the frame, arms crossed, smiling his sexy, crooked smile.

"Hi, handsome. Come on in."

"Thank you, love." He crossed the threshold, leaned down, and kissed her on the cheek. "Want to give me a tour?"

"Sure, there's not much to see, though."

He took her hand and said, "You said this place was an important part of your life. I want to see you through it."

Her stomach did a back flip, and she hoped he didn't notice her sweaty palms. She led him through the kitchen and out onto the lanai. The small dunes were peppered with sea grass that rustled in the breeze like strands of hair and beyond was the Gulf of Mexico, the waves gently lapping the soft white sand. The sun was a rippling orange orb floating just above the horizon.

"It's just beautiful," he said. "So peaceful. I see why it's important to you." She felt him give her hand a light squeeze, then he lifted it to his mouth and kissed the back of it. Martha started back inside, but he didn't move. She looked at him, and he said, "Let's sit out here for a bit, listen to the gulf. It's lovely."

They sat on the love seat, and as she snuggled in the crook of his arm, her stomach untwisted and the sweat on her palms dissolved into the sea air.

He looked down at her. "Tell me about your family."

"What do you want to know?"

"Do you have any siblings?"

Martha rolled her eyes. "A younger sister. She's the worst." Her hand went to the hook-shaped scar beneath her eye.

Thomas laughed. "I want to hear all about it. A little sibling rivalry is good for the soul, don't you think?" He reached over and brushed his thumb across the scar. "Did she give you this?"

Martha nodded. "She threw a picture frame at me when we were little."

"Well, that wasn't very nice now, was it?" He leaned over and kissed the scar. "I think it's beautiful. It gives you mystery and character. Why did she throw a picture frame at you?"

Martha pushed herself closer to him. She hesitated, remembering that day so clearly and wondering what to tell him. "Well, I slapped her."

Thomas grinned. "So, you deserved it?"

"I...guess I did."

"I'm sure she's a royal brat and deserved every bit of your wrath and more."

Martha smiled and wished the adults in her life had seen it the same way. "She absolutely did."

They sat in silence for a while, watching the sun as it began its descent, closing in on the horizon. Thomas asked, "Do you know the story of Selene?"

Martha turned to him. He brushed a strand of hair off her cheek, and she leaned into his touch like a cat. She nodded and again felt the wet heat in her eyes. "My mother and I used to collect shells on the beach. She always told me they were gifts from Selene, the little girl in the moon."

"She was known for her beautiful and bright hair. It shone in the night sky like a shooting star." He pushed her honey hair behind her ear and leaned in, his lips lingered on her ear, and he said, "Just like yours. You're a goddess."

She shivered in delight; the tears vanquished by his words. He remained at her ear, barely grazing it with his lips. Hot jolts of pleasure shot through her. She was like paint waiting for him to splatter her on his canvas.

Martha leaned in so close her lips were barely touching his. She skimmed his cheek with her lips and made her way to his ear, pausing with heavy breath. "If I'm a goddess, you're my god."

She wrapped her arms around his neck, swung a leg over his lap, and straddled him. As she pressed into him, she felt his growing desire. Martha flinched as he put his hands inside her sweatshirt. His icy touch turned her skin to gooseflesh. She kissed him and said, "Let's go inside."

He pulled away from her and pointed to the gulf behind her. "Patience, love. Let's watch the sunset. Maybe we'll see the green flash."

"Okay." But the heat between her legs said something different.

He put his hands on her hips and pivoted her back onto the sofa, slung his arm around her shoulders, and pulled her close. She rested her head on his chest.

The sunset was beautiful—it always was. There was no green flash, but as the last of the fire fell below the horizon, he kissed her on the top of her head. "Thanks for indulging me. That was something special. Now where were we?"

She nodded. "I think we were headed inside."

"Were we? Shouldn't we stay out here a little longer?"

Chilled by the December gulf breeze and anxious to get to the bedroom, she said, "Okay, but let me grab a blanket."

"Hurry back, love."

She ran inside, tripped over the threshold, and nearly face-planted on the kitchen floor. *Be cool, Martha.* She grabbed a blanket and yelled out to Thomas, "Do you need anything while I'm in here?"

"Just you."

She wrapped the blanket around her and returned outside. "Do you want to share?"

"No, love, I like the chill. This weather is perfect for me." She sat back in the crook of his arm. "Tell me about your parents."

"Not much to tell. My dad's an attorney and my mom died when I was seven."

"I'm so sorry about your mother. That must have been so difficult as a little girl."

"It was. I miss her every day. Her mother—my grandmother—moved in with us to help my dad. He travels a lot for work. Practically lives in Atlanta. I think it was his way of dealing with the loss of my mom. But it seems to have stuck, so he's only home about once a month."

"He's a lawyer, you said?"

She nodded. "My mom was too."

"That's why you're going to law school next year?"

"Yep."

"I'm not sure how I feel about you leaving me." He leaned in and kissed her. His hand traveled between her legs. She let out a gasp and her body tensed as the beginnings of the rush she craved spread through her. She wasn't sure how much longer she could hold out. He had such willpower, and she felt like a horny teenager.

"Really?"

"Really. I've quite fallen for you, Martha Lee." Before she could respond, he said, "This is new to me. I've never dated a student before. I think we could really have something special here."

Martha felt the heat in her cheeks. Was she falling for him, too? Thoughts of Jake flooded her mind. Thomas was supposed to be a fling, so she'd never told him about Jake.

He put a finger under her chin and tilted her face up. "It's okay, love. You don't have to say anything. I just want you to know how I feel. And that I'm not some sleazy professor hitting on his students just to get laid."

Martha hid her smile and bit her lip. "I wouldn't have invited you here of all places if I didn't feel something. I don't know what it is, but I like it."

"Well, I'm glad we got that out of the way. What else do you want to know about me?"

She thought for a minute. "What about your family?"

"My family, hmm. Well, there's not much to it. I was an only child, and my parents are long dead. It's just me."

"You're lucky you didn't have any siblings."

"We always want what we don't have, don't we? I always thought it would be nice to have a little brother or sister around."

"You can have mine, but I'm sure you'd be ready to give her back after the first fifteen minutes."

He chuckled. "If you say so."

"Have you ever been married?" She worried he might have a wife hidden somewhere, and she wasn't interested in children.

He took his time answering. "I had someone a long time ago. She was... my everything."

Martha felt a pang of jealousy. "What happened?"

"She was murdered. I've never really gotten over it." Martha was stunned silent. *Murdered.* "Enough of the depressing talk. Ask me something else."

She took his right hand and caressed his index and middle fingers. They were too short, unnaturally stubby, and the nail bed was barely there.

"Brachydactyly," he said.

"What's that?"

"A genetic disorder."

She took both of his hands in hers. The left was perfect, his fingers long, his nails buffed. He could be a hand model with that one. But the fingers on his right hand looked like they'd just stopped growing at different times. He kept the nails buffed, but they were misshapen.

She kissed each finger. Then she put his cold hand inside her shirt, and he caressed her breast in a way that drove her crazy. They kissed for a long while. She let him explore her mouth, her ears, her eyes with his tongue. She tried to relax and savor and feel every bit of his touch. He took his hand out of her shirt and ran it through her hair. She draped her legs across his lap and leaned back into his chest.

He broke the silence. "You said your grandmother lives with you?"

"Yep, Nanny. She's great."

"Is she an attorney as well?"

"No, she's an art teacher at Vision Prep."

"An artist, is she?"

"She is. Got all the talent and then kept it to herself. She's the one who lives with us. Since my mom…"

He pulled her close. "You don't have to talk about it. I don't want our time together to make you sad."

She shivered under the blanket. "I'm okay." She didn't want to fall apart in front of him. She'd never opened up to anyone like this before and realized her body was responding to more than his touch.

His voice was the same, low and melodic, as he'd talked of his lost love and his deformed hand. His gray eyes never lost their intensity as he listened to her spill everything in her heart. It was a raw intimacy, like she was peeling off her clothes and rather than exposing her body, it was her naked soul. Maybe true intimacy was a connection of two souls tangled up in each other.

"You know what would make me happy?" Martha asked.

He kissed her neck. "I do."

Before she realized what was happening, he was on his feet, scooping her off the sofa. She put her arms around his neck and kissed him as he carried her across the threshold and to her bedroom. He pulled her shirt over her head. She pulled her jeans off and reached for his pants. He stopped her and held her at arm's length, staring at her naked body. "You're so beautiful."

His words took her by surprise. If she hadn't already been naked, his stare would have made her feel that way. She broke the connection and moved to unbutton his pants. He kicked his shoes off and let her slide his pants off.

Martha pulled him down to the bed and on top of her. She lifted her hips and arched her back, her body begging to join with his. He teased her and refused to give her what she wanted, driving her mad. His mouth and hands worked together to ignite every inch of her body. He kissed her neck, biting her hard enough to make her yelp. His hands were in her hair, caressing her head and her face with a feather touch as his mouth lingered on her breasts.

She was breathless as he moved, never stopping. His hands were on her shoulders, almost tickling. His tongue playing with her belly button, biting a hip bone. He was like a snake, slithering and tasting its way around every inch of her, pausing at the tender spot that made her writhe in ecstasy. His tongue was so gentle. She grabbed him by the hair and drove her hips into his face, needing her release, but just as she was about to climax, he paused and pulled away.

Panting and breathless, she teetered on the edge of a bliss she'd never known. And as much as her body wanted him to push her from the cliff from which she hung, she felt a connection with Thomas she never knew was possible and her mind wanted to stay in this stasis forever. He had complete control over every aspect of her being and in those moments, as much as she wanted her release, she knew it would pull her out of this new and magical space, where she would happily stay forever.

He made his way back up to her mouth and continued to tease her with his fingers. When he kissed her, she tasted herself in his mouth.

She couldn't stand another minute without him. He granted her wish, and as she fell, every inch of her body tingled in a timeless ecstasy. Thomas's powerful arms squeezed her tighter. She wrapped her legs around his back and pulled him deeper into her, willing her body to take her to Nirvana. As she felt his body go rigid, she let herself slip from the cliff into blissful oblivion. She felt his gasp more than heard it, and she hoped his pleasure was as intense as her own.

She floated back into the soft pillow of reality, and as she lay on the other side of euphoria, she wondered what had just happened to her. Thomas was still inside her. His breath was cool on her neck. She hugged him as he started to move. "Don't go. I want to stay like this forever."

He kissed her and said, "It has to end sometime, love."

***

The next morning, she woke with him hard against her back. She was still wrapped in his arms, and he was fondling her breasts. She rolled over, and he pulled her on top of him. It didn't take long for her climax to begin. He hugged her tight as they moved together in a harmony reserved for those connected at the deepest levels.

She lay on top of him, catching her breath as he ran his fingers over her back.

He stopped and pushed her up. "We really have something special, don't we? I know you feel it. And I don't just mean the sex, though that's been pretty special too."

She couldn't do anything but nod her head.

He caressed her cheek. "I haven't felt this way since…well, since my last partner, the one who died."

Her emotions were in such an uproar, she couldn't help the tear that fell and landed on Thomas's chest.

"Don't cry, love."

She sniffed, feeling stupid. "Sorry, I don't know why I'm so emotional." She knew exactly why. Thomas and Jake. She didn't know what to do.

"I'm sorry, love, but I've got to get back to New Orleans. Don't think I'm a cad."

She sniffed again and wiped her face. "I don't. I'm so happy you came. And yes, I feel it too. I've never felt anything like it. I'm not sure how I'll survive winter break without you."

"Maybe you can sneak back early."

She nodded. "I can do that for sure."

He got up. "I'm going to take a quick shower."

"Okay, you want breakfast or coffee or anything?"

He kissed her. "No, thanks, babe." He pinched her nipple and disappeared into the hallway.

CHAPTER 2

Martha had gone back to sleep after he left, and when she woke, the sun was already high in the sky. She'd planned on going home after Thomas left but decided to stay another day. She was going to have to face reality soon enough. So, wanting to remain in this limbo where she could still pretend she was a little girl, she pulled out her copy of *The Black Stallion* and went out on the lanai to read about Alec Ramsey and The Black.

The blanket was still on the sofa from the night before, and she wrapped herself in it. She stared at the pages but couldn't focus. She closed it, put it in her lap and said aloud, "Mom, am I royally screwing up my life?"

Martha waited for an answer but got only silence. She closed her eyes and breathed in the cold salt air and pretended she was a child again, a child who still had a mother. She longed for those days of innocence, the time before her mind was clouded by sex and conquest.

She remembered asking Nanny about sex and laughed aloud. She'd probably only been twelve or thirteen. The only part of the conversation she remembered was about making yourself vulnerable. She guessed the degree to which you made yourself vulnerable with someone was equal to the hurt of a betrayal. Now twenty-one, she understood the complications of relationships. She wondered how her parents, or anyone for that matter, stayed married. And for the first time, she wondered if she was cut out for marriage. She had to do something about Jake.

Nanny always told Martha she thought her sister Raven would be the one she'd have to worry about. She wasn't wrong often, but she sure missed the boat there. Raven was as big a prude as Martha had ever known.

Her hand involuntarily went to the hook-shaped scar under her eye at the thought of her sister. She thought of Thomas kissing her scar and smiled.

She tried to think of Jake, but couldn't. She tried to go back to her book, but like a slow dense fog, thoughts of Thomas rolled into her mind. His captivating laugh, drinking wine and discussing Socrates, looking into his eyes as they made love all over his apartment. And last night. What he'd done to her, what he'd made her feel, was hard for her to even comprehend. He was mysterious, smart, and so handsome. She even loved his deformed hand.

Until yesterday, she thought she understood the situation. She was graduating in a few months and moving on with her life. She never expected to be blindsided by one of her flings. Thomas was now her drug, her addiction, a necessity like food or water. He was her nourishment.

She wasn't ready to step out of this feeling of wonderment and go back to reality, but she felt her phone buzz. She grabbed it, willing it to be Thomas.

Miss you already, love.

Her stomach flipped. She snapped a picture of one of her breasts and sent it to him, saying she wished he was still here. She watched the three dots wiggle at the bottom of her screen, then nothing.

As she put her phone down, it buzzed again. Her smile faded as she looked at the screen and saw a message from Jake.

Hey, babe, haven't heard from you in a few days. Everything okay?

She responded, *I decided to stay at the beach another day.*

The three dots wiggled, and he responded, *Want me to come down?* A winky face and an eggplant emoji followed.

Martha rolled her eyes, irritated at his immaturity. She wanted to ignore him, but knew she had to respond.

No – crying face emoji – I've got to head home in the morning.

He immediately sent back three crying faces.

There was a time when she would have swooned over this text exchange. Martha had been smitten with Jake from the first time she laid eyes on him, and they'd been together since she was sixteen. Well, there'd been a few blips along the way, but for the most part, he'd been her ride or die. But now there was Thomas, infecting her brain and body with his essence. The pit constantly in her gut was as big as the quandary she found herself in.

Her phone buzzed again. She glanced down at the screen; it was from Thomas. *Counting the days until I can kiss that and the rest of you again xoxo.*

Martha groaned out loud when she read it. She stopped herself from responding. She needed to be cool. After last night, and this morning, that would be difficult. It had only been a month since they'd started seeing each other and just last week, he'd been her professor.

After texting her dad and Nanny to check in, she dozed off on the sofa.

RAVEN –
HODIE
DISCIMUS
CRAS
DOCEMUS

CHAPTER 3

Raven walked toward Vision Prep's old stone buildings that loomed in the distance. The pre-dawn fog gave the buildings an eerie look that reminded her of the black-and-white Hitchcock movies her parents used to watch. Fitting for a school that taught young witches to master their craft. She smiled and let the mist swaddle her.

Raven and her little basset hound, Daisy Mae, got to the arched stone trellis that spanned the footpath running between the ancient stone walls marking the school grounds. She jumped, as she did every day, and tried to slap the school motto *Hodie Discimus Cras Do-cemus*—Today We Learn, Tomorrow We Teach—etched across the arch. Her natural jump didn't come within a foot of the sign. She spun up a hover spell and tried again.

"Yes!" she said as she floated back to the ground, her hand tingling from the cold stone. To her dog, she said, "Everything's better with a little magic, don't you think, Daisy Mae?"

The founders of Vision, Morgana and Agatha, had escaped the Salem witch trials and fled as far away from the misogyny of Salem and the Puritan northeast as they could get. Their dream was to create a place where witches and non-witches would learn to respect all people no matter their color, religion, magical or sexual orientation, or any other trait a person could have. They settled in what was the Mississippi Territory (and a century later became Alabama) and got to work manifesting their vision. Three hundred and some years later, their dream was a thriving boarding school for both witches and mortals alike.

Raven's hoodie wasn't enough to keep out the chill of the winter air. She picked up her pace and hurried to get inside the Witchery. She closed the door behind her and as always, her fingers tingled as the centuries old magic of the building ran through the young witch like electricity.

The sound of a door closing caused Raven to jump. Instinctively, she spun a stun spell and squinted to see where the noise was coming from. She looked at her phone: 5:45. Too early for anyone to be here. The spell pulsed in her hand, the vibrant strands of magic ready to do Raven's bidding. Daisy Mae ran off toward the sound, and Raven followed her.

Raven let the spell dissipate when she saw Rosie James standing outside of the art room. Rosie was a junior—a year younger than Raven—and she only knew her by sight. Daisy Mae jumped at Rosie, her short legs landing on the girl's belly.

"Don't hurt me!" Her hands shot in the air, and she backed into the wall.

"Daisy Mae! Off! What are you doing here, Rosie?" Daisy Mae ignored Raven and danced around Rosie's feet, sniffing her shoes. Raven called Daisy Mae again and said to Rosie, "Don't worry, she just likes to sniff."

Raven walked over and knelt down to grab Daisy Mae by the collar, repeating herself. "What are you doing here so early?"

Rosie looked down and stammered. "I...thought I left my chemistry book here yesterday."

"Really? I'll let Nanny—I mean Ms. Black know and see if she found it."

"Oh, okay. Thanks." Still pressed against the wall, she moved toward the door.

Raven could see her face was pale, eyes puffy and bloodshot like she'd been crying. "Are you okay, Rosie?"

"Yes, I'm fine. I just need my book so I can finish my homework."

"Okay. Don't worry about Daisy Mae. I've got her. You don't have to be afraid."

Rosie nodded and trotted away and out the door.

"That was weird." Raven shrugged and went over to the little kitchen area, heated some water, and made a cup of tea. Daisy Mae settled into her plush little bed in the corner of the main room.

Tea in hand, Raven sat at the table to wait for her advanced spells instructor, Ms. Tengos, to arrive. A copy of *American Dirt* Ms. Tengos must have left behind lay on the table. Raven had read it for her Social Studies class. She leafed through it and some photographs fell out on the table. Just as she picked them up, Ms. Tengos, Nanny, and someone she didn't recognize came through the door chittering like angry birds. They startled at the sight of her.

Daisy Mae looked up at the commotion, sniffed the air, and put her head back down.

"I didn't realize you were here," Ms. Tengos said.

Raven looked at her phone. It was 6:00 a.m. "I'm right on time. I think you're late." She crossed her arms.

Ms. Tengos looked at Nanny and the other woman. "We can talk about this later."

"Talk about what?" Raven asked.

"You can field this one," Nanny said to Ms. Tengos.

The strange woman turned to Raven. "You must be Raven. I've heard a lot about you. I'm Fala. It's so nice to finally meet you."

"Hi, Fala."

"See you later, Raven," Nanny said. "Fala, let's go to my office."

Nanny and Fala started off to the back of the Witchery. Raven remembered Rosie and yelled, "Oh, Nanny, hang on a sec."

Nanny stopped. "What is it, Raven?"

"Rosie James was in the art room when I got here. She said she thought she left her chemistry book in there. She looked like she was crying."

Raven caught the look Nanny traded with Ms. Tengos.

"She's from New Orleans, isn't she?" Ms. Tengos asked.

Nanny nodded. "Thanks, Raven."

Raven turned her attention to Ms. Tengos, who had gone over to Daisy Mae and was rubbing her belly. The dog had rolled on her back, ears splayed out like Dumbo and one hind leg kicked at the air in rhythm with Ms. Tengos's petting. "Who was that woman? Fala?"

"She's a Choctaw witch who sometimes helps us find vampires."

"What were you talking about?"

"We think the wards around the town are breaking down. There is an eclipse coming soon, and that's the perfect energy to refortify them. It wouldn't bode well for us if the vampires could get into Vision."

"Why not? We could just kill them. It might be kind of fun for me to put all this training to good use."

Ms. Tengos shook her head. "Raven, this isn't a game. The last thing I want is Mathias coming into Vision."

"I know about Mathias. I pay attention in class. Maybe he's dead. He's been gone for, what, three hundred years?"

"Don't be a fool, Raven. Have you been going through my things?" Ms. Tengos stood at the table, looking at her book and the pictures.

"Well, I was early."

Ms. Tengos gathered the pictures and put them back in the book. "Did you look at these?"

Raven shook her head. "Can I help with the ward spells?"

Ms. Tengos nodded. "It would be good for you to learn."

Raven gasped. "Awesome."

"Let's get started."

CHAPTER 4

After her lesson with Ms. Tengos, she left Daisy Mae at the Witchery—Nanny would take her home at lunchtime—and met up with her best and only friend, Ranjit, to head off to class. "Want to come over for dinner tonight?"

"Of course. Anything is better than dorm food, especially Nanny's cooking."

"Cool. Meet me at the Witchery after school? I have the little ones today last period."

"Can I watch? I love to watch you get flustered with all those little girls."

She fake punched his arm. "No way."

Ranjit laughed. "See you later."

They went in opposite directions, Ranjit to history and Raven to non-magical math. She had been told all her life that she was a witch like no other Nanny or Ms. Tengos had ever encountered. She loved her magic and had been dedicated to the practice since she was a toddler. But as adept as she was with her magic and her weapons, and with her fundamental knowledge of vampires—the threat they posed and even how to kill one—she had no real-life experience with anything outside of Vision.

Ms. Tengos didn't want her to leave their protective bubble for fear she'd be attacked by a vampire. "There is a long and deep history between the witches and vampires, and it's not safe for you." She told Raven this all the time.

"But Martha." Always her response. "And Dad."

"Martha is away at college, and she poses no threat to the vampires. She can barely conjure a spell, much less kill a vampire. When it's time for you to go to college, we'll discuss this. You must have a strong mind. I've told you they can get in your head and manipulate you if you're not careful."

"You say that all the time. You realize I'm almost eighteen and graduating this year, right? And how do the vampires know she's not a threat?"

"Martha may not be a powerful witch, but she has a sound mind. Now enough. Go study."

It was always some variation of this conversation. She loved Vision and her home, but she itched for more. Raven wanted to travel, study abroad in Europe, go back to India with Ranjit. She'd settle for Nashville or New Orleans; they were as foreign to her as another country.

She'd be eighteen soon enough, able to make her own decisions. She'd secretly been applying to colleges in California with Ranjit. He was brilliant and would have to decide which elite school he wanted to attend. It was a longshot for her, but she kept her fingers crossed she'd get accepted to Stanford or Berkeley or NYU. She'd also applied to American University simply because Martha was going to law school there in the fall and she loved to annoy her sister. She wondered if the adults in her life thought she was just going to stay in Vision and keep teaching six-year-olds.

Her phone buzzed. An email from Ticketmaster to reserve Eras Tour tickets for Atlanta. Her phone buzzed again with a text from Ranjit. *Did you get the email???*

When the presale for the Eras Tour started, she and Ranjit had tried to buy tickets. Her father and Ms. Tengos would have to let them go if they had tickets in hand, and her father could chaperone them in Atlanta. But the demand broke Ticketmaster, and they'd failed. Even her magic couldn't fix the debacle.

As she started to respond to Ranjit, she saw him running across the small quad. She ran to him, jumping up and down like she was on a pogo stick. "You need to calm down. You're being too loud," she sang.

Ranjit grabbed her hands and jumped with her. "OMG, OMG, we're going!!!"

"I've got to go to class. Let's get this done."

They both opened their identical emails. Each had the option to buy four tickets at varying prices.

"Should we buy two each?" Ranjit asked. "It says they aren't guaranteed."

"You can invite Stephen if we have extras."

Ranjit blushed. "I could. Who will you bring?"

"Doesn't matter. I can figure that out later. Let's just get this done." She scanned the email. "What seats should we pick?"

Ranjit gave her a look. "Do you need to even ask? Best available."

"It's a lot of money."

"Two things. One, it's the Eras Tour! And two, my parents won't even notice it on their credit card. I can get yours too."

She smiled. "Thanks. I can pay you back in installments. Should you just order four so they're all together?"

"What if I don't get them? Let's just do two and two and one of us should get them." He held out his hand. "Give me your phone."

She handed it to him, and he put in the request, handed her phone back, then did the same on his phone. "Done! And don't even think about paying me back. Consider this a token of my appreciation for all the time I've spent at Chez Beaumont."

"Thanks, Ranjit. That's really sweet."

"Whatevs. It says we should hear back within five days."

"Fingers crossed. I think we're late for class now."

"Worth it!"

She gave him a hug. "Thank you. See you later."

CHAPTER 5

Last period of the day, she went back to the Witchery to teach first grade girls Elemental Basics. She'd been teaching elementary and middle school girls for two years. It was something she genuinely enjoyed, and if she had to work, this was a great way to make extra money.

There were six girls in this class, and being the little witches they were, they could definitely get on her nerves. It was almost winter break, and the girls, who were restless with excitement, had difficulty focusing on their lessons. Raven raised her hand and pretended to spin a spell. The girls stopped everything and stood in silence.

"Does anyone know this spell I'm conjuring?"

They shook their heads in unison. She continued to hold her hand out, giving the girls the illusion she was conjuring. "This is Miss

Raven's specialty." She paused for effect and heard a gasp. "That's right, fear this spell."

One of the braver girls asked, "What does it do, Miss Raven?"

Trying not to smile, Raven pursed her lips. "This will hex you into a permanent and unsolvable math equation." There was a collective gasp. "Sounds awful, right?"

"Yes, ma'am."

Raven put her hand down and heard a collective sigh. "Okay, are we ready to have some fun before break?"

"Yes!"

"Everyone line up against the wall." She could feel their nervous energy. A low current of electricity was making the room hum. "Let's conjure some snow and have a little winter wonderland of our own."

The girls had barely conjured rain, so Raven had her work cut out.

By the end of class, there was a mixture of snow, rain, sleet and even a little hail on the floor. Both teacher and students were laughing so hard they couldn't talk.

After class, she headed to the main room. Ranjit was talking to Ms. Tengos and a strange woman wearing a Vision Prep hoodie walked away from them, heading toward the classrooms. She looked familiar, and Raven smiled at her.

"Who are all these strangers here today? Am I missing something?"

"No, maybe you're just starting to open your eyes," Ms. Tengos replied.

Ranjit turned to Raven. "I'm starving. You ready to go?"

"Yes."

The little students were filing out behind her, and she heard one of them say, "Miss Raven's got a boyfriend." Accompanied by a lot of giggling.

Ranjit laughed and put his arm around Raven. He pulled her in and kissed her cheek.

She leaned into his kiss and clenched her teeth. "Too bad you play for the other team."

Ranjit let her go. "Too bad for me? Good one."

Raven rolled her eyes. "Can we go, please?"

They got to Raven's house, and Nanny was in the kitchen drinking a glass of wine. "Hi, Nanny. Ranjit's going to stay for dinner. Is that okay?"

Nanny put her glass on the counter and picked up her purse. "No need to ask. You're always welcome, Ranjit. I need to run to the store though. The cupboards are bare."

"Thanks, Nanny." Raven reached for a tomato and popped it in her mouth.

"Yes, thanks, Nanny!" Ranjit yelled as she stepped into the garage.

"We have to tell her about the concert, right?" Raven asked.

"Let's wait until we have tickets in hand. Something I've always wondered is how Nanny can be your grandmother and look so young?"

"Magic." Raven laughed.

"I guess that was a dumb question. Why does she always wear a scarf?"

"She had surgery when she was a little girl, thyroid or something, so she covers the scar. Just ask her. It's not a secret, Sherlock. I'm going to change. I have little witch residue on my clothes. It makes me want to giggle and act like I'm six again."

"Don't let me stop you. Go."

Daisy Mae followed her upstairs. She went into her room and stopped short. Leaning against the wall was a painting of her mother. She gasped at its beauty. She knew it was from Nanny and could see the magic pulsing within it. But what that magic was, she had no idea. It looked to be an oil painting and brought the image of her mother vividly to life. Swirls and peaks gave it texture. In the background, an eddying ocean of deep blues and greens accentuated the unique blue of her mother's eyes. The bust reminded her of the cameo ring Martha wore sometimes. Her mother's honey-blonde hair contrasted sharply with the sea around it, a perfect match for the gold filigree frame.

She stared at the picture. Her mother had died when she was only three and her memories were captured in photos and stories Nanny and her father told. When they were little, Martha would torment her with the relationship she'd had with their mother, something Raven would never know or understand. Martha had inherited her mother's beautiful hair and eyes. It was a constant reminder to Raven she was somehow lesser than her sister, the ugly duckling with no mother to speak of. But this painting seemed to make her mother real, and Raven felt a tingle of something like hope.

Daisy Mae sniffed the picture, and when her nose touched it, she barked and jumped back like she'd been shocked.

Raven absently petted her dog. "It's okay, girl."

She ran her finger along the frame and felt the familiar charge of magic. Kneeling before the painting as if in worship, she looked into her mother's eyes. She teared up, her heart swelling with a longing for this woman she'd never known who had etched a piece of herself onto Raven while she was nothing but an acorn in her womb—a connection that survived even death. That maternal imprint contained a fragment of all the mothers that preceded her own, a strength passed on from mother to daughter, giving all who came before her a kind of immortality.

A knock on the door startled her out of her reverie. She wiped her eyes and turned to see Ranjit.

"Hi, you coming back down?"

Raven stood and stepped away from the painting. "You've seen this?" She crossed her arms and gave her best *humph*.

Ranjit nodded and averted his eyes. "Sorry, Nanny asked me if I thought you'd like it."

"I'm not mad. Go away so I can change."

"Well, you said you were coming to change about thirty minutes ago. I'm hungry, so can you get a move on?"

"You mentioned that. Is Nanny back? I'll be right down."

"Yes, and dinner's ready."

Jeez, where did the time go? Ranjit left, and she changed into sweats and a Rolling Stones T-shirt. She ran back downstairs and went straight to Nanny, wrapping her in a hug.

"Oh, Nanny, it's beautiful. Thank you."

"I'm glad you like it. Think of it as an early Christmas present."

"I *love* it."

"You're welcome. Can we eat now?"

As they passed around the giant bowl of rice and quinoa with lentil salad, Ranjit said, "I feel like I should know this, but how come only girls at Vision Prep are witches?"

"It's a fair question," Nanny said. "It's a female gene. At least as far as we know today, it's an exclusive club for women."

"That sucks for us guys. Was Mrs. Beaumont like you and Ms. T?"

"When she was younger, she was a strong witch—though not as powerful as Raven here. But she had two daughters; they stole her powers." She winked at Raven.

"What does that mean?" Raven took a bite of her food.

"If she'd had sons, her powers would have remained mostly intact, but with daughters, they absorb the powers of the mother."

Ranjit nodded. "So, after you have kids, you aren't a witch anymore?"

"No, we'll always be witches, but after birthing daughters, powers can fade with age. We have to work hard to keep them."

"What if you don't have kids at all?"

"Our powers stay intact with sons, and a witch can live a long life if she doesn't have children and continues to practice her craft."

"I didn't know that." Raven grabbed a lingering piece of bread and took a bite. "What happens if you stop practicing?"

"Your powers fade. If a witch has a son, often they give up their powers, so they don't outlive their child."

Raven nodded. "So if I don't have kids, will I be immortal?"

Nanny shrugged. "We're not immortal, but we can live long lives."

"That's reason enough not to have kids."

"Wait," Ranjit said. "If you're Mrs. Beaumont's mother, how come you still have powers?"

Nanny chuckled. "It wasn't easy. There was a time I thought I might lose my powers, but Ms. Tengos helped me get through and keep them."

"Tell me about Fala," Raven said.

"Who?" Ranjit asked.

"A Choctaw witch I met this morning."

"Nothing really to tell," Nanny said. "She has a special gift and helps us determine if, say, a serial killer is actually a vampire or a human. Things like that."

"What is it?" Raven asked. "What's her gift and how come I've never met her before?"

Nanny shrugged. "Timing, I guess. As far as her gift goes, that's not really your business."

"What's the magic in the picture?" Raven plucked a lone tomato off her plate and popped it in her mouth.

Nanny smiled. "Let's clean up this mess and go find out."

"I can't stay for the show," Ranjit said. "It's almost curfew. I need to get back to the dorm."

"Nanny can call and let them know you'll be late."

"No, I have homework, and I think you need to do this on your own. Call me later and tell me about it?"

Raven nodded.

"Bye, Ranjit," Nanny said. "Thanks for your help with this."

"Anytime." He vanished out the front door.

They cleaned up the dishes and went upstairs to Raven's room. Standing in front of the picture, Nanny said, "You know painting is my gift."

Raven nodded. Nanny was unusually serious. Even Daisy Mae was behaving.

"First, you must promise not to tell Martha about this, no matter how mad you get at her."

"Okay."

"You can use this painting to see your mother."

"How?"

"Touch it."

Raven touched her mother's face, and her fingers tingled with the familiar spark of magic. They disappeared into the painting and an intense energy flowed up her arms. Daisy Mae gave a low growl and backed away as Raven jerked her hand back and looked at Nanny. "What the heck? What is it?"

"I paint pictures that can transport certain witches through time and space. You're one of those witches. Think you're ready for that?"

"What do you mean I'm one of those witches?"

"Remember the tests I did on the day of your first art class? I find out who can paint magic and who can use magic paintings to...move around time and space."

Raven vaguely remembered the tests. "So, this is a thing? It's not like our gifts?"

"Painting is my gift. The ability to go through the paintings is something different. We don't know what allows some to go through. One of the many mysteries of witches."

Raven nodded, taking in this flood of new information. It seemed she learned something new and weird about being a witch every day. "Who else can go through?"

"That's not for me to discuss. I don't even tell the students initially. It's a conversation I have with their parents. I let them decide how to proceed. Time travel is quite a big deal."

"Time travel. Wow."

"This painting will take you through time to visit your mother when she was still alive."

"Why now?"

"I think you're ready, mature enough to handle it. And it's time you got to know your mother. I can set an intention when I paint and create something specific. I'll show you some of those another time. But, sometimes," she nodded toward the picture, "it just happens, and I don't have control over what I'm creating. I go into a bit of a trance and can be as surprised by the result as anyone."

"Can you come with me?"

"I can paint them, but I can't go through them on my own. I could go through with you, but I think you should do this on your own."

"I can take people with me?"

Nanny nodded.

"So, I'll be time traveling? What if I touch something that changes the world as it is today, you know, the butterfly effect?"

Nanny grinned. "That's not how it works. You can exist in that time with her. You just become a part of the timeline. Think of time as a wheel that spins around and doesn't really change. It may pick up some dirt and debris along the way, but it plods along doing its thing, going around and around. It's not like the movies. If you see yourself, it's fine, you're just a little dust on the wheel. Enjoy your time with your mother, okay? Once you go through, your time is limited. Are you ready?"

Raven wasn't at all ready, but she nodded anyway. Dust on a wheel didn't sound too appealing.

"What do you mean, my time is limited?"

"You won't have control over how long you stay and when you can come back, you'll just get pulled back to our time. It gets better the more you go through, you can learn to control it."

Raven nodded. "Wait, why can't I tell Martha? Can't she go through?"

"She can't. You can never tell her about this, okay?"

Raven nodded and turned her attention back to the painting. She touched it again. The swirls had a velvety feel and undulated beneath her fingers, beckoning her in. Once again, her fingers melted into her mother's face, then her hand, and her arm disappeared as if being eaten by some monster lurking behind the mysterious picture. There was a slight tug from the other side, and then her full body was passing through. Her dinner roiled in her gut.

She was immersed in an eddying but viscous sea of the unknown. It enveloped her body like a warm glove and pushed her along in some unseen current. The weight of her body was gone and with it, she realized, her senses. She was aware of her thoughts, now somehow calmer. Her distractions and worries were gone, and she just *was*. She wondered what had happened to her body and if this was what it was like to die. Maybe this was what it was to achieve enlightenment. Had she arrived in Nirvana? She didn't sense any other beings and thought what a lonely existence this would be—why was there so much hype around this stuff? Raven appreciated the calm in her mind, but she wasn't so sure about not having a body. How could she do magic in this state? And what would even be the point? She guessed she was timeless and helpless. Until she wasn't.

The swirls took shape, and she realized she could squint. She shivered and the hair on her arms stood on end as a cool breeze passed through her. Raven hugged herself, rubbing her arms, wanting to make sure they were really there. She could make out vague shapes and shadows dancing ahead and thought *maybe I'm in Plato's cave*. Then gravity returned, and the weight of her existence pulled her into the past.

She gasped. Sitting in the overstuffed rocking chair covered with Chinese blue tapestry that sat in Raven's bedroom was the beautiful woman from the painting she'd just gone through.

Raven mouthed the word, "Mom."

Her mother looked up. "Rae-Rae! I was wondering when you'd show up."

Raven noticed the blanketed bundle in the crook of her mother's arm and took a step backwards.

"Don't be frightened, sweet girl. Come, say hello to your baby self."

Her feet were heavy, and she didn't trust her legs to get her the short distance to where her mother sat.

Her mother got up, gently placing her baby self in her crib and walked over to Raven—who was still unable to move—wrapping her in a warm hug. She folded her arms around her mother, buried her face in her soft hair, and breathed her in. If only she could bottle that smell. Her eyes burned and her chest heaved as a sob escaped.

"Aww, Rae-Rae, I'm so happy you're here. You've grown into such a beautiful young lady. Now you can visit me whenever you want."

Raven's hands tingled, and she suddenly felt like she was fading, becoming less solid. "Mom!"

Her mother pulled back and touched Raven's cheek. "It's alright, honey. The first time is always awkward. I love you."

The words were faint in her head, and she was being sucked into the great vacuum cleaner of the universe. She had a new affinity for all the bugs in her world that had experienced the same sensation, and she'd never look at the family Dyson the same way again.

The return trip brought no philosophical musings, no feelings of weightlessness, nor any sense of being outside time. After being sucked up by God's vacuum, she simply fell back through the painting and onto her floor as if the past were vomiting her back to her own time.

She tried to stand up, but the room seemed to spin. "I'm going to puke."

Nanny grabbed her arm and helped her to the bathroom. Raven collapsed on the floor in front of the toilet and spilled her guts. Nanny held her hair and rubbed her back as Raven rested her head on the toilet.

After a few minutes, the spinning slowed down. "Thanks, Nanny. I think I can stand now."

"Hold on to me, just in case."

Raven took Nanny's outstretched hand and pulled herself up.

"Let's get you to bed. We can talk about this in the morning, okay?"

"Bed sounds good."

With Nanny's help, she made it to her bed and crawled in, still fully clothed. Daisy Mae jumped on the bed and gave Raven's face a lick, then spun around twice and snuggled up against her.

Just as she was dozing off, her phone dinged with a text from Ranjit. *We're going to Atlanta!!!*

MARTHA – THE DILEMMA

CHAPTER 6

Martha and Gretchen were sitting on their balcony overlooking the Uptown neighborhood of New Orleans. It was February, but Martha felt the warmth of spring trying to break through the chill in the air. She loved New Orleans and would be sad to leave.

"Did you decide what you're doing for spring break?" Martha asked.

"My sister is taking my nieces to Arizona to see the Grand Canyon. I think I might tag along; I've never been out west before."

"That sounds like so much fun. Can I come too?"

"Of course, but I thought you were doing something with *Thomas*."

"I mean, we talked about going to his hunting lodge, but nothing ever materialized, and I don't want to appear needy. I think I'm going home, though. My dad's coming to help me get some of my stuff moved out. I can't just leave it all for him."

"Jeez, what *is* a hunting lodge and who has one, anyway?"

Martha shrugged. "I know, right?"

"What about Jake? Shouldn't you be seeing him?"

"Ugh, Gretchen, I don't know what to do. His spring break isn't for another couple of weeks. Indiana in March? No, thank you. He wants to come here, by the way, for his break."

Gretchen shook her head. "Jake's a good guy, Martha. You should break it off with him or the professor. Probably the professor, don't you think? You're different when you're with Thomas."

"What do you mean, different?"

"Nothing I can put my finger on. You just seem off, not your normal self. Honestly, it's like you're under a spell." She laughed. "He's not some kind of witch, is he?"

Martha chuckled. "I doubt it. There aren't any male witches. I think I'm just smitten. I keep thinking it'll run its course, like with Dr. Daniels and Dr. Parker, but it never does."

Gretchen laughed. "You and your professors."

Martha grinned. "Are you slut shaming me?"

"Yes! Someone has to."

Martha crumpled the Starbucks napkin on the table next to her and threw it at Gretchen. It fluttered to the ground, not even close to hitting its mark.

Gretchen giggled, then got up and went inside. When she came back, she had two shot glasses, a cut up lime, a plate of salt and half a bottle of Patron—all neatly arranged on a silver tray.

"Aren't you the little Martha Stewart." Martha pointed to the tray. "Where did that even come from?" Then she saw the friendship bracelet draped over one of the shot glasses. She laughed and picked it up. "Illicit Affairs. Nice one." It was peppered with hearts and broken hearts. "Where did you find this?"

"I made it, special for my bestie."

"I love it." She slipped it on her wrist.

"I found the tray at a yard sale. Swanky, right?" She poured them each a shot. "Momma would be so proud, except for the tequila part of course. What should we drink to?"

"Being single."

Gretchen laughed. "A state you'll never know or understand." She raised her glass to Martha's. "To sluts everywhere!"

They went through the ritual—salt, tequila, lime.

"I needed that. Thanks, friend."

"Seriously, Martha. You can't keep this up. Do you see a future with Dr. Hottie? Talk to me. What's going on in your head?"

Martha considered the question. There was really nothing going on in her head. She was just following Thomas's lead. He took her to cool places around the city, old churches, abandoned buildings, little cemeteries. He called it NOLA's hidden history and had endless stories and details about each place. He took her out to dinner, they cooked together, they did things that normal couples do. It hadn't been like this with her other professorial flings. They'd been interested in sex only, and she'd been happy to accommodate.

She'd let her ego take the lead the first time when her economics professor, Dr. Daniels, suggested coffee to discuss Martha becoming an economics major. He was handsome, smart, and only thirty-one.

A good bit older than Martha's nineteen, but she loved the idea of dating a man so mature. Coffee led to dinner and wine, and from there it was a no-brainer. After her second semester as a freshman and plans to stay on campus for the summer, Peter went to England for a year as a visiting professor at the London School of Economics. Their whirlwind fling ended when Martha dropped him off at the airport where he swore he'd text her every day.

They kissed goodbye, and she never heard from him again.

The following year was Dr. Parker. He was a bit more brazen than Peter and ten years his senior. There was no offer of coffee or a plea to major in anthropology. He'd invited the class to his home for dinner at the end of the semester—something he did with all his classes. Martha hung around after everyone else had gone—at his request—for a nightcap. That was the first of many nights she spent with David. Again, she stayed for summer school, and they spent the next three months glued at the hip. By the time fall had rolled around, Martha grew bored with him. They had nothing in common, and she missed Jake. Things died out by the time autumn classes started again.

She and Jake had been on again, off again those first couple of years she was at Tulane. She knew the timelines crossed and at the time she didn't care because she also knew those professors would fade into the background and Jake would be there. Her ride or die.

She'd never told him she'd been with anyone else and had no idea if he had. Martha didn't want to know, though hoped he had. Their experiences with other people would make them closer. They had been together so long and only been with each other when she left for college. David and Peter had made her appreciate Jake even more, and it was why she'd pushed for them to make the distance work.

Her fascination with older men had run its course. Martha didn't want to be taken care of or molded into some creation of theirs, like an essay or book. Her days of being mindless arm candy were over.

Then Thomas came along. He'd been her philosophy professor first semester of junior year. He was older, but everything about him was different. He never pursued her. Never wore her like an Olympic medal. He saw *her*. Treated her like a peer, not a student.

Of course, she'd found him attractive. That was the extent of it, until one night before Thanksgiving break, they bumped into each other picking up carryout at the local Thai place. He suggested eating together would be much less sad than going home alone and asked if she wanted to join. They went back to his place and shared their curry and Pad Thai and talked and laughed.

Martha made the first move. She couldn't stop herself from kissing him. He was the moon, and she was the tide, helpless to do anything but be drawn into him. That first kiss had been magical, and she got lost in time. Everything that happened after had been like a dream and somehow otherworldly.

For another month, she was still his student, a line she hadn't crossed before. Martha didn't care. She'd let him take her in his office. They couldn't keep their hands off each other, like a couple of high school students looking for every opportunity to be together without their parents finding out.

Once the semester had ended and winter break had passed, they didn't hide their relationship. She didn't expect it would last and never told him about Jake. Four months later, she faced as big a mess as she'd ever created.

She shared these thoughts with Gretchen, who responded by pouring two more shots of Patron. "Here's to making good decisions."

Martha raised her glass. "Damn straight." And, ignoring the salt this time, they drank. "I'm sure there's a song for this." She pulled out her phone and queued her Taylor playlist. "Who better to help figure this shit out?"

Gretchen laughed. "Hail Taylor! A song for everything!" She poured two more shots as "Babe" started playing out of the Bluetooth speaker they had on the patio. "This song is Jake singing to you."

"Cringe. But you're pretty spot on. You know, if it weren't for you, Jake and I might not even be together."

"I was just helping a friend out. If it hadn't been me, you would have ended up together, eventually. The universe has a funny way of making things happen."

The tequila was making Martha sentimental. "No, really Gretchen, I don't know what I'd do without you. Our friendship transcends all these boys. You're my real rock. You know that, right?"

Gretchen laughed. "You're drunk!"

Martha hiccupped. "Yes, I believe I am. But that doesn't change what I said."

Gretchen grabbed her hand and squeezed it.

"Best friends forever!" Martha poured two more shots. Her phone vibrated on the table. She picked it up and looked at the message. It was from Thomas. She showed it to Gretchen.

"Don't respond. Let tonight be about us."

Martha nodded and turned her phone off as "You All Over Me" played.

"Yikes," Gretchen said. "Another song from Jake to you. Don't worry, by the time we finish this bottle, we're going to have your love life figured out."

Martha laughed. "And tomorrow we'll have no memory of anything!" They clinked their glasses and drank.

For a while, they sat in silence, listening to the sounds on the street below and watching the sun fall behind the trees.

Gretchen broke the quiet. "Have you thought about what you'll do if Jake proposes?"

"That's a buzz kill. Thanks."

"Sorry, but what kind of friend would I be if I didn't get you to think about this stuff?"

Martha whined. "Didn't you just say tonight's about us?"

"I did, didn't I? Cheers to us."

CHAPTER 7

Martha woke the next morning to the bed spins. She had to pee, but didn't know if she could make it to the bathroom. Vomiting was a possibility. She pulled herself out of bed and crawled on all fours to the toilet in time for the tequila and bile to make its way out.

She lay there, arms hugging the toilet rim, face buried in the crook of her elbow, when she felt a hand on her neck. It gently pulled her hair back. It wouldn't be the first time Gretchen held her hair while she puked, but then she felt soft lips on her neck.

"Good morning, darling. I got worried when I didn't hear from you last night."

Martha's stomach did another flip, and she felt it lurch. She wasn't sure there was anything left to come up.

Thomas, still holding her hair, rubbed her back with his free hand.

She was too hungover to care he was seeing her at her absolute worst. Even Jake hadn't seen her like this.

"Come on, love. Can you stand?" He put his hands under her arms and lifted her up.

She moaned. "Just kill me now." She pushed him out of the bathroom and took a minute to brush her teeth and splash her face with cold water. Looking in the mirror, she groaned. She grabbed a hair clip and put her hair up, deciding that was the best she could do under the circumstances.

She headed to the kitchen, where Thomas was making tea and toast, and settled onto a bar stool.

Martha noticed a bag filled with takeout on the counter. "What's that?" Maybe he'd brought breakfast and realized the state she was in.

"It was sitting outside your door. You must have ordered it and forgotten about it." He put the plate of dry toast and a mug of Earl Grey in front of her. She took a bite of toast and had a vague memory of craving Thai food. The thought of it now brought a fresh bit of bile to the back of her throat. She put the toast down.

"Eat."

Martha forced another bite.

After she finished, she felt somewhat human. "Why are you so great?"

He walked around the bar and put his arms around her. "I'm falling in love with you, Martha Lee."

She gasped, and suddenly the hangover was forgotten.

He put his arms around her waist and lifted her off the stool. She loved the way his arms felt around her. Their mouths locked, she wrapped her legs around his waist and drove herself into him. They moved like this, as one, back to the bedroom and fell onto her bed. The sex was as good now, if not better, than it had been at the beach. She still felt like she transcended to a new plane of existence every time.

After they finished, he said, "I'll leave you to get some rest, love. Text me later."

She smiled. "Okay."

It was well past noon when she woke. She got up and showered and brushed her teeth again. What day was it? She wondered if she was still drunk and grabbed her phone to check, hoping she hadn't missed a class.

Her phone was still powered down. She pushed the button and waited for her home screen to appear.

Thursday.

Phew, no class today.

Then she saw the slew of texts from Jake. "Shit."

She went searching for Gretchen, but she was nowhere to be found. Martha took a deep breath and went out to the patio. The remains of the night's debauchery still littered the table. They'd finished the tequila.

She wondered if they'd solved her love triangle.

Martha plopped down, her stomach in knots again. Without reading the texts, she called Jake.

RAVEN – SHE'S SO BASIC

CHAPTER 8

Raven and Ranjit sat in her room, the painting of her mother still on display. Daisy Mae slept on the floor between them. Leaning against her bed, Raven absently played with the dog's floppy ears.

"It was so cool. And my mother is so beautiful, her hair smelled like spring. I wish I could bottle her scent. It was almost like she was expecting me."

"Wow. What a great gift." Ranjit touched the painting.

"Can you feel anything?"

"Nope, not a thing."

"I had no idea Nanny could do that. I knew painting was her gift but didn't realize it was *that* kind of magic. Makes me wonder what else she can do."

Ranjit rolled his eyes, "I'm sure there's nothing else, no other weird, secret magic she and Ms. T have been hiding from you."

Raven smirked. "Sarcasm is your strong suit, you know. She told me if I work really hard, I can control my time there, like I won't just get sucked back without any control."

"Work hard is the key. Not your forte."

"I'm going to ignore that. Come with me to the Witchery. There's something I've been meaning to do. I think Ms. Tengos is gone for the day." She got up and headed downstairs. Ranjit and Daisy Mae followed. "Let's get some snacks first." In the pantry, she grabbed packs of trail mix and stuffed them in the pocket of her hoodie.

"How could you survive without your snacks?"

"Don't ask me for any if you're going to be like that. Ready?"

Ranjit nodded, and they left the house for school. It was Saturday, so she hoped there wouldn't be too many people around.

Raven broke into a run. "Come on, Daisy Mae."

"Wait up," Ranjit called after her.

Raven turned. "No, keep up."

She arrived at the Witchery and was opening the magic lock on the door when Ranjit caught up.

He panted. "What's going on?"

"The other day, I got here early, before Ms. Tengos, and Rosie James was in the art room."

"So?"

"She said she thought she'd left her chemistry book there. But she was lying."

"How do you know?"

Raven shrugged. "I just do. I want to look around the art room and see what she could have been looking for."

"Did you tell Ms. T?"

"Yes, I told her and Nanny." The door opened, and they hurried inside to the art room. Raven went to open the door and realized there was no knob or lock.

"Should it be like that?"

"I'm not sure."

Ranjit shrugged. "Why don't you try unlocking it like you unlock the main door? You have a spell for that, right?"

"Why not?" Raven spun up the spell and nothing happened.

"I guess that would be too easy. But how could Rosie get in?"

Raven shrugged. "No idea. I wish there was a TikTok or YouTube video for magic spells."

"Maybe there is?" Ranjit pulled out his phone. Raven watched as he typed in, *how to pick a magic lock*. "We're not magicians, but there is some cool stuff here I might check out later."

Raven ignored him, intent on the screen. "Wait, that one that says 'invisible.'" She touched the screen, and a video popped up. Ranjit hit play and turned his phone sideways so they could see it better.

"Pause it." Raven tapped the screen to pause the video. She could see the spell as the witch spun it, but without the ability to touch it, she could only guess its contents. She conjured what she thought was a good replica and cast it at the door.

A knob with a lock appeared.

"Wow, Raven, that was—"

"Shhh." She tapped the video again to play. Next was a spell that wove itself into the workings of the lock and released it. Raven captured the elements of the spell. "If this works, shame on Nanny and Ms. Tengos."

She cast the hex and watched the strands of energy work their way through the lock. After a series of clicks, the door opened. "Let's go see what Rosie was so interested in."

"As a *muggle,* could I watch that video and perform the spell?"

"I don't think so. I'm not sure all witches could get the spell right from a video."

"Rosie managed." Ranjit grabbed her arm. "Are you sure this is okay?"

"What kind of trouble could we possibly cause?" She wrenched her arm free and went through the door.

"Said every person who died in a horror movie, ever. Come on, Daisy Mae, let's see what your mom is going to get us into."

Raven created a magic torch so they could see in the dark. Ranjit found a light switch and turned it on. "Sometimes the good ole fashioned way works, too."

Raven rolled her eyes. She'd been in this room a million times but tried to have a fresh perspective. "Do you see anything weird, Ranjit? Out of place?"

He shook his head. "I wouldn't know what to look for." He pointed to a door at the front of the room. "Where does that go?"

"I don't know. My classroom is next door, but it doesn't connect."

They walked to the door, and Raven tried the knob. Locked. "Can you pull up that video again?" He held the phone for her while she mimicked the spell again. The lock clicked. "Shall we?"

They walked in together, Daisy Mae still at their heels. The door clicked behind them. Raven jumped at the noise.

"What's the point of a magic door if it doesn't close itself?" Ranjit asked.

"This room shouldn't be this big. We'd be in my classroom now." She searched the wall for a light switch and couldn't find one.

"Wow." Ranjit shined his phone flashlight around the room. "Raven. Turn on your flashlight."

She fished her phone from her pocket and turned the light on to reveal a mural of what appeared to be Vision. Not as it was today, but the early days. A woman sat on the grass facing the lake, her long, honey-colored hair blowing in an unseen breeze. She leaned on one hand, head tilted back, as if absorbing the sunlight. The lake reflected the forest behind it and a great blue heron stood, one leg cocked, on the opposite shore.

Raven looked closer at the woman in the painting and touched it. She jerked her hand back. "Ranjit, it's magic, like the one Nanny painted of my mother."

"It's beautiful. I feel like I could get lost in it. Look at the detail."

She looked at the other walls. They were covered with paintings as well, but not murals. These were all framed. Rolled-up canvases filled a row of cubbies against one wall. "Ranjit, look at these." She ran her fingers over each of the paintings hanging on the wall. "They're all magic. Nanny told me she had a lot, but this? Wow."

"Look, what are these clothes for?" He pointed to the table in the corner of the room. On it lay a pair of blue jeans, a Vision Prep hoodie, and a pair of pink Nike slides.

"Odd, I have no idea." She touched the hoodie, and a tingle traveled up her fingers.

"You really had no idea this room was here?"

"Nope. I want to go through all these paintings."

"Maybe you should ask Nanny first what they are before you go jumping through them."

"Let's go through the mural."

"How can I go?"

"I don't know. Hold on to me. Let's see if it works. We'll get pulled back when our time is up. Put your arms around my waist." She grabbed one of his hands and with the other, grabbed onto Daisy Mae.

"Raven, you shouldn't bring Daisy Mae."

"She'll be fine. You ready?"

"Raven, if something happens to her, you'll never forgive yourself. Leave her here."

He was right. "Well, I'd also never forgive myself if something happened to you. Are you sure you want to come?"

"Hell yes. Let's go."

She squeezed his hand and stepped into the painting, feeling the same out-of-body experience as before.

When they came out on the other side, Raven saw the lake in the distance. It was exactly like the mural, except the woman wasn't there. She wondered if Nanny could see them in the mural if she entered the room.

"Ranjit, are you okay?" He lay on the ground, motionless. Raven dropped to a knee and touched his face. "Ranjit. Please." She thought he was breathing but wasn't sure. "Oh, shit. Ranjit. Please wake up."

His eyes fluttered. "I feel like I had the crap beat out of me. Let me sit up." She helped him. "Oh, that's not better at all. Where are we?" He turned his head and threw up in the grass. "Sorry, I don't know where that came from."

"Same thing happened to me when I got back from seeing my mom. You okay?"

"Maybe you should've mentioned that. Let me see if I can get up." Raven stood, reached for his hand and pulled him up. "Okay, I think I can walk on my own."

Raven pointed to the lake. "It looks just like the mural, right?" She put his arm around her shoulder to support him.

"Look over there." He pointed to structures that looked like houses. A steady stream of smoke oozed from one. "That's where your house would be, right? And look, that must be the school."

Raven nodded. "Maybe that's Agatha's place."

"Let's head that way." He wiggled free of her. "I'm okay."

She paused and looked around at what was, in her time, a whole town. But here it was just a wide-open space. "This is crazy, right? We're standing in the middle of town."

Raven's fingers tingled and the feeling of not being fully there was setting in. She looked around to grab Ranjit, but he'd kept walking and was out of her reach.

"Ranjit!" She tried to move toward him but felt the pull and couldn't. "Ranjit! Get over here! Hurry!"

He turned, and the look on his face frightened her. She held out her hands, and he ran toward her. He grabbed her hands, and she squeezed with all her might.

They were back on the floor of the secret room.

"Shit, that was close. Are you okay?"

Ranjit nodded. Daisy Mae danced around them and stopped to lick Ranjit's face.

Raven heard a gasp and looked up; Rosie stood over them.

"Rosie? What are you doing here?"

Her face was pale. "I was looking for Ms. Black. And this door was open. I thought she might be in here."

"On Saturday?" Ranjit replied. "That door was closed. How did you get in?"

"I need to ask her about the assignment, for, for next week. I've got to go."

Before Raven could get up and go after her, she was gone. "What the hell?"

"Second that. Isn't she the reason we came here?"

"Yep. What's she up to?"

"Maybe she's going through the paintings?"

Raven pondered this. "But, why?"

"Same reason we are, because she can. She's curious."

"Didn't she seem off, like she was scared?"

"Maybe it was because she got caught again."

"What do we have here?" a new voice asked.

Raven startled and gawked at Ms. Tengos. "Where did you come from?"

"I guess there is no issue taking someone through the picture with you. I hope you're not permanently damaged, Ranjit."

"How did you know we were here?" Raven asked.

"It's a magic lock. How do you think?"

Ranjit laughed. "Of course. You have some kind of alarm built into it, don't you? *You* put the TikTok out there."

"Astute of you, Ranjit."

Raven was confused. "So, you already knew about Rosie? What's going on?"

Ms. Tengos nodded. "I'm not ready to answer that yet. I will tell you that we knew someone was trying to break into the art room so we put the video out there and a magic alarm on the door so we could catch the person. We guessed it was Rosie, but we wanted to talk to her. So, if you see her in here again, please stop her—even if you have to use a stun spell—until I arrive. It's important I speak to her, and I'm afraid your little *experiment* may have cost me the opportunity."

"Is she in trouble?" Raven asked.

"I'm afraid her family might be."

"You think someone is using Rosie for the paintings?" Ranjit asked.

"And her ability to travel through them," Ms. Tengos said.

"She can go through them, too?" Raven asked. "Is that why you made the video to access this room?"

Ms. Tengos seemed to think this over, but didn't answer.

Raven let it go. "What is this room? There's a lot of magic in here. There has to be at least one hundred paintings."

"Please don't go through them all. It could be dangerous, okay?"

"Who's the woman in the mural?" Ranjit asked.

Raven stopped herself from speaking and watched Ms. Tengos touch the picture, her eyes glazed over as if in a trance or lost in a memory. Her hand wasn't penetrating the painting.

"You can't go through," Raven whispered.

Ms. Tengos shook her head. "Sometimes magic is cruel and ironic. It's Agatha, of course."

"I guess I should've known that. Why can't you go through?"

"If Agatha can come through," Ranjit said. "Doesn't that mean there has to be a painting on her end?"

Raven glanced at Ranjit. "Good question. Wait, *can* Agatha come through? Who painted it?"

Ms. Tengos nodded. "All questions for another day. We have a bigger issue at hand. I think Rosie took one of Nanny's paintings. Nanny will have to do a proper inventory to know for sure."

"But, why?" Raven asked.

"I'm not sure. There are other forces at work here."

"Like the wards?"

"So much more than just magic."

"Are those clothes for Agatha?" Ranjit asked.

Ms. Tengos looked at the clothes. "Yes."

Raven looked at the outfit, then caught a reflection in the pile of clothes. "Is that a cell phone?"

Ms. Tengos nodded. "So she can call me or Nanny when she comes through. You both know time is limited. She's able to control it, but still..."

"Then why the clothes?"

"We never know how long she'll have. She likes to see the town, her creation."

"Why doesn't she just take them with her?"

Ms. Tengos shrugged.

"Wait, why is this a secret?" Ranjit asked. "Shouldn't she be coming to your magic classes and meeting the students?"

Ms. Tengos stared at him. "It's best people don't know about this magic. Imagine if the government knew? You see, Ranjit, you went through, and you're not a witch. I don't want anyone to know that, okay?"

"Are there any other girls with Nanny's gift?"

"We've found a few over the years, but none with as strong a power as Nanny."

"Wait, if Nanny can't go through, who painted the mural in the 1700s? Did she have someone take her back in time to paint it, like Raven took me?"

"Not today, Ranjit." Ms. Tengos rose and ushered them out of the room and locked it back up. They left the Witchery together. Dark clouds churned in the distance. "You two had better get going before you get caught in the storm. We'll discuss this later, after I've had time to process."

Ranjit started to respond, but Raven put a finger to her lips. "Let's go to my place and sit out the storm. Daisy Mae, let's go!"

Thunder rumbled in the background, and lightning flashed in the distance.

CHAPTER 9

They ran the short distance to her house and stepped inside just as the rain started to spatter. Heavy drops plinked like stones against the windows.

They sat in front of the bay window in the living room, looking over the backyard and lake. The rain came down harder. Thunder cracked above them, and the house absorbed the storm's vibrations.

Raven held out her hand and spun a storm spell. She'd been able to see spells as she and any other witch spun them for as long as she could remember. It was her gift, *sua potentia*. The spells were like balls of electric yarn, colorful and vibrant, twisting and turning until ready to be cast. If she didn't understand a spell, she could touch it and absorb its essence. Raven learned at a young age, if she touched what she called "the witch's strand," she could step into the mind of the witch casting the spell. She could see the witch's problems, her fears, her desires.

This was helpful in her teaching. She could see if a spell was incorrect and by touching it before it was cast, she could tell the student exactly what was wrong and how to fix it. Raven could also "catch" a spell that was cast, as if she were catching a softball. She could let the spell dissipate or she could redirect it.

She studied the spell in her hand. It was writhing in anticipation of its purpose.

"Earth to Raven."

She let her spell dissipate and peered at Ranjit. "Sorry. Lost in my head again."

"Shocking."

The storm seemed to reach a crescendo. Thunder and lightning united like two lovers in their intensity. The rain curtained the landscape, disrupting the view of anything beyond it. The rhythmic beat of hail bouncing off the roof added to the cacophony.

Ranjit shook her by the shoulders. "Raven, snap out of it."

She looked at him. "What? Sorry, this storm. Don't look at it. Experience it with all your senses. Close your eyes and feel the vibrations of it in your bones. Let the sounds wash through you. We're connected to it, you know. Here, come with me." She stood up and held her hand out for him.

They walked to the patio door and stepped under the protection of the awning. The storm raged beyond. Raven tried a spell that would form a protective bubble around them, like a giant umbrella. She grabbed Ranjit's hand again and, knowing he'd protest, said over the din of the noise, "Trust me."

They stepped into the storm.

The rain pummeled them with dramatic force. Ranjit jumped back under the awning. "What the heck, Raven?"

She joined him, drenched. "Oops. I'm still working that one out."

She tried the spell again, going over it in her hands, touching the strands and trying to understand what she was doing wrong, knowing she was missing something.

Growing more confident, she cast the spell and stepped into the storm again. The rain pelted her.

"Dammit." She went back under the awning and sat down in a chair. Ranjit had gone inside, so she absorbed the sounds of the storm once more. Beneath the chaos, she heard the birds chittering in the trees, angry at the interruption to their day. The frogs, enjoying the splatter of the rain, knew when it was over, they'd dine on mosquitoes, fat with fresh blood.

As they always do, the tempest retreated, overtaken by the sun and the wind. Cicadas resumed their song, frogs croaked, birds tweeted, and the squirrels came down from the trees on their never-ending search for food. Raven felt the subtle transitions in her deepest self and was a little sad the storm had passed.

Ranjit came out holding a towel, his hair a disheveled mess. He sat next to her, eating an apple.

"Where's mine?" Raven asked, taking the towel from him and drying her face.

"Are your legs broken?"

She giggled. "No, just paralyzed by my failure."

Ranjit laughed. "Maybe you shouldn't take yourself so seriously."

"Want to go down to the lake now?"

"Why not? We're already soaked."

They took their shoes off and walked barefoot to the dock. They sat on the edge, the damp wood soaking through their jeans, feet dangling just above the water. Ranjit was taller, so he kicked water at her.

Raven chuckled. "I don't think you can get me any more soaked than I already am."

He smiled. "Just a little payback."

A rainbow peeked from behind the retreating clouds. Raven nudged Ranjit and pointed to it. "Beautiful, right?"

Ranjit nodded.

They watched the life by the lake go on around them. Time seemed to stand still and move quickly all at once. She loved sunset by the lake, the way the pastels blended together as they coalesced into the close of day. It reminded her that no matter what she did, it would all blend in the end as a beautiful swirl of color.

Ranjit elbowed her. "What's going on in that brain of yours?"

"I'm just enjoying the sunset. Those colors, they're like the music of the sky."

"You're so poetic."

"Thank you. Wasn't that a spectacular display of nature? A perfect way to spend an afternoon?"

"It was pretty cool. I'm not sure it beats time traveling through a painting, though. You know you check out when there are storms, right?"

She lay back on the dock and closed her eyes, enjoying the last of the day's sun. "I do. It's important to connect with nature. It's a reminder to just take a step back from our everyday nonsense and reconnect with what's important. Even squirrels take a break. Be more like a squirrel, Ranjit. Our time traveling experience isn't going anywhere."

Ranjit lay back next to her and took her hand. "If you say so."

"Have you asked Stephen yet?"

"No, I can't get up the nerve."

Raven rolled her eyes. "The concert is going to be here before you know it. Do you want me to ask him for you?"

"Have you told your dad and Nanny?"

Raven didn't respond.

"The concert is going to be here before you know it. Do you want me to tell *them* for you?"

"Don't be such a snark. But maybe we should consider it. A loose version of *Strangers on a Train.*"

Ranjit laughed. "Nothing at all like *Strangers on a Train.* But you might be onto something."

"We could just sneak off to Atlanta, leave a note."

"Not a brilliant plan, but we could. Who are you going to bring? We have four tickets."

Raven shrugged. "I probably won't ask anyone until I've told Nanny. Maybe she'll want to go. Maybe she'll *insist* on going."

"We have to have this done by the end of the weekend, okay?"

"Fine. I want you to be there when I tell her. I think she's more likely to agree if you're there."

"Shake on it."

Raven hitched herself up on an elbow, held out her hand, and they shook. "Have I ever told you, I'm a conduit for all the elements? I think that's why I'm so connected to storms."

"What does that even mean?"

"Nothing can block my powers. Most witches have only one element. To use magic, we need all four. Ms. Tengos's element is fire, so as long as she has the other three around her, she can be the conduit for fire. Nanny is water. It's not really a big deal anymore because we have access to all the elements all the time. But the one thing I remember from my history classes is that during the witch trials, they didn't allow fire in the prisons, to keep the actual witches from escaping. The vampires used witches to put wards up around the prisons to prevent magic."

"How could they do that?"

"They would threaten the witch's family to manipulate them."

"Jeez, is that what's going on with Rosie?"

Raven shrugged. She had a hard time buying into the fear and drama Nanny and Ms. Tengos held toward the vampires.

The rainbow was gone, and the last rays of the vanishing sun twinkled off the surface of the lake, creating prisms of light that bounced around like little stars.

She sat up, conjured a fire, and let it float in front of them, over the water. "I wish you could see what I see when I conjure. It's even more beautiful than a storm."

"Must be pretty special then."

She spun another fire spell and let it marinate in her hand. "My primary color changes depending on the spell I'm spinning up. So, this spell in my hand is for fire. My primary color is red. Give me your hand."

"What? Why?"

"Just give me your hand."

He hesitated, then sat up and gave her his hand.

She put it on the spell resting on her own. "Can you feel that energy?"

He shook his head. She took his index finger and put it on the red strand. "What about now? This is me, my essence."

He pulled his hand back. "Did you feel it?"

"I felt something. It was weird. Kind of like going through the picture."

"Interesting."

If she conjured a storm, her strand was blue; a spell that pulled from the earth turned her strand a vibrant green and one that pulled from air was yellow. She knew this was unusual and had asked Ms. Tengos about it. "Ms. Tengos called it basic. I'm a Basic Witch. Sounds insulting, right?"

Ranjit laughed. "Really? Basic?"

Raven blushed. "Maybe it's a language thing."

"Maybe. Can I call you BMW? Basic Mother Witch?"

She punched his arm. "No."

"Sorry, it's just so funny after what happened earlier—when you totally failed to make that protective bubble."

"It has to do with the purity of the elements or something. I can control all of them at the simplest level, elemental or something, I don't know. A witch needs control of the elements to create magic. In order to control the elements, we need access to our base element, but since all elements are my base, I always have magic. Ms. Tengos said this was a problem in the *old days*."

"How do you determine what your element is?"

"It's based on your zodiac sign."

"Wait, what? Then how are you all the elements?"

"Well, Nanny and Ms. Tengos told me that some Pisces have traits of all the signs because they are the end of the zodiac, including all the elements."

"Can you pull fire from electricity?"

Raven shrugged, "Probably. Want to find out?"

"Let's not."

Raven laughed. "Don't you trust me?"

Ranjit glanced at her. "No offense, but I definitely don't trust you."

"Nanny is home. Should we—"

"How do you know she's home?"

"Witch's sixth sense."

Ranjit rolled his eyes. "Okay, let's get it over with."

They got up and walked back to the house. Nanny was in the kitchen putting away groceries. Raven and Ranjit sat at the island, and Ranjit said, "Hi, Nanny. Raven has something to tell you."

Nanny put a bunch of bananas in a bowl. "Does she?" She looked at Raven. "Out with it."

"Well, Ranjit and I have tickets for the Eras Tour in Atlanta."

Raven braced herself for the verbal beat down, but Nanny just took the green apples out of her shopping bag and arranged them next to the bananas. "When is the concert?"

"April 29th."

"Did you get a ticket for me?"

"Um, yes. I did."

Nanny stared at her. "Really?"

"I did. I figured you wouldn't want us to go unsupervised."

"Well then, we've only got two months to get ready. Ranjit, do you have someone you're bringing?"

"Stephen Halloway."

"But he's too chicken to ask him," Raven said.

Nanny nodded. "Well, you'd better hurry up."

Raven felt like she was bursting out of her skin. "Ranjit, go now. Find Stephen and ask him. Call me immediately or just come back over. I want *all* the details."

Raven forced him out, then hugged Nanny. "Thank you."

Nanny squeezed her. "You don't really have to take me. Don't you have someone you'd like to invite?"

"Nope."

"Okay. Then help me put the rest of this stuff away."

After the groceries were put away, Nanny said, "Let's sit outside."

They walked out to the patio and sat under the awning.

"I have more good news for you," Nanny said.

"Really? What?"

"I'm going to New Orleans to help Martha pack up some of her things during spring break. I thought you might like to visit New Orleans and see Tulane. That's where your mom went to school, you know?"

"I know. Martha mentions that every opportunity she can. Can Ranjit come? He was supposed to meet his parents in London, but they backed out. He's pretty bummed."

"Of course. Martha will have a conniption fit, but we don't have to tell her."

Raven laughed at the thought of how mad Martha would be to see her and Ranjit. "Thanks, Nanny. That will be so fun!"

Her phone buzzed. She looked down at it. "Well, Ranjit has a date for the concert."

CHAPTER 10

A few days later, during a harrowing class with the little witches, Caroline's gift of defying gravity revealed itself and she spent most of the class floating and giggling.

"Look at me, Ms. Raven! I'm floating!"

This wasn't an uncommon occurrence in class, though this was the first time Raven had seen anyone float and all she could think about was Pennywise encouraging his victims from the storm drains with, *We all float down here.*

She shuddered at the thought.

A week after she finished reading *It,* she'd started seeing red balloons around town. She'd been eleven and had enlisted Ranjit to help her find Pennywise.

"Ranjit, it's real. Pennywise is real. We have to find it and kill it."

He'd laughed, and she glared at him. "Oh, you're serious?"

Raven had collected the red balloons and had them in her closet. She'd tried to put on a brave façade for him, but was truly terrified. She found another one in the Witchery and showed him. "I have three more of these at home. Children are going to disappear. We have to do something. Let's go back to my house. I want to map out the locations where I've found them."

They walked to her house. She got the balloons from her room and a sizeable piece of printer paper to draw out a map.

Nanny came in as they were creating the map and saw the balloons. "I was wondering what those balloons were for."

Raven and Ranjit both stopped what they were doing and looked at her. "What do you mean?"

"Martha has been hiding them around town."

"What?!"

"Well," Ranjit said, "at least there's not a child-eating monster in town."

Raven flushed with anger at the memory, then was pulled back to the present by Caroline yelling.

"Ms. Raven, I can't get down!"

She was nearly to the ceiling. Raven twirled up a magical rope, lassoed Caroline around her waist, and pulled her down.

"You be careful with this, or you'll end up in outer space!"

She thought that was a pleasant note to end class on and excused the little witches.

She'd seen plenty of gifts manifest themselves. Girls who could converse with animals. Converse with the dead. Some were painters like Nanny, but none could paint pictures used for time travel. Ms.

Tengos's gift was telepathy. Raven learned early on it was no use lying to Ms. Tengos because she really did know everything.

Raven had yet to find another like herself, a witch that could see, touch, and manipulate spells *and* have power over all the elements. She laughed as she thought she had the market on being basic. She didn't know what Martha's gift was. Her sister was so anti-witch she wondered if she had one at all.

She walked into the art room. Ms. Tengos and Nanny were staring at something on the desk. Graphic pictures of dead people.

"What are those pictures, and why do you have them?" She saw the folder on the desk next to them with her name on it, the .note still in place. "You left those for me to look at?"

Nanny and Ms. Tengos exchanged a look. Ms. Tengos gave a slight shrug of her shoulders. "Not my best decision."

"You think? You could have at least given me a head's up."

"I'm sorry. But here we are, and this is something you need to learn."

"Remember Fala?" Nanny asked.

"Yes, the Choctaw witch?"

"These are police photos," Ms. Tengos said. "Murder victims."

"Gross, why do you have them?"

"Fala finds the killers and determines if they're vampires."

"How does she do that?"

"She can put herself in the body of a bird," Nanny replied.

"She's even cooler than I thought. So, what does she do? Fly around and watch the killers?"

"That's exactly what she does," Ms. Tengos said. "If they're vampires, we kill them."

"What are these in the pictures?"

Nanny took two of the pictures and put them side by side. "Which one is the work of a vampire?"

Raven studied the graphic pictures and felt her stomach churn. She took a deep breath and looked closer. One was a woman in an alley behind a dumpster. Her head was at an unnatural angle, and she was badly decomposed. The other was also a woman in a shallow grave in a wooded area. Her throat was slit. She was naked, her skin caked in blood.

"I would guess the one with all the blood is the vampire's work."

Ms. Tengos shook her head. "You would be wrong."

Raven looked at the pictures again. She pointed to the woman without blood. "What's the sign it was a vampire?"

"A vampire's bite is poison as well," Nanny said. "The effect is this rapid decomposition of the body. Also, the lack of blood on the victim is a sign there is no blood left. Most vampires won't leave a bloody corpse. If they're feeding, they will suck it dry. We often find their victims with broken necks. It doesn't seem to be intentional, more a consequence of their bloodlust. Also, a vampire won't take the time to bury a body. That's likely a human trying to hide the evidence, if you will."

"What will you do to the killers that aren't vampires?"

"We'll send an anonymous tip to the police or FBI and let them handle it."

"That's dumb. You should kill them, too."

"It's not our way to take the lives of humans."

"Even if they're mass murderers?"

"Yes."

"I still think that's dumb. How many people do they kill between the time you report them to the police and when they get caught? What's that word... vigilante? Be a vigilante."

"Don't you need to pack for New Orleans?" Ms. Tengos asked.

Raven gave up her cause for vigilantism and went back to being a teenager. "Yes. I've got to find Ranjit."

PART II
THEN

AGATHA – A WITCH'S LOT

CHAPTER II

Agatha sat in the corner of the cell, head buried in her skirts, and sobbed.

A woman in the cell next to her spoke. "They did the same thing to me." The sound of a kind voice caught her attention, and, for a moment, she lifted her head and looked at the woman.

"Pardon?" Even in her devastation, the societal pressure engrained in a woman from birth to be polite came through.

"They did the same thing to me. Those two men. They'll die for their actions. I promise."

Agatha tried to focus on the words, but only heard *men* and *die*. She glared at the other woman and tried to unjumble her head.

"Come over here to me." Agatha pulled closer to the wall and away from the stranger. "It's okay. I'm not going to hurt you. Come here and give me your hand."

Agatha didn't want to touch or be touched, but she eased further out of her mind and looked at the woman beckoning her, testing her own mental stability.

She had long dark hair, and her skin was a beautiful olive color. It looked like she had blotches of dirt on her face, but it may have been the creepy shadows. Her eyes appeared black as coal in the dark cell. Her hand reached through the bars, fingers wiggling. "Come here, it's okay." Agatha noticed a strange accent.

She uncurled herself, scooted out of the corner, crawled across the disgusting floor, and sat next to the woman.

"Take my hand. It's okay."

Agatha, unable to meet the woman's gaze, raised her hand and did as she was told. A charge ran through her fingers as they touched. Literally shocked, she stopped crying and looked her neighbor in the eye. *You're a witch,* she thought.

"Yes. I'm a witch," her neighbor said, and squeezed her hand.

You can hear me?

"Yes, I can hear you."

Agatha held the woman's hand like it was a tether to her sanity. She leaned against the bars and realized what she'd taken for dirt was, in fact, a giant bruise marring the lovely face before her. Closing her eyes, she let sleep take her.

As she woke, she was in the groggy state between slumber and wakefulness, absent of problems, stress, and trauma. Waking life bled into sleep's bliss of forgetfulness, and the physical discomfort she felt sitting on the damp floor of her cell was confusing at first. Then it all came rushing back. Her stomach lurched, and she spewed yellow bile all over her skirts.

This started another round of tears. She couldn't even wipe her mouth. She leaned against the bars again, exhausted, drool falling down her chin. The other witch's hand was in her hair, stroking it through the bars, her touch still electric.

"I'm so tired of men," the woman said. "All they want is power. Those two bastards who violated us had nothing, so they took what wasn't theirs to create a false sense of pride and ownership. The power they thought they had over us made them feel like kings when they're nothing but common thieves. They kidnapped us—and probably many other women—and sold us like slaves to the jailer who had power over them because he was the one with the money. But he got that money from someone who has power over him and up the chain it goes.

"They have nothing of their own, so they steal women's bodies and use them for their pleasure. They're probably spending all the money they made on us in the pub. Once their hangovers wear off, they'll go back to feeling like the little trolls they are until they find another woman to kidnap and rape. Make a little money. The cycle continues.

"I'm only twenty-two, but I feel like I've lived a lifetime. So many men have used me as those two monsters did. I lost count. This new world, a change of scenery, a new life. I thought the madness would stop. But evil resides in the hearts of men everywhere."

Agatha realized her jaw hung slightly ajar as she listened to her neighbor's rant. She had no idea how to respond, so she said the first thing that came to mind. "Your powers don't work either?"

"No, they don't. There are wards in the prison to prevent us from using them."

"Wards?"

"Yes, they can't have us using our powers to escape."

Agatha's heart sank, and a fresh round of tears started.

"By the way, I'm Morgana."

"Morgana. That's a beautiful name. I'm Agatha."

"I know you must be in great pain. It's not physical, but feels like your soul is trapped in a deep well, unable to function."

Agatha sniffed. "Yes. I feel like there's a very heavy cloud wrapped around my mind."

"It's worse than any physical pain and there's no relief. At least for bodily pain, there are medicines and tinctures."

Agatha nodded and felt the hot tears warm her cheeks. She dozed off again. Morgana was there when she woke, stroking her hair and whispering soothing words in a strange language through the darkness.

"They did this to you, too," Agatha said. "How can you be so calm?"

"This was not the first time."

"That bruise on your face? Did they hit you?"

"Yes. They'll suffer for what they've done."

"My husband. How can I ever face my husband again?"

Morgana squeezed her hand. They sat in silence for a while, and Agatha tried to push the thoughts of James away. Her anxiety was palpable, and she didn't know what to do with the flood of feelings passing through her mind.

"I'm from across the ocean," Morgana said. "Poland. I was in prison there, too."

"Did you have your powers while you were in that prison?"

"Not at first. I was there for some time before I could use my powers and escape. From what I've pieced together, the vampires use witches to put wards around the prisons to prevent us from using our powers."

"Why would a witch agree to that?"

"Because the vampire threatens to kill her family if she doesn't. They keep fire out of the prisons too, as a fail-safe. We need fire, or a guard. I can manipulate the mind of a guard to bring fire."

"What do you mean, manipulate the mind? How can you do that if you don't have your powers? What's a vampire?"

"It will be easier if I show you." As she held Morgana's hand, Agatha saw into Morgana's mind in a detail so intricate Agatha could feel this witch's experiences like her own. She saw the massive hunt for witches in her country and the devastation it caused for families everywhere. The loss of Morgana's husband and child brought tears to Agatha's eyes. Instinctively, she rubbed her belly.

She saw Morgana accused of being a witch and the prison she was in for nearly a year. Human prisoners escorted out of the jail and later returned to their cells, dead and decomposing. This was "proof" they were witches and had been consorting with the devil.

Morgana let Agatha's hand go. "Cassius is responsible for those dead people. He would take them out to the woods to hunt them and feed on their blood, then bring their rotting corpses back to the jail. This is what he did to my husband and our child."

"He fed on their blood?"

Morgana nodded. "This is the nature of the vampire. Give me your hand again, and I'll show you how I killed him."

Agatha let Morgana take her hand and saw Morgana use her telepathy to manipulate a guard to bring fire into the prison. Cassius walked with the guard past Morgana's cell as the guard lit his pipe. The moment there was fire, Morgana conjured a stun spell and hit the vampire with it, freezing him in his tracks.

The guard realized his error and looked at his pipe like a lover who had betrayed him. Before he could react, Morgana blew out the bars from her cell with such force he was impaled by one. His pipe dropped to the ground, the tobacco glowing as it scattered on the dirt floor. She stepped into the debris, stared at the still-living guard, and kicked him in his privates. Then she spat in his face.

She looked around for a weapon, saw an axe, and summoned it. Grinning at the vampire, she said, "Remember me?" In seconds, the axe sliced through the air, cutting right through the demon's neck. The head sat in place with a stunned expression fixed on its face. The thin red line across its throat was the only evidence of her act.

She tapped the head with the axe to make sure it was severed through, and it tumbled to the ground. The body stood for a moment, unsure how to proceed without its head, then glowed an eerie yellow color from the inside. She stepped back, not knowing what to expect.

As the body lit up, the head exploded into ash. The body looked like an oblong sun with legs, quite beautiful really, and then it, too, burst into what looked like a million shining stars, and was gone, as if it never existed.

Agatha pulled away. "Was that real?"

Morgana nodded. "That was a vampire. They have senses like wild animals, hunt like wolves, and have the strength of a bear. They feed on humans and drain them of their blood. A witch's blood is poison to the creatures and our scent is repulsive."

"You refused to put the wards up? So that's why it killed your family?"

Morgana nodded. "He found another witch to put up the wards and threw me in prison to rot. Likely a monster will show up here hoping to hunt one or both of us. It's best if we can escape before it comes. It'll be angry we're both witches and may kill us for sport. Do you know where the jailer is?"

"No."

"I've only seen him twice. In Poland, there was always someone around. But our town was much bigger."

"Wait. I've never seen or heard of these vampires. They exist everywhere?"

"I think they do. I've met and killed quite a few since Cassius, but all in Europe."

"Morgana, is that your gift? To get into the minds of others?"

"My gift?"

"Your gift. Mine is communicating with animals."

"I don't follow. What do you mean?"

"*Mea potentia*. All witches have a special gift, something specific to them. We all have our powers and magic, but we also have our gifts. You showing me what's in your mind and being able to influence the guard has got to be magic, right? If you can do that, we can figure out a way to our freedom. Maybe I can get a rat or a bird or something to help."

"Wait, you talk to animals?"

"That's what you took from everything I just said?"

Morgana looked at her and smiled. "Where should we start?"

"We have everything but fire. Can't wait for someone to come; we could be dead before that happens."

"Could you have a bird bring us a burning stick or something? All I need is a spark."

Agatha's face lit up. "I bet I could." She glanced around at the windowless keep. "Let's see if I can summon a rat."

She tried every spell she knew to call some animal to her aid, but to no avail. She didn't know how much time had passed, but she was exhausted.

"I haven't seen a sign of life in here since I arrived," Morgana said. "Vermin were rampant in my other prison. Prisoners ate them if they could catch one, out of sheer desperation. You should rest. We can try again later."

Agatha nodded. "Did I understand you? The witch hunts were brought on by the vampires so they could have a steady stream of food without raising suspicion?"

"That's what I witnessed. That's why I'm alive. At least where I'm from, they weren't interested in real witches, so we were just stripped of our powers and left to die."

CHAPTER 12

Agatha woke to a tickle on her leg. She looked down and saw two rats. Their paws were raw and bloody, but next to her lay the remnants of a burning stick. It was still hot to the touch, and she wasn't sure if it would work. She picked up the rats and cradled them in her arms, petting their heads, thanking them.

"Morgana," she hissed. "Wake up, Morgana!" She put the rats down, reached through the bars, and grabbed Morgana's hand. It seemed like an eternity had passed since she'd been in this version of hell. There was no way to tell the passage of time.

Morgana startled when she grabbed her hand. Her eyes grew wide. "How?"

Agatha showed her the injured rats. "My rats came through for us. They had to dig their way in. See if it works."

Morgana stuck her hand through the bars and touched the charred wood with her index finger. The wood glowed and then a flame bloomed like a phoenix rising.

Morgana looked up. "And then there was fire."

Tears welled in Agatha's eyes. "We have to heal these little rascals before we do anything, okay?"

Morgana stuck her hands through the bars. "Give me one."

Agatha passed one rat to Morgana and used the beautiful burning stick to summon her magic.

When they finished, the rats scurried off. "Should we fashion a key to let ourselves out?" Agatha asked.

Morgana looked at her and laughed. She blew out the door of her cell and stepped out, turning to grin at Agatha. "A bit more efficient and feels great."

Agatha laughed and followed suit. She felt invincible as the bars burst at the seams and crashed into the cells across from her.

Morgan looked at her. "See what I mean? Put that anger to good use. Let's get out of here. We might not want to make as big of a commotion leaving, just in case someone is out there."

Agatha gave the door a push, and it opened.

"Well, that was easy," Morgana said.

Agatha was delighted to see the sun falling just below the horizon. Still, after being in the dark for so long, the fading light was blinding. She closed her eyes and inhaled the freedom.

Morgana summoned a wind spell.

"What are you doing?" Agatha asked.

"Just making sure everything works. We have some payback to dole out. Do you want to go home to James and let me deal with those pigs?"

Agatha considered it. Until now, revenge wasn't a concept she understood. It would be hard to see the men who kidnapped and raped her. Getting home to James was all she could think about. But she thought about hurting those men, and excitement pulsed in her gut. "I want to make them pay."

Morgana smirked. "That's my girl." They headed to the only pub in town, where they guessed the pigs were probably still spending the money they'd made off the sale of the two witches. "Glamor me up. Like a prostitute. I'll go in and entice them out here."

Agatha couldn't face them in a public setting. Not that facing them in private was any better. She wove the spell and smiled as she transformed her new friend. Morgana's cheeks were the pale pink of roses, and her pouty lips the color of blood. Her hair shimmered like a lake in the moonlight and flowed down her back.

"One last thing." Agatha tightened up Morgana's bodice and gave her ample cleavage. "There. They won't be able to resist you."

"Good. Go into the woods and wait for me. Be ready, okay?"

Agatha hesitated, suddenly scared again.

Morgana took her by the shoulders. "You're going to be fine. This is the first step to healing."

Agatha nodded, then Morgana was gone. She was alone. Alone with her pain again. Alone knowing she'd have to face her attackers. She closed her eyes and tried to breathe, paralyzed with fear, as if a stun spell had been cast upon her. She heard Morgana in her head. *I've got them. Be ready.*

She saw them through the trees and gasped. How could Morgana do it? The two men followed Morgana like lost lambs who'd found their shepherd. Morgana laughed like they'd told her a joke. Agatha's guts twisted, pushing bitter bile into her throat. She swallowed hard and kept it down, resisting the urge to run away. Morgana caught her eye and gave the slightest of nods.

Agatha kept hidden in the trees as her new friend led the men toward her hiding spot in the woods behind the pub. Morgana said in her mind, *They think we're prostitutes.*

Morgana stopped once out of sight from the tavern. She shot the stun spell so fast Agatha didn't know what had happened. She struggled to move from the safety of the trees. Hiding was more pleasant than facing the men who had violated her. Morgana strolled over and pulled her from her hiding place to face the pigs who'd caused her so much shame.

Morgana spun a spell that removed the glamour from her face. She was now the bruised and battered woman they might recognize. "Take a good look, you trolls. Remember me?"

She kicked the tall one between his legs. Agatha saw the pain reflected in his eyes. Morgana peered at her. "Kick him again."

When Agatha's foot connected with his crotch, she felt a jolt of power. Pockmarks covered the short, chubby man's face. Drool made his pouty lips glisten. His cloudy eyes filled with terror as they caught the reflection of the fading sun through the trees. She moved to him and kicked. She kicked again, and again, and again. Gasping for breath, she felt the shattered pieces of her dignity reconnecting.

Morgana laughed a manic sound. "I warned you both about the dangers of fucking a witch. You brought this on yourselves, you worthless trolls." She looked at Agatha. "We need to get going. How do you want to punish them?"

"Isn't *this* punishment?"

Morgana shook her head. "This is healing."

Agatha pondered, and a smile found her lips.

They heard the rats before seeing them. The women stood and watched tears form in their rapists' eyes as the first rat crawled up the tall man's pant leg. A sea of chirping grey swarmed the men, and Agatha walked up to each man and spat in their faces. "Rats feasting on rats. I hope we were worth it, boys."

Morgana grabbed her arm and pulled her away. "Let's go."

They retreated further into the woods. Agatha paused. "The stun spell might wear off before the rats kill them. Should we release them, give them a chance to run away? Or should I call the rats off?"

Morgana stared at her. "After what they did to you? No way. Let your rat friends have the meal of their lives. But you decide. Better be quick though; they'll be dead soon."

Agatha remembered the men taking turns with her body. Disgusting sour breath in her face. Rotting, black teeth biting her breast. The pig-like grunting as they used her body for their pleasure. She hoped their deaths were long and slow. "Okay, let's go."

"Lead the way. Oh, I grabbed some bread from the pub." Morgana pulled two small loaves from her skirts and handed one over.

Agatha led them through the woods, chewing on the bread. "I think there's a stream up here. I need a drink and a little rest."

They walked in silence. When they arrived at the stream, Agatha asked, "How do I face James after what they did to me? How do you go on living with that horror?" Morgana took her clothes off. "What are you doing?"

"Washing that filth away. You'll feel better if you do it too. Trust me, the water is healing."

"Did you hear what I just said?"

"Keep living. What happened is part of who you are now. I know that sounds horrible, but it's the truth. What those men did to you doesn't define you, but it will always be with you. So, you live. When that anger bubbles to the surface, and believe me, it will, respect it, acknowledge it, and appreciate the strength you now have because of it. If you don't, they win."

Agatha was grateful for this witch. Morgana had saved her life. She still didn't know how she could face James. *I can cross that bridge when I get there*, she thought. After shedding her clothes, she followed Morgana into the stream. The water was indeed healing.

She stepped out of the stream and sat naked on a large rock, enjoying the warmth of the summer air against her wet skin. Morgana joined her. The sky was clear and full of stars.

"We have to leave town," Morgana said. "Tonight. Get as far away from here as possible. You realize that, right?"

"What? Why?"

Morgana took her hand. "Agatha, they arrested us as witches. We broke out of prison and killed two men. They might not connect us to that, but we can't take any chances. They'll hang us on the spot."

Agatha knew it was true, but didn't want to believe it. "I wish there was somewhere we could go and just be safe."

"Me too. My mother told me about this place in Bohemia, she called it *raj*. I think the English called it *paradise*. A magical place where everyone lived in harmony with each other and with the earth. I never understood the significance until I went to prison. People fear what's different, and Mother said this was a place without fear or greed or hatred."

"We should go there."

They sat without talking, the sounds of the woods surrounded them.

"Does James know about that boy growing in your belly?"

Agatha rubbed her belly, the slightest bump beginning to show. "No. I was waiting for the right moment. It's been three months, and I still haven't figured out how to tell him. Especially now."

"You've got a lot to deal with in the next hour." She stood and held her hand out.

Agatha grabbed it and stood up. "What are those marks?" She pointed to what appeared to be scars on Morgana's inner thigh.

Morgana looked down and touched the lines on her legs. "A reminder. You've got other things to worry about. Focus on James, not my leg."

"I'm not sure I'm ready."

Morgana put on her clothes. "Time's up. If you want to stay with this man, you've got to tell him. Get dressed and lead the way."

Agatha picked her dress up, slid it over her head, and picked up her shoes, not putting them on. "Do you know who accused you? My neighbor, Humility Parsons, accused me. She probably saw me in the garden talking to animals or creating tinctures with my herbs. They killed my pig." Her voice cracked as she said this, heat flooding her eyes. This was the first time she could grieve her little Moo. "They said she was here to do Satan's bidding through me. I had that pig since I was five years old. Saved her from a butcher's axe, but I couldn't save her from those savages."

Morgana stopped and looked at Agatha. "Show me where that bitch lives."

"We're almost there."

They walked further and Agatha pointed. "This is my home. Humility lives there."

"If James is half the man you say he is, he'll be nothing but thrilled you're safe." She leaned in and hugged Agatha. "You've got this."

CHAPTER 13

Agatha watched Morgana disappear. She walked up to a faint light coming from the kitchen window and looked inside. James sat at the kitchen table with his head in his hands. She thought he was crying.

Once she stepped inside, she'd no longer be able to pretend everything that had happened to her was a nightmare. It would become the new reality she'd have to introduce to her marriage. The thought of creating a new life without him tugged at her heart and she rubbed her belly. She didn't want his decision to be swayed because of her condition, so she'd wait to tell him—or not, if he no longer wanted her.

She forced herself to go inside. "James." He started when she touched his shoulder. "James, it's me."

"Agatha! Oh my God, you're here. I was so worried." He stood up and put his arms around her. She buried her face in his neck. He pulled away, and she flinched as he brushed her hair off her face. "What did they do to you?"

"You'd better sit down."

She sat across from him, took his hands in hers, and told him everything.

When she finished, he sat in silence. She wished she had Morgana's gift.

"Say something, James."

"You've had a hell of a couple of days. We're going to get through this. But we have to leave. Now. When they realize you're not in jail, they'll come for you. I can't have that. I've been fighting all day to get you free; no one would listen to me. They all believed Humility. Where is this Morgana?"

"She went to Humility's."

He smiled. "I like this woman. I'm going to get the wagon hitched and ready. Grab the things you want to take."

"James. Wait. There's something else."

"What is it?"

"I'm pregnant."

He beamed. "All the more reason to get out of here."

James disappeared out the back door. She went to their bedroom to put together her things.

Agatha looked around at what had been her home, so familiar, but now so different. The smells were overpowering, and the sounds were off their normal key. Maybe she was different and now her perception of everything ran through a filter that hadn't existed before. Her senses were sharper. Everything she perceived seemed to have an edge, like she was balancing on a knife's blade.

She went back to the kitchen and was gathering food when she *felt* her name and realized it was Morgana in her head.

Agatha, we need to go. The sun will be up soon.

MORGANA – DEATH OF A VAMPIRE

CHAPTER 14

Morgana, Agatha, and James had been on the road, heading south, for about a week when they came across a man in distress.

They traveled mostly at night, the days too hot for the women to stay hidden in the wagon.

It was dusk when the man burst through the trees. "Help! Help! It's coming for me!"

Morgana saw Agatha spinning a spell. "Wait. Let me deal with him. But be ready, okay?" Morgana approached the trembling, towering man with dark skin and rippling muscles.

He waved something in his hand, breathing so hard he had difficulty speaking. "Help me, please. I'm a free man. Here's my papers. The demon is coming for me."

"Give me your hand," Morgana said. He held his hand out and she touched it. "Show me this demon."

He only peered at her.

"In your mind, show me the demon in your mind."

Then she saw a beautiful woman. The image shifted and changed into the demon she was. Fangs. A vampire. Her first female of the species.

"Come with me." Morgana led him to the wagon. "James, give him some water. Agatha, come here."

Agatha hurried over. "He speaks the truth. It's a vampire hunting him."

Agatha gasped. "What do we do?"

"Stay here. I'm going to kill it."

"You can't go alone. Let me come with you."

Morgana pointed to her belly. "Keep your baby and yourself safe."

Morgana headed into the woods where the man had just come from. In Europe, she had learned a vampire had a nose like a dog and would smell her approach. As soon as she had that thought, she heard a hiss.

She had to act fast. While moving, she conjured a stun spell with one hand and summoned a stick with the other. It floated behind her, carving itself into a stake, wood shavings dropping on the soft bed of leaves. The last of the sunlight filtered through the trees, giving off an eerie glow. A light breeze rustled the woods. Morgana's senses heightened, *feeling* the vampire's presence more than seeing her. She had one shot and hoped the vampire wouldn't expect magic. She thought of her husband and child dying at the hands of Cassius. Her time in prison. Now facing yet another vampire, her first in the new world. Her anger intensified.

"Give him to me, witch," the vampire said. "He's mine. A runaway slave. You've no right to him."

Morgana had no response to the abomination standing before her. She sent the stun spell.

Vampires were fast, but Morgana's spell was faster. At close range, the vampire had little chance. She was a fly trapped in a spider's web. Her beautiful face froze mid snarl, the tips of her fangs hiding behind full, red lips. Long blonde hair swirled under her wide-brimmed hat. Morgana had to look up to meet her rage-filled green eyes.

As she knew she would, the vampire tried to enter her mind and get Morgana to release her. She learned of this ability in Europe during her prior kills, but because of her own gift of telepathy, was immune to this subtle power. She touched the vampire's hand, shocked to see this creature had lived for many centuries, maybe a millennium.

"He'll come for you," the vampire said.

Morgana took a step closer, about to drive the stake into her heart, but felt another presence. Like she was being watched. A slight resistance, as if someone or something brushed her arm. Morgana focused and plunged the stake into the vampire's heart.

She stepped back as the vampire's insides glowed. She'd been caught before in the explosion of a dying vampire, and while she was proud of her scars, she didn't care to have fire rain down on her.

Morgana enjoyed the spectacle of a vampire death, the initial glow as the internal organs heated like a kindling fire. The eyes came next. When they began to melt, the end was near. Usually there was a death scream when the internal organs exploded that echoed in her head long after the thing turned to dust. She took another step back as the glow intensified and the beautiful green eyes slid down the face like paint on canvas.

As the vampire before her went up in flames, Morgana felt an intrusion in her mind, a wailing inside of her head. Confused. Angry. Utterly devastated. She thought the vampire had entered her mind, but the fire disappeared. Ash scattered with the wind. The intruder slipped away.

The stake dropped to the ground with a soft thud, unaffected by the fire. Putrid smoke dissipated in the breeze. The shape of feet singed the earth. Morgana kicked at the leaves, dispersing evidence of the vampire's existence. There was no variation in a vampire's death. She often wondered what it was about vampire anatomy that caused such a display.

She picked up the stake and raced back out of the woods to the group.

Morgana found the man, who told them his name was Immanuel. "She's gone. We don't have to worry about her coming after us. Were there others that will come looking for her?"

Immanuel's demeanor relaxed when he heard the news. "I don't know if her partner will come. I don't think he was a demon like her, and he seemed sickly the past few weeks."

"Well, we should go. I don't want to take any chances." She looked at her friend, whose belly seemed to grow every day. "We need to find a permanent place we can settle before that baby comes."

"Immanuel, get in." James pointed at the wagon.

"Thank you, sir. I'm going north. I have family up there and that's where I was headed before Alma came after me."

"Can you tell us everything you know before you go?" Morgana asked.

Immanuel shared his story. He'd been a slave on a plantation in the Southwest Territory, called Stoney Ridge, his freedom purchased by a group of Methodist Missionaries. His master's decision to accept the missionaries' offer and grant his slaves their freedom had infuriated his only son, Seth.

"Master Seth was not a kind man, and his partner, Alma, was a living evil. I think Master Seth wanted to marry her. A match made in hell. Her lips looked like she painted them with fresh blood each day. It was rumored that if a slave went missing, Alma had made a meal of them."

"Alma," Morgana said. "Is that who was chasing you?"

Immanuel nodded. "Even though I was a free man, Master William, Seth's father, was kind, and paid us a fair wage, so I stayed on. I was one of the few. Then he died. I'm sure she killed him. I knew it was time to leave, so I went to say goodbye to Master William. He looked so…I don't know how to describe it."

"Withered?"

"Withered, yes, like a walnut. He'd only been dead a day or two. It wasn't right. I never felt scared in a church before. That's where his coffin was. But that time was spooky. The light in the stained-glass windows was all wrong. And when I saw Master William, it was too much. I ran outside and threw up. That's when I heard her. She stood in the church's door smiling at me. Her teeth were like spikes. My mother told me stories of the blood-sucking monsters when I was a child. I never believed they were real."

He paused and stared off into the distance.

"Run," Immanuel said.

"What?"

"Run. That was all she said to me. So, I ran for my life. Every now and then, I'd hear her laugh. I knew she was hunting me. Then I found you."

Morgana took in his story, grilling him for details about Seth and Alma. She wondered about Seth. She didn't have any knowledge of how vampires lived, more focused on killing them than extracting information. *Was Alma referring to Seth when she said, "He'll come for you?"*

After she made a few more stakes and insisted Immanuel take them with him, they said their goodbyes and continued moving south.

CHAPTER 15

That night, while Morgana thought the others were sleeping, she pulled out her dirk and pulled up her skirts.

She sliced a line across the top of her thigh and winced at the pain. After letting it bleed for a moment, she touched the open wound. "Alma."

Morgana concentrated on the kill and how it went down. She removed her finger to let her skin weep its bloody tears, then used magic to close it and seal in the memory.

"What are you doing?" Agatha asked. Morgana tried to pull her skirts down, but Agatha stopped her. She ran her finger over the scars. "What are they?"

"The vampires I've killed."

"You've killed eight vampires?"

Morgana nodded. "All in Europe—mostly Poland—until today."

"Why do you do it? It must hurt."

"I like the pain. I know that sounds weird. It's a reminder I'm still alive. The sting of the knife against my skin is a rush and I can feel the life inside me. I can see the life in me as my skin parts and blood flows. And I know this life is a gift I won't take for granted."

Morgana took Agatha's hand and pressed her finger on the top scar. "Can you feel it?"

Agatha pulled her hand away. "Cassius."

Morgana nodded, took her hand again, and pressed it on the next one.

"Marten?"

Morgana nodded. "I use magic to heal the cut and infuse the memory inside the scar. Can you see their deaths?"

Agatha nodded, and Morgana let her feel the rest of the scars.

"In my life before, when I had a husband and a baby, I took it all for granted," Morgana said. "I don't want to make the same mistake again."

CHAPTER 16

As they traveled south, Morgana kept occupied by fashioning stakes out of sticks and branches they came across. She made sure everyone was armed with plenty to spare. Morgana knew Agatha was a strong witch, probably stronger than she was, but her pregnancy made her vulnerable.

The memory of the intruder in her mind still rattled her. Someone was in there trying to stop her from killing Alma. That had never happened before. When she killed Cassius, no one seemed to notice when he was gone. The townspeople probably celebrated his disappearance. She hadn't stuck around after her other kills, but there had been no mental resistance.

Next night, Morgana told Agatha about the presence in her head when she'd gone to kill Alma.

"Do you think it was Alma trying to make you stop?" Agatha asked.

"If she'd been alive for a thousand years, she was a strong vampire. I was in *her* head. She tried to get into mine, but I'm immune, and this was different. I'm nearly certain it wasn't her. I just don't know. But it felt... like a man. And her words. *He'll come for you.* Maybe the presence was the *he.*"

"I know nothing of these creatures or the full realm of their powers. Obviously, they're not immune to magic. You say they can communicate through their minds, as we can. And maybe she summoned one of her own for help? Your stun spell only works on them physically, not mentally. If they have mental powers, we'll need to come up with a stun spell for the mind as well."

Morgana nodded. "If it was some other entity, how did he get in my head?"

Agatha shrugged. "Maybe because you have the ability. Or maybe this Alma simply had masculine energy and that's what you felt, her resistance."

"I guess that makes the most sense."

"Whatever that thing was, it's dead now. You killed it. And it doesn't look like there's anything coming for vengeance."

"I know, but I can't shake this...this feeling. We can't just brush this off and ignore it. I'd rather be paranoid and be right than think everything's fine and have some crazy vampire coming after us. If it were just me, I wouldn't care, but there's you, the baby, and James."

"You're right, let's just find our place to settle and figure out a plan."

"How are you doing?" Morgana asked.

Agatha took Morgana's hand. Agatha's lingering pain rushed through her like daggers to her soul. She wished she could take the burden of it.

"Don't you dare feel sorry for me," Agatha said.

CHAPTER 17

A few weeks later, they came upon the lake in what was then the Mississippi Territory. Morgana knew as soon as she saw it.

This was the place they would settle.

She stood with Agatha at the edge of the lake, the sky a collage of purples and pinks as the sun set behind the trees across the water. A great blue heron stood like a statue, one leg cocked, waiting for its prey. Fish jumped, ripples spreading out in perfect circles. A bullfrog croaked.

Morgana took Agatha's hand and squeezed it.

Agatha looked at her. "We're home."

James cut down trees while Morgana and Agatha used magic to build shelters that would eventually turn into their homes. Morgana insisted they put up wards to create a magic perimeter and fortify it from intruders, specifically vampires.

"How do we go about that?" Agatha asked.

"We have to set up some kind of boundary, at least around the houses."

"Didn't you say that vampires have to be invited into a home before they enter? We'll be safe inside our houses, right?"

Morgana nodded. "We could set up the town to be like our home, to keep the vampires out."

"The wards will have to be connected to each other, almost like walls of a home."

"This is new magic to me. Do you have any spells for something like this?"

Agatha shook her head. "We're going to have to figure it out."

CHAPTER 18

They created the magic that would fortify their new homes.

Morgana wanted to use the power of the sun, but Agatha wanted the energy from the moon. They agreed elements from both the sun and moon were needed to weave in the fabric of their spell, but they had difficulties getting everything just right.

"The moon and the sun will cross paths soon. An eclipse," Agatha said. "We can pull both energies at once."

"How do you know that?" Morgana asked.

"I chart the movements of the skies."

Morgana laughed. "Of course you do."

"I've been thinking about the Paradise your mother told you about. What did you call it? Raj?"

"Yes, Raj."

"What if we built it here?"

Morgana glanced at Agatha. "A place where witches can practice their craft without fear of persecution, from humans or vampires."

Agatha grinned. "Women can live without fear of men."

Morgana moved to her friend and took her hands. "What happened to us in Salem will *never* happen here. We will be the protectors of all women. We can make our paradise a place of healing." Morgana wiped a tear from Agatha's cheek.

Agatha sniffed and wiped her nose. "A school. We should start a school. We can take care of the broken, but teaching children to be good and free of prejudice and hatred will have value beyond measure. Don't you think?"

Morgana beamed. "I guess we'd better make this perimeter bigger."

"We should mark out the boundaries of what we expect this town to be five hundred years from now."

The witches fashioned a map of the area. Agatha drew a pentagram around the area they proposed to be their new home. She touched each of the five points. "The wards go here." She touched the center of the circle. "The school goes here."

Morgana studied the map. "That's pretty big. When is this passing of the moon and sun happening?"

"In the next few days. We'll have to have our spells ready; I think we're close."

"We've got our work cut out for us." She leaned over and hugged Agatha. "Let's head back and help James. We can probably get things done a lot quicker with magic."

Agatha laughed. "That's a fact."

That evening, James asked what they'd been doing all day. Morgana explained the idea of outlining the area they wanted for the town and how they would use it to keep the vampires out.

Then Agatha piped in about how they wanted to create a safe place for anyone, but especially those groups that suffered persecution—witches, slaves, and anyone else that came along.

"Agatha came up with the idea of a school where we can teach children respect for everyone," Morgana said. "A place without hatred and fear."

"You've been busy. That's quite a vision!" James replied.

"It is. Agatha is brilliant."

James put his arm around his wife. "I already knew that." He kissed her head and rubbed her belly. "Your first student."

Morgana laughed. "The pressure is on.

PART III
NOW

MARTHA – A MAN OF WEALTH AND TASTE

CHAPTER 19

"What are you doing here?" Martha was furious to see her sister get out of the car with Nanny.

Raven smiled. "Ms. Tengos and Nanny thought we should visit the big city."

"Did it have to be *my* big city? Who's we?" Then she saw Ranjit step out of the car. "Seriously?"

"Enough," Nanny said. "I've no interest in listening to you complain all weekend. Your father is stuck in Atlanta, and I thought you sisters could use some good bonding time. Now, let's look at your apartment and see what we can clear out."

"Fine." She led the way up the stairs to her apartment. The door was open, and Gretchen stood in the entry.

"Gretchen!" Raven cried as she sprinted up the stairs, pushing Martha out of the way, to give her a hug.

Martha clenched her jaw, stifling words that would get her in trouble with Nanny. Gretchen had taken a liking to Raven back when they were in high school. Martha wasn't keen on sharing anything with her sister, especially her friends.

They all went inside, and Nanny said, "Well, Martha, looks like you haven't done a thing."

Gretchen laughed. "Would you expect anything less from Queen Martha?"

"Gretchen!" Martha laughed. "That's why I asked you to come help." She looked at Nanny with what she hoped were pleading doe eyes.

Nanny ruffled her hair. "I know, child. We'll get this done in no time."

Gretchen smirked. "You have until June, so no rush."

Martha and Gretchen had been in this apartment for two years, and Martha had a way of collecting stuff. She wanted to get a head start on clearing out as Gretchen had someone taking over Martha's portion of the lease in June.

Gretchen grabbed her keys. "Raven, Ranjit, want me to show y'all around New Orleans? I don't want to be around for this debacle."

Martha wanted to vomit when Raven and Ranjit looked at each other in unison and said, "Yes!"

"Cool, let's go." She looked at Martha and Nanny. "Y'all have fun. Maybe we can meet up for dinner tonight?"

"That would be splendid," Nanny said. "It'll be lovely to catch up."

"Bye, Gretchen." Martha purposefully ignored Raven and her dorky boyfriend. She led Nanny to her room. "I guess we can start with my closet."

"Do you have any boxes?"

Martha grabbed the boxes she'd put on the balcony. When she returned, Nanny was conducting a magical orchestra of clothes. Martha sat back and watched. She looked at her own inept hands and felt a pang of sorrow she hadn't practiced magic more. Nanny finished in no time.

"Thanks, Nanny. I couldn't have gotten this done without you. Want to go for a walk and get some lunch? There's a cute café around the corner."

"Sure. I've worked up an appetite."

When they'd settled in their booth and ordered, Nanny said, "It's been a while since we've talked, dear. Tell me what's going on with you."

"Where to begin?" She sipped her coffee. "I broke up with Jake."

Nanny's eyes widened slightly as she registered the words.

She felt the tears welling in her own eyes as Nanny took her hands. "Oh, Martha, are you okay?"

The reality of what she'd done hit her head on. It was so easy to forget when she was busy with school and Thomas. Since his initial declaration of love, they'd been spewing it back and forth at each other like a tennis rally. She was disgusted with herself and loved it at the same time. She'd never felt so alive before. But in this moment, confessing her sins to Nanny, she felt ashamed of how she'd treated Jake.

"I met someone else. It just kind of happened." She looked at Nanny, wishing she'd tell her what a fool she was, but she only nodded.

The tears fell as she poured everything out that had happened over the past six months.

Nanny reached across the table and took Martha's hands. "Martha, I'm so sorry you're hurting. I have to ask, though. Are you really ready to give up Jake for this philosophy professor you haven't even known for a year? You and Jake have done so much to make things work. I'm not trying to sway you. I just don't believe you're thinking clearly right now. Jake is in Indiana; Thomas is here in your daily life. And have you thought about what you're going to do when you go to DC in the fall?"

"Nothing will change. Thomas says he can teach anywhere. I guess he's got plenty of money from his parents' estate or something, so that's not a problem."

"He's going to uproot his life in New Orleans and move to DC for a twenty-one-year-old student?"

Her words were a knife to Martha's heart. Fresh tears dampened her cheeks. "Jeez, Nanny. Do you have to be *so* honest? When you say it like that, it sounds ridiculous."

"It *is* ridiculous. If it were Gretchen in this situation, what would you tell her? I know it doesn't matter what I say. You have to figure this out on your own. And *that* is why I will always be completely honest with you."

Martha nodded. She wasn't sure what to think and wondered if she'd made a mistake breaking up with Jake. Maybe she should have let things with Thomas fizzle out.

Nanny interrupted her thoughts. "One more thing. It's never a good idea to jump from one relationship to another and not take any time for yourself. Even with Jake, you've had time apart. Your relationship has been tested and survived. Your time with this Thomas is a drop in the ocean compared to what you've been through with Jake. Sorry if I sound like a broken record, but my point is, how do you even know who *you* are anymore? Don't lose yourself over some man you barely know."

"That's a lot to think about."

"It's a major life decision, Martha. You're a grown woman now. Time to make grown woman decisions."

Martha nodded. "Adulting sucks." She sipped her coffee. "Do you want to meet Thomas?"

Nanny laughed. "Adulting does suck. And no, I don't want to meet Thomas. If you're still together this time next year, we'll celebrate right here in New Orleans. How's that?"

"That's fair."

Martha wasn't sure what she'd expected from Nanny. Maybe it was her brutal honesty. She had a lot to process, but she didn't have to decide right now, did she?

Their food arrived, and they dug in.

After eating, Martha said, "I won't be hungry for a while."

"Same. That's okay. I'm glad we had the time together to catch up. And Martha, please don't take what I said the wrong way. It doesn't matter to me if you're with Jake or Thomas, I just want you to do right by yourself. Okay?"

Martha nodded. "Thanks, Nanny."

"What's everyone doing for spring break?"

"Gretchen is going to Arizona, of all places."

"Oh, that'll be fun. What's Thomas up to?"

"Well, he invited me to his *hunting lodge.* It's near Natchez."

"Hunting lodge? Are you going to be hunting?"

Martha laughed. "I hope not. I'm not even sure what a hunting lodge is, but that's what he calls it."

"Sounds romantic." Martha gave her a look and they both laughed. "Look, Martha, if you want to spend some time with Thomas over spring break, I'm fine with that. I just want you to be thinking clearly about your relationships."

"Thanks, Nanny. I can still have some fun before I leave for law school, right?"

"Of course you can. Should we head back?"

They left the café and headed back to Martha's apartment.

"Oh, is my car ready?" Martha asked.

"Yep, it's ready for the long drive to DC. I almost let Raven and Ranjit drive it out here for you."

"What?"

Nanny laughed. "Just kidding. You're just going to have to come home with us to get it."

"That's the plan."

They got back to Martha's place, and Nanny said, "I'm going back to the hotel for a shower and a nap. I'll come back around dinnertime, and we can go out with Gretchen. Sound good?"

"Sounds perfect. I could probably use a nap as well."

They paused in front of Martha's building, and she gave Nanny a big hug. "Thanks for listening, Nanny. I needed your sage advice."

"You're welcome, dear. I'll see you later."

Martha went upstairs to her apartment and napped until Gretchen got back with Raven and Ranjit.

She woke and saw a text from Thomas wanting to know if he should come by or if she was too busy packing.

She responded, *Yes!*

Just seeing a text from him sent everything she and Nanny had just talked about out the window.

He responded, *Is your Nanny there?*

No, she's gone back to the hotel.

Oh, too bad.

You can come anyway and meet my awful sister and her friend.

He responded with a thumbs up.

Ten minutes later, he arrived at Martha's place.

She ran over and threw her arms around his neck. He nuzzled her ear. "Hey, baby."

"This is my sister Raven and her friend Ranjit. They've been stuffing their faces with beignets at Café du Monde."

Gretchen laughed. "I don't think they're going to be up for dinner tonight."

"Not so fast, Gretchen," Ranjit said. "I want to eat as much as I can while I'm here." He walked over to Thomas and shook his hand. "Pleasure to meet you, sir."

"It's so nice to meet you, Ranjit. And Raven, how good it is to finally meet you as well." He extended his hand to her, and Martha was horrified when she hesitated to take it. She gave Raven a look. She responded by quickly grabbing his hand and mumbling something Martha thought might be "Nice to meet you." Then she disappeared into the bathroom.

Thomas looked at Martha, obviously puzzled, and Martha said, "See what I mean?"

Thomas gave her the slightest nod. "Well, I just wanted to come by and say hello and meet Martha's family. I only have a few minutes. As always, I'm drowning in papers. I'm so sorry I didn't get to meet Nanny."

"Me too. She did all of my packing for me and needed a nap."

"Well, it was nice meeting you, Ranjit." He looked around, then yelled, "Bye, Raven, so nice to meet you."

"Sorry, she's just rude," Martha said. "And socially awkward. I'll walk you out." She took his hand, and they walked down to his black G-Wagon. "So, you still want me to come to your hunting lodge over spring break?"

"I do." He leaned down and kissed her. A chill ran down her spine as she pushed herself into him.

"I can't wait to get you alone. I've got to go home with them tomorrow, but I'll get my car and head your way as soon as I get all those boxes put away. Probably Monday."

"I'll be waiting patiently."

She kissed him again. "Love you, babe."

"Not as much as I love you."

"Happy grading." She kissed him one more time, then headed back to her apartment.

Raven sat at the bar in the kitchen with Ranjit eating beignets.

"What the hell?" Martha said.

"We got some to go," Ranjit said. "They're so good. Do you think Nanny knows how to make them?"

"You're swine."

Gretchen shot her a look. "Be nice, Martha."

"I feel dirty after shaking your boyfriend's hand," Raven said. "What's wrong with his fingers anyway? They're creepy. Why would you leave Jake for that guy?"

"Well, at least I have a boyfriend, twerp. And, for your information, he's got brachydactyly."

"Sounds disgusting."

"Your turn to be nice, Raven," Gretchen said. "Jeez, you two are really annoying to be around. And the man can't help it if he's got a birth defect."

Martha's phone buzzed. A text from Nanny. "Nanny is on her way back. Are you two going to eat dinner, or can we just leave you both here?"

Ranjit grinned. "My stomach is a bottomless pit."

CHAPTER 20

Nanny, Raven and Ranjit had stayed at The Chloe, and it was all Raven talked about the next morning as Nanny packed up her Bronco with Martha's stuff. She was sure it wouldn't have fit without Nanny's magic, especially with Raven and Ranjit in the back seat.

Raven said to Gretchen, "We had a suite and when we got back last night, our beds were turned down and there was chocolate on our pillows. Chocolate! We ordered room service this morning and they brought it in on a cart with a white tablecloth and all the food was covered with these silver dome thingies. Nanny, what was the thing in the bathroom called?"

"A bidet."

"Yeah, a bidet. It cleans your butt for you."

Gretchen laughed. "Thanks for the visual Raven. I know what a bidet is!"

"Raven, can you shut up already?" Martha said. "I get it. It's a fancy hotel. Get some culture." She hated the person she was around her sister, but she couldn't seem to help herself.

"Whatever, Scarface."

Nanny stopped what she was doing. "Raven! How many times do I have to tell you not to call your sister that?"

"Well, she has a scar on her face, so."

"Don't push me this morning. I'm not in the mood. Next time you say a word about Martha's scar, I'm going to take it personally. You make fun of Martha's scar; you make fun of mine." Nanny touched the scarf covering her own scar. "Are we clear?"

"Yes, ma'am."

Nanny rarely took Martha's side and by the look on Raven's face, Martha thought she was shocked, too.

Nanny went back to packing the car.

Martha just wanted to get on the road. She turned to Gretchen. "Have fun in Arizona. I wish I was going with you."

"There's still time, if you change your mind." They hugged. "Have fun with Dr. Hottie. But please don't do any hunting while you're there, promise?"

Martha laughed. "Pinky swear. I'll see you next week, right?"

"Before that, I'll Facetime you from the Grand Canyon. I'm going to need a break from Heidi's twins. I love them, but, well, they're kids."

Martha laughed. "Drive safe, friend. Tell Heidi I said hi."

"Will do. You be safe, too. Raven! Come give me a hug. Ranjit? Do you have a hug for me?"

Raven trotted over and threw her arms around Gretchen. "Thanks for everything."

Martha watched as Gretchen said her goodbyes. "Thanks for everything, Nanny. Good luck with this motley crew on the drive home."

"You sure you don't want to come along and keep the peace? I'll pay you."

"I'd rather deal with my toddler nieces than these two."

"Wise choice."

Martha trotted over to the Bronco and sat in the front seat. Everyone else was already in their places.

They drove away and from the back seat, Raven said, "What's with that guy Thomas? What about Jake?"

Martha turned around and glared at her sister. "First of all, my relationships are none of your business. But if you must know, Jake and I broke up."

"That guy is creepy. And he's so old. He's like, older than dad old. And his hands."

"Fuck off, Raven. And he is not. He's not that much older than me, actually."

"Martha Lee," Nanny said. "One more time and I'm going to hex your mouth shut. Apologize to your sister."

Martha hesitated, but Nanny slowed down and pulled into the Target parking lot. "I'm sorry for telling you to *fuck off*."

Nanny pulled into a space and put the Bronco in park. She turned to Raven. "Now you."

"Me? I didn't do anything."

"Raven. Apologize or you're *both* going to have a hard time talking for a while."

Ranjit elbowed Raven.

"I'm sorry for calling your boyfriend creepy."

"Thank you," Nanny said. "Now, I don't want to hear a peep from either of you. Like Gretchen said, you're worse than dealing with a couple of toddlers."

Nanny put the car in gear but paused. She looked at Martha. "What's wrong with Thomas's hands?"

"He's got a birth defect. It's called brachydactyly."

Nanny nodded. "He has both of his hands?"

"Yes. His fingers on one hand are stunted. That's what brachy-dactyly is."

Nanny pulled out her phone. "Can you spell it for me?"

"Why?"

"Never mind, I found it."

"Nanny, what are you doing?"

Even Raven had leaned forward to look at Nanny's phone.

Nanny put her phone back in the console and looked at Martha. "Is there any chance Thomas is..."

"Is what?"

"Never mind, for now. Before you run off to Natchez, let me do some research."

CHAPTER 21

Next morning at breakfast, Martha munched on some fruit with Nanny. "Can we go get my car this morning?"

"I forgot all about it. Let's get it now."

Martha laughed. "Can I at least get dressed?"

"Of course, but I need to get to school, so hurry."

"It's spring break. Why do you have to go to school?"

Raven came running down the stairs looking half asleep, Daisy Mae at her heels. Even though she was Raven's dog, Martha adored her. "Daisy Mae!" She jumped off her stool and got on her knees to play with the goofy basset hound.

"Martha, get moving and meet me at the car," Nanny said.

"Bye, sweet Daisy Mae." After giving the dog one more scratch between her ears, she ran upstairs and put on a pair of jeans and a

Tulane hoodie. She looked out the window and saw Nanny in the front yard talking to someone.

She sprinted downstairs to see who the mysterious visitor was, but she'd vanished.

"Where'd she go, Nanny?"

"Who?"

"The woman you were talking to. She looked like Mom. I thought maybe it was her ghost stopping by or something."

"Oh, Martha. No, if it were your mother, do you think she'd be here to see me?"

Martha laughed. "I guess not. Was it Agatha?"

"Get in the car."

They got in the car and Nanny started it. Then she turned to Martha, "It was Agatha. She comes to visit sometimes."

"Okay. Care to elaborate?"

"No, not now."

"You can be infuriating, you know that, right? Have you done your *research* yet?"

"No. That's why I'm going to school this morning. Don't go any-where until I tell you it's okay."

"What's this all about? Why all the mystery, just because Thomas has a birth defect?"

"Just be patient with me, okay? It's probably nothing."

CHAPTER 22

That evening at dinner, Nanny said, "Martha, I need you to hold off going to see Thomas for a few days."

"Why? This is ridiculous, Nanny. You said I could go."

"Can you just wait a few days? Will that kill you?"

Martha stared at her food and moved it around on her plate with her fork.

"Martha, answer me."

"Yes, ma'am."

"Yes ma'am, you'll wait a few days?"

She looked up and saw Raven smirking. She used her middle finger to scratch her nose and nodded. "Why can't you just tell me what's going on?"

"Give me a day or two and I'll tell you everything, okay?"

She nodded again. "May I be excused?"

"Yes."

Martha took her plate to the kitchen and dumped the uneaten remains into the trash before storming up to her room.

She flopped on her bed. "Hey Siri, play Taylor Swift." "The One" started playing and she instantly thought of Jake. "Hey Siri, pause."

Her phone buzzed. It was Thomas. *Hey babe.*

Even a text from Thomas didn't pull her out of her funk. What the hell was Nanny's issue with her going to Natchez?

She slammed her phone face down on the bed. Hot tears welled in her eyes. She felt like a petulant teenager. She was twenty-one and could do what she wanted.

Taking a deep breath, she went into the bathroom and filled the tub with steaming water and some ten-year-old Mr. Bubble from under their sink. She knelt beside the tub and stuck her hand in the water, her Scorpio nature refusing to let the heat beat her. She stepped in and submerged herself, her body absorbing the heat and clearing her head.

Martha knew Nanny wasn't trying to punish her or be malicious, but why wouldn't she want Martha to go to Thomas's?

She tried magic to summon her phone, but frowned at the clattering she heard in the bedroom. She submerged herself once more, enjoying the lightheaded feeling that came from holding her breath.

When the water cooled, she got out and dressed. Her phone lay on the floor next to her bedside table. She picked it up and was surprised she'd been in the tub for an hour. No more texts from Thomas. She needed to tell him she wasn't coming tomorrow.

She sat on the edge of her bed and decided maybe she *would* go tomorrow. What would it hurt if she snuck out before everyone was up?

Hey babe, when do you want me to come?

Three dots wiggled on the screen. *Yesterday*

LOL how about tomorrow morning?

Perfect. I'll send you the address later.

She packed a bag, hid it in her closet, and went downstairs.

Ms. Tengos was there with Nanny, watching *Breaking Bad*.

"I was going to see if you wanted to go to the movies with me," Martha said. "*Breakfast at Tiffany's* is showing. But I see you're pre-occupied with Walter White. Are you looking for a magical meth recipe?"

Nanny and Ms. Tengos shushed her in unison. She laughed at them, but they didn't notice.

It was a beautiful evening, so she walked to the theater. As she approached, she saw Raven and Ranjit buying tickets. What were they doing here?

One of her guilty pleasures was sneaking into the theater. Her *gift* was the one bit of magic she had complete control over, and she grinned as she walked right past the ticket window. The pimply teenager working at the window didn't even look up. Skipping the popcorn, she headed straight into the nearly empty theater. She sat behind her sister, hoping she could listen in on their conversation. Raven was going on about one of her students whose gift appeared in class. The previews started, and they fell silent.

Martha smiled. Her sister didn't even know she was there. She leaned forward and blew on the back of Raven's head. Her sister swatted at her hair and turned around. "What the hell?"

Ranji shooshed her, and Martha grinned.

After too many ads and previews, Audrey Hepburn appeared on the screen, walking the deserted, early morning streets of New York City, eating her breakfast, and gazing longingly in the window at Tiffany's. Martha had read the Capote book so many times she could recite it. She loved the perpetual loneliness of Holiday Golightly. The Holiday on the pages never gave up on her dreams. She traveled the world and stayed uncaged. She wouldn't give it all up for a man as she did on the screen

After the movie ended, she spotted Raven and Ranjit outside the theater. "Come on, Ranjit," Raven was saying. "She sold out for a guy. The only redeeming part of that ending is she gets Cat back. And she doesn't deserve him after she threw him out of the cab."

"It doesn't matter what you say," Ranjit replied. "No one can out-shine Audrey Hepburn. She brings Holly to life!"

"Oh really? I'm going to tell Jen Aniston you said that."

"You wouldn't."

They were headed home and Martha, bored with their conversation, went in the other direction, taking the long way. She wanted to enjoy the pleasant night.

When she got home, there were no signs of Nanny, Ms. Tengos, or Walter White.

She went up to her room to lie down and heard the bluesy sounds of the Rolling Stones playing in Raven's room. Ugh. They were

Thomas's favorite band. How could Raven have that in common with him?

Country music was her thing with Jake. He was like an old and favorite pair of jeans—comfortable and dependable. She wanted to stop thinking about him, but couldn't seem to do it. They had a rich history together and forgetting him would be like forgetting herself for all those years. She had no idea how to cherish the memories and let him go at the same time. Her heart panged with something.

Regret or excitement?

CHAPTER 23

Martha was up with the sun, left a note for Nanny, and hit the road. Nanny would be furious, but she'd get over it. She tried to focus on Thomas, but Jake kept creeping back in. This was the problem with being alone with her thoughts.

"Hey Siri, call Gretchen."

She hoped she wasn't on the plane yet. Martha was just about to hang up when Gretchen answered. "Hey, everything okay?" She sounded out of breath.

Martha chuckled. "Everything okay with you?"

"Yep. You couldn't have called at a better time. We're at the airport and both little Mona and Mary just had big meltdowns. You're my escape. What's up?"

"I'm driving to Thomas's. And I'm having all these thoughts about Jake. Did I fuck up?"

"I wouldn't say that. You just have to navigate life around the choices you make. Sounds like you need to do your pros and cons."

"I know. Great time to be worrying about my life choices. But, yes, pros and cons would be great. Do you have time?"

"We don't board for another thirty minutes, and this saves me from my demon—I mean *adorable*—nicces. Hit me, but please pay attention to your driving."

"Okay. Thomas, pro. He's established. Has a condo in New Orleans. A hunting lodge inherited from his parents. He's a professor. We share a love of philosophy—the ancient Greeks, in particular. We have the best conversations. He's so deep, and I love his mind.

"He's lived in New Orleans his whole life—but will move to DC with me, and he's never been married. Did I ever tell you he had a long-term partner who died? He won't open up to me about it, but I can tell he's still hurt by the loss."

"No, you never told me about that. Yikes. I'm not sure that's a pro. I'm also not sure that a man his age never being married is a pro either. Fear of commitment."

"Good points. Anything else?"

"The amazing sex should be a pro, right?"

Martha laughed. "Definitely. Okay, cons. I can't think of any."

"I just gave you two. Would you like me to add to my list?"

"Sure."

"You've not even been together a year. You think you know him, but how well can you know anyone in just six months? Also, when you're with him, you kind of lose yourself. It's like you're in a perpetual lavender haze, but you've been together too long for that. Where does the sex haze end and the actual relationship begin?" Martha thought about this. She didn't believe their relationship was all about sex, but Gretchen had a point. She suddenly felt sick. "You still there? I didn't mean to upset you if I did."

She saw a sign for a rest stop.

"No, let me call you back. I'm feeling sick. Pulling into a rest stop."

"I hope you're not pregnant."

"Why would you even put those words out in the universe? I'll call you back."

Martha opened her door and threw up. *Where did that come from?*

She sat in her car for a few minutes with the door open, waiting to see if anything else was going to come up.

Confident the vomiting was over, she got out of the car and walked around, hoping the fresh air would make her feel better.

Martha used the bathroom, then stopped at the vending machines for a water and a Coke, thinking it might settle her stomach. She sat at a picnic table and took a long sip. Once she felt better, she thought about seeing Thomas. Did her pros and cons list really matter? Thomas was all she cared about right now. But she did still have a slight pull of guilt for disobeying Nanny. This was shaping up to be a year of massive fuck-ups.

She drank the rest of the Coke, threw the can in the recycle bin, and got back on the road.

Gretchen called back. "Hey, you feeling better?"

"Yeah. I had a Coke. Think I needed some caffeine or something. I got sick. What if I am pregnant? That would really suck. Do you think I could sue my IUD company?"

"Let's hope it's just nerves. And no. I'm sure they have some sort of clause in there protecting them from those pesky unwanted pregnancies. Maybe Thomas has super sperm."

"Not helping, Gretchen."

"Want to give me your pros and cons for Jake? I'm boarding in ten minutes."

"Let's do it. Jake is at Purdue. I mean, couldn't he have stayed in the south for college? And he studies math and engineering. I hate math. We have little in common, except for music."

Silence on the phone.

"You still there?"

She heard Gretchen sigh. "A school in the south. Really? Maybe you could have gone to a school in the mid-west."

"I know, but I went to Tulane because my mom went there, and you're there, and it's still in the south. He could have gone to Vanderbilt or even Texas A&M. He was accepted to both."

"Purdue is one of the best engineering schools in the country. And he's from Indiana, for fuck's sake. You're really reaching here, Martha. If you don't want to do this, it's fine. Just go enjoy your time with Thomas. This conversation can wait until after spring break."

"Are you mad?"

"Of course I'm not mad."

"Okay, my heart's just not in this."

"Maybe that's all you need to know. Maybe you and Jake ran your course, and you just needed Dr. Hottie to see it."

Martha considered this. "Maybe. It would explain my ambivalence."

"It would. But that doesn't mean you should jump from Jake to Thomas and get all serious. Just see where it goes. I think Nanny was right about him not going to DC with you. By the way, American University is also not in the south. Jeez, Martha, that's weak. And you want to be a lawyer? You might never live that one down."

"I'm just going to have fun this week and see how it goes. Thanks for listening. Have fun and tell Heidi and the twins I said hi. Love you."

"Love you too, bye."

"Gretchen, wait."

"What?"

"I have something else to confess."

"Out with it. Let's wrap this up. I've got a plane to board."

"Nanny told me I needed to wait a few days before I left, and I left anyway."

Gretchen sighed. "This is what I'm talking about, Martha. You do stupid shit like this when he's involved. Look, I've got to go. What's done is done. Just go have fun, okay?"

CHAPTER 24

T he lodge was in the middle of nowhere. She turned off the main road and maneuvered her Fiat down several miles of dirt road lined with ancient looking tupelo and cypress trees. The road was littered with scaly cypress cones that crunched beneath her tires. Finally, Google announced she'd arrived. Thomas was waiting for her outside. She left her bag in the car and ran to this man she'd fallen so madly in love with, melting into his embrace.

"Come on, love. I have a surprise for you."

He led her inside and whisked her to his bedroom. On the bed lay two pairs of handcuffs. Her heart jumped, and she glanced at him. "Handcuffs?"

"I thought we'd have some fun this week."

She froze and instinctively put her hands behind her back. She wasn't prepared for this.

Thomas came closer and kissed her ear. "Are you afraid?"

Martha was helpless against him. "A little."

He smiled. "Good, a little fear turns me on. Trust me?"

Trusting him and letting him handcuff her to the bed in the middle of nowhere were pretty much mutually exclusive. But she brushed her nerves away. "Let's do it."

"This is going to be fun." He wrapped his arms around her and kissed her again.

He took his time undressing her, kissing her all over as he did. She moaned as his lips brushed across her skin. "Oh, God, please don't stop." He buried his face between her legs, and the release she felt was almost too much to bear. She collapsed on the bed like a rag doll. He lifted her limp body and positioned her at the head of the bed, snapping the handcuffs in place.

"I had these braces added just for you." He tugged the handcuffs.

She just smiled, not really hearing his words as she enjoyed her post-coital fog.

He stood and caressed her breasts. "You really are lovely."

Her phone rang, snapping her out of the sex haze. He pulled her phone out of her purse. "It's your Nanny, shall I answer?"

Martha looked at this beautiful man who took her to places she'd never experienced. Nanny would be worried; she should have texted her when she arrived. As she stared into Thomas's eyes, nothing else mattered but him. She shook her head, and he silenced the call and tossed her phone back into her purse.

Her head was still swimming, but she spread her legs instinctively, beckoning him. She looked at him again, wondering what the delay was, and realized he was still dressed. "Thomas. What are you doing?"

"I have one more surprise for you, love. I'll be right back." He disappeared behind a door in the panels of the wall.

Sensing something was off, she looked around the room. It was massive and manly. There were no windows in the room and the bed on which she lay was a canopy. Towering oak posts held it together. This room was nothing like his chic condo in New Orleans. On the wall hung disturbing paintings. They seemed Old Testament biblical, exuding suffering and death. Devils and demons feasted on sacrificial animals and people. It wasn't just the artwork, the *feeling* in the room was heavy.

Martha pulled at the cuffs. She remembered reading *Gerald's Game* and hoped Thomas didn't have a heart attack while she was handcuffed to the bed. She took a deep breath and tried to shake the weight of the air bearing down on her. But even thoughts of sex couldn't pull her out of her escalating fear. She tugged at the cuffs again, wanting to be done with this game. Terror slithered through her veins.

Thomas popped his head out of the door with a wide grin. "Look who I found creeping around your apartment after you left."

Martha saw who he had, then turned her head and vomited.

PART IV

THEN

MATHIAS – VENGEANCE

CHAPTER 25

The steady rhythm of the carriage wheels soothed the pain exploding in Mathias's mind.

He said to his driver and faithful servant, "What does mortality mean to you, Jesse?"

Jesse turned to look at Mathias. "Mortality? I'm not sure what it means."

"Oh, Jesse, I'll make a scholar of you yet. Mort is Latin for death. Mortality is an Old English—and perhaps French—word for a human. Basically, it's a descriptor for humans. You're all going to die, Jesse. But vampires, we can be immortal and live forever."

Jesse nodded. "I understand, sir. But you're going to see about Miss Alma, right? And she's dead?"

"Astute of you, Jesse, yes. How can someone who is supposed to be immortal, die?"

"I guess she wasn't immortal then, sir."

"You brilliant simpleton. That's exactly my quandary. Why has my immortal partner gone and gotten herself dead?"

Jesse only nodded.

Mathias shifted his attention back to the wheels grinding in the dirt and the thundering of the horses' hooves.

"You know, Jesse, I've been alive for thousands of years. Alma's death is a reminder of the fragility of our lives. Do you know we don't age and the only way for a vampire to die is by another's hand—or their own?"

Jesse turned again and looked at Mathias. "You mean a vampire can kill itself?"

Mathias nodded. "It's rare, but it happens. Eternity can be a long time for some, and the sweet promise of nothingness can be a stronger pull than going round and round on the wheel of life.

"If they go into the sun, will that kill them?"

"As we age, our sensitivity to the sun wanes, and it's no longer deadly, just uncomfortable, like a rash. Now, a young vampire could die from sun exposure, but mostly they're just maimed like a burn victim, and it rarely happens twice. We also have incredible healing abilities. So, if a vampire gets burned, the wounds will heal rather quickly. If you were burned in a fire, Jesse, your scars would be with you for life."

Jesse nodded at his master again.

Mathias continued. "However, there's no antidote for a stake to the heart, no cure for a puncture from silver, and no remedy for a beheading. When death comes, all the expired vampire's 'relatives' feel it. A disturbance in their minds, like the ripples from a pebble tossed into a lake. A direct parent or child feels the disruption strongest. But no matter the relation, the death of one of our own is an unsettling reminder of the fragility of life."

Alma's absence from the world was like a boulder in a puddle. First was the sharp awareness something was missing. Then the realization shook the very essence of his being. He'd lost many children over his long life, and he'd felt the agitation in his mind each time. But with all his loss, until now, he'd never experienced a physical pain so great it dropped him to his knees.

Jesse's voice brought him back to the present. "If she's dead, sir, then why are we going to Master Seth's plantation?"

"I need to know what happened to her. If I stand on the spot where she died, I can see her last moments."

"Your powers, sir, you have so many. I don't know what to say."

"Then say nothing, Jesse."

"Yes, sir. I remember Master Seth when he came to visit you. A real handsome one, that man."

Mathias sighed. He didn't want Jesse's banter for the long hours ahead. But it was better than being alone in his own head missing Alma.

Mathias remembered that visit as well. Seth had captivated Alma with his handsome looks and evil nature, but also his money. They'd met at a slave auction, and he'd taken to her immediately. She'd gone with him to Stoney Ridge, Seth's father's plantation, to see if it could benefit them. She'd seen the potential in bringing Seth into the family and adding his plantation to their already exorbitant assets.

Her flippant attitude and infatuation with Seth had stirred an ache in his gut, and he almost forbade it. He wasn't fond of sharing Alma, but didn't want his emotions to interfere with a good turning.

"What's it like, sir?" Jesse asked.

"What's what like?"

"Turning into a vampire."

Mathias thought about this for a moment. Jesse wanted to be a vampire, but Mathias knew he didn't have the mind for it. He'd likely go crazy. "The turning is a slow and delicate procedure. A vampire's bite is poisonous to humans and has the potential to kill them. My old friend Martin was bewitched by a young lady back in Cyprus several thousand years ago. Alma had only been with me for a short time. This young lady, I've forgotten her name, Mary, Mona, Magdalena, some holy M name. Anyway, Martin started the process, biting her and, without swallowing her blood, mixed it with his own saliva and blood."

"How did he do that?"

He remembered the first time he'd sunk his teeth into Alma's neck. The rush of her blood in his mouth. The rush of his own blood to his cock. His desire for her unbearable. He had to pull away without accidentally draining her or swallowing her blood. It had been torture.

"First, he bit her and took her blood. Then he spit it into a bowl or something, cut his own wrist and mixed his blood in with the changeling's blood. He had to do this at least once a day and feed it back to the changeling. This process—the blood loss—is draining on the parent as well. So we choose those who we want to join us carefully.

"The changeling is in a state of insanity and pain as they suffer through the physical and mental transformation from human to vampire. They require constant care and attention, like a human infant. They should simply wake up a vampire after three or four weeks. If they don't, as happened with Martin's lover, they have to be put down. Martin was devastated."

"Put down, sir? Like a horse with a broken leg?"

"He broke her neck. She was mad, her blood tainted and useless. Such a waste."

Jesse fell silent, and Mathias slipped back into his memories.

Alma had been persistent, and Mathias finally agreed to let her bring Seth south to his own plantation so the two could meet. Seth was everything Alma said. Although he showed the right amount of reverence—or perhaps it was fear—toward Mathias, he had a smarmy charisma that could charm the petticoats off the primmest of ladies. Physically, he had a strong build with sandy blond hair, a sly and crooked smile, and eyes as blue and deep as the sea. When Mathias looked into those eyes, he understood Alma's attraction and saw Seth's potential as one of his children.

He'd explained the process, then asked Seth, "Why do you want to become a vampire?"

Seth smiled his charming smile. "Immortality, of course."

Mathias had wanted to kill him on the spot. "Immortality is not guaranteed."

Seth shrugged. Alma started to say something, but Mathias threw her a look. She nodded and remained silent.

"Alma and I met in Greece, over two thousand years ago." Mathias paused and put his hands in his pockets to keep them from knocking Seth's head off. "We haven't lived as long as we have for the sake of living forever. In our time together, we've lost many children. So, eternal life, it's not a guarantee."

Mathias's fangs pulsed, and he'd ached to drive them into Seth's throat. He felt the cringe fly off Alma like a dagger. He took a breath and gathered himself, and he saw her face relax.

Something shifted in Seth's demeanor. Maybe he sensed the dangerous line he'd crossed. "My apologies, Mathias. I mean you no disrespect. I want to learn from you both. Expand my mind. I want to be like you."

Mathias wasn't fooled by Seth's flattery, but he'd appreciated the turn of attitude. He noticed the awe in Seth's eyes.

"Alma was the last vampire I turned. All these years, she's been enough for me. We're a team. We look out for each other." He paused and sipped his goblet of blood. "If immortality is your motivation, you're better off staying human."

Seth bowed. "Alma has shared the danger with me. I'm prepared to take the chance."

Mathias had sent him on his way and granted Alma the permission she'd sought. Now, she was dead.

The turn of the wheels brought him back to the present and the absence of his love. He punched the door of the carriage so hard his fist went right through it.

Jesse slowed the horses. "Everything all right, sir?"

"I'm fine. Just keep driving."

"May I ask you another question, sir?"

Mathias reached under the seat for the basket filled with port, cheese and bread. He pulled the cork out with his teeth and drank the port straight from the bottle. "Ask away." He handed the bread to Jesse. "You hungry?"

He took the loaf of bread and set it on the seat. "Thank you, sir. What's going to happen to Seth? Will you have to kill him?"

Mathias took another swig of the port and smiled. "I can take over his turning. Alma started the process about three weeks ago, so he's almost there. If he's not already suffering from Alma's absence, he will be soon. But I can make sure he gets through. I think I should let him live to honor Alma's memory, unless he's stuck as a halfling, then I guess I will have to kill him. What do you think, Jesse?"

"Seems like if Ms. Alma wanted him to be a vampire, you should finish it for her."

Mathias drank again, finishing the bottle. He tossed it out of the carriage, watching the shadowy countryside pass by, and breathed the crisp air. He took in the smells from miles away, among them humans. "Do you think this is all my fault, Jesse?"

"No, sir."

"If I had forbidden her from turning Seth, she'd still be alive. She'd be here, with me, not turned into a puff of smoke. I'm not against taking the blame. I haven't been alive for as long as I have for shirking my responsibility."

"Sir, I don't think there's any way you can blame yourself for this."

"Want some port, Jesse?"

"No, thank you, sir."

"Suit yourself." He pulled out another bottle and drank. "You humans have always been at the mercy of the greater species. Humans are to vampires what chickens are to humans. The purpose of a chicken is to serve its humans with eggs and meat. So, humans are to vampires."

He drank again. "If humans are left unchecked, the population will grow out of control. If they're allowed to think too much on their own, they get crazy notions about freedom and living their lives in peace and without the fear of vampires."

He offered the bottle to Jesse. "Drink with me."

Jesse obliged and sipped from the bottle.

"Over my lifetime, humans somehow learned to kill us. Entire groups of men would hunt and destroy my brethren. Do you know why this is?"

Jesse shook his head and handed the bottle back to Mathias. "No, sir."

"Because Jesse. Humans need a cause, something they believe is greater than themselves. This is humanity's fatal flaw; it's also the key to their manipulation. I see it as my duty to create causes that don't involve killing vampires." He drank again. "When a human belief is challenged—particularly a religious one—they're quick to forget their vampire foe and turn to killing each other simply because they don't share the same deity. It gives them a false sense of control. I relish in the wars of humans. They're so distracted and consumed by the war; so busy killing each other over their ridiculous ideas they never notice the destruction vampires bring in war's wake. Women and children are fair game, their deaths chalked up to the brutality of the 'other side.'"

He scoffed aloud at the stupidity of it all. "Like their beliefs matter; they'll all end up dead, eventually. And just like chickens, they're oblivious to the control the greater species has over them. Their gods will never come to their rescue."

"Why are you telling me this, sir?"

"I'm trying to distract myself from thinking of Alma, so humor me Jesse and just listen. You can ask questions later."

"Yes, sir."

"I've knelt in the oldest of churches and prayed beside the holiest of Christians. Performed the Salah as if I were a genuine believer in Muhammad. I've meditated with Buddhists feigning the quest for enlightenment. And I've spent Passover with Jews and partaken in their Seder like I care about their exodus from slavery at the hands of Egyptians."

He drank again, but the bottle was empty. He tossed it out the window; the crash rang in his ears as it shattered on a rock.

"I actually witnessed the Jews flee Egypt. I did these things not because I have any respect for these abominations called religion. But in the name of research. I want to understand my prey and what drives their madness. Despite their words of peace and love, they're always willing to fight each other to the death. So, Alma and I used this knowledge to provoke hatred and war everywhere we went."

The port was kicking in, dulling but not eradicating his pain.

"I have broods all over the world. Do you know what a brood is, Jesse?"

"No, sir. I don't."

"You're getting quite the education tonight, aren't you? A brood is a group of vampires. Like a gaggle of geese or a murder of crows."

"I see."

Mathias fished around for another bottle of port, pulled it out of the basket and took a long pull, relishing the rush and enjoying the lightheadedness the alcohol brought. "Every few centuries, Alma and

I would gather the broods together to come up with new ideas about how to indulge our hedonistic lives."

He looked out the window at the passing trees and their shadows in the darkness. The blade of sadness was still sharp. It cut through the fog of the port as he remembered the great witch hunts that had been Alma's idea.

"What's hedonistic?" Jesse asked.

Mathias sighed and drank. "It means pleasure. Indulgent pleasure."

"Thank you, sir."

"Alma came up with the idea to stir up the witch hunts. That caught on like wildfire in Europe. It kept us going for centuries. The irony is the blood from an actual witch is poison to a vampire. A witch's scent is repugnant to us. You humans think garlic keeps us away? That's a joke. Get a vial of witch's blood to wear around your neck.

"The European broods infested their communities with the idea witches consorted with the devil, and their souls needed to be freed from his hold. A vampire had its pick of the town. All it had to do was say the girl, boy, woman, or man had been seen doing something unnatural and just like that, they were thrown in prison, no questions asked. The number of humans, and even some dogs, *accused* of witchcraft continues to feed us.

"The townspeople got in on the fury as well, and occasionally an actual witch would end up in the prison. At first, this presented a problem for the vampires, as the actual witches could use their magic to escape and wreak havoc. Witches are a small percentage of the population, so it rarely causes problems. We learned who the witches were and forced them to build wards around the jails to prevent the use of magic by threatening their families. Are you following, Jesse?"

"Yes, sir. Well, you're saying you accuse humans of being witches and then feed on them. You're not hunting actual witches, right?"

"That's correct, Jesse. Sometimes things backfired, and a witch ended up in prison and found her magic within the prison. This just happened in Poland. Cassius was a brazen fool and got himself beheaded. Good riddance to him. Do you go to church, Jesse?"

"Yes, sir, doesn't everyone?"

"I don't."

"I meant humans, sir. All humans."

"I know what you meant, Jesse. As I said before, your religious beliefs make your kind so easy to manipulate. You go to church and kneel before your god, pretending to be holy and good. Showing your faces in church because people will talk if you don't, and we can't have that. Do you believe in God, Jesse? Or do you go to church because if you don't, you'll be ostracized?"

They sat in silence for a moment, as Mathias supposed Jesse was trying to think. "Well, sir, I don't rightly know if I believe. I've been taught my whole life that we have to be good so we can go to heaven. My parents always used God to scare me. And if he's so scary, how can he be so good and kind at the same time?"

"I knew you could do it, Jesse. That's a well-thought-out response. God is simply a tool used for manipulation. Your parents manipulated you, the church and governments use God as social control, like your parents, just on a larger scale. They tell you it doesn't matter if you live a miserable life now; you'll get the spoils of heaven after you die. What a load of horseshit. Why shouldn't you enjoy your life while you're alive? This compassionate God wants his people to live in squalor and be miserable? Where is the logic in that?"

"You're right, sir. It makes no sense."

"I often wonder at the self-righteous hypocrisy of men who kneel before their God on Sunday, yet Monday through Saturday buy and sell their fellow men, treating them like animals because their skin is a different color? They throw innocent men, women and children in jail because someone accuses them of consorting with the devil. They disrespect their wives often to the point of physical abuse. Frighten their children with the scary-yet-loving God. This suits me just fine. I can exploit all these flaws and prey on their ignorance. Therefore, I agreed to let Alma turn Seth. His father is a plantation owner. The slave trade was to be our next big venture."

"It's brilliant, sir."

The smell of the humans was getting stronger. "Thank you. You know vampires live for the thrill of the hunt? It's one thing to feed on blood, but the smell of human fear is an aphrodisiac, the hunt is foreplay and the kill an intense climax. It's quite sexual." He smelled the sudden sweat coming from Jesse's apprehension. "Don't worry, Jesse, you're too valuable to me alive."

"Thank you, sir."

Mathias took another long pull from the port bottle.

"What do you know about reason and passion, Jesse?"

"Sir?"

"What is driving me to take this trip, Jesse?"

"To find out what happened to Alma?"

"Yes, but why do I need to know?"

"For revenge, sir? Understanding?"

"It's more than that. It has nothing to do with logic or reason. I'm driven by sheer passion. I can feel the echo of her under my skin like blood flowing through my veins. It's almost like her essence is pulling me, like a compass needs to point north. I need to see Alma's death. I've never felt like this before over the death of a child."

"Maybe Alma was more than just your child. Maybe you're soulmates."

Mathias laughed. "Soulmates? Vampires don't have souls."

"All due respect, sir, how would you know?"

Mathias tipped the bottle up to take another drink and paused at Jesse's words. Some of the maroon liquid dribbled out onto his white shirt, flowering like a bloodstain.

"What are you saying, Jesse?"

"Well, you're alive, sir. How could you know if you have a soul or not? Alma was human before, maybe she still had her human soul."

"You're making a leap, Jesse, that God actually exists. And you're forgetting, I've never been human."

"Yes, sir. And you're making a leap that he doesn't. People have always believed in God. You just said so yourself. All over the world, they believe in some sort of god. Seems like he has to exist. Who is to say that we don't all have souls, animals, plants, people, even vampires like you?"

"I also said God was the reason humans go to war and kill each other. And vampires take advantage of the chaos. If there is a heaven, it's not for vampires."

"Sir, wolves, hawks, cats, and even dogs, hunt and kill for nourishment. It's not wrong or evil when they do it. Perhaps it's the same for you. You need human blood for nourishment, so you hunt."

"I appreciate what you're saying, Jesse. But even if there is an all good and compassionate God reigning in heaven, he's not going to let me in. I'm sentient, understand right and wrong. I lack what you humans call a moral compass."

"I don't know what sentient means, sir. I'm just saying, hunting is in your nature. If that's the case, how can it be wrong in the eyes of God?"

"Well, Jesse, you make a compelling argument. But on that note, I smell humans and I'm quite hungry. Why don't you let me out and head back home?"

The port sloshed in his rumbling stomach, and his fangs quivered in anticipation of the hunt.

Jesse slowed the horses and stopped. "Are you sure, sir? How will you get to Stoney Ridge?"

"Don't worry about that."

CHAPTER 26

Mathias got out of the carriage and sniffed the air like a dog. The scent of humans stirred a familiar arousal. He vaguely heard the wheels crunching the earth as Jesse pulled away and disappeared into the forest.

The smell of this new land, America, was untainted and wild, so different from the old and dank towns of Europe. It was fresh. The Louisiana Territory was perfect for a new beginning. Beautiful. Untamed. Virtually untouched. The ideal location. He and Alma had built this dream together.

Mathias breathed in the dead leaves beneath his feet and the ones still hanging on to life in the surrounding trees. The precarious balance between the two had always fascinated him. He smelled the wolves and their fear of his own scent, and the carrion of some long dead animal, picked apart by its killer and then the vultures and worms and ants. The cycle of life continued around him. He wasn't a part of it. He stood on the outside of that circle and watched it go on.

His kind took. They didn't give back as other living creatures did, even in death. They took life to sustain themselves. If a vampire was to die, its end was quick, and nothing of its existence remained for the nourishment of other species. Just a poof of smoke and they were gone. No meal for the wolves. No corpse for the scavengers. This complete form of narcissistic self-indulgence was why they had the power they did. They were a ruthless breed of sociopaths—a word Mathias didn't know at the time but would come to love centuries later—living their lives in complete sensual pleasure.

He closed in on the humans now, two of them, man and child. The sweet smell of their blood mingled with the embers of a fading fire and horses.

The blood of the youth was the sweetest delicacy. It didn't matter if it was female or male. Their innocence intensified their raw fear as they faced certain death, and the fear sweetened the taste of their blood. They weren't much to hunt, their peril slowed them. An adult was better for hunting, but the spoils weren't as sweet. It was a matter of mood, but Mathias was hungry, and the anticipation brought his fangs to life.

He moved quickly and with stealth. It was simply the nature of the vampire. He was upon the camp in minutes. His presence agitated the horses, so he let them loose to maintain the quiet and then sat down in front of the dying fire.

Mathias stoked it a bit with the toe of his boot, the flame returning in a flash before settling back down to a dull glow. He waited for the elder to sense his presence and drag himself from his dreams to face a living nightmare, but the anticipation was too much for Mathias. He added some dead leaves to the fire. The crackle stirred in the man, and Mathias watched as he pried his eyes open. The boy, blond curls framing his pale face, was the picture of innocence. His little chest rose and fell in the slow steady rhythm of deep slumber.

The man startled and reached for the boy. Mathias was fast, dragging the man to his feet. "You want to watch the boy die?"

The man shook his head.

Mathias let him go. "Then run." He flashed his fangs for good measure. The man turned and ran into the woods. Mathias knelt beside the boy, stroking his hair in anticipation of the sweet dessert he would make. He enjoyed the fire longer, not because he was cold, but to indulge his senses with the smell and the snapping of the charred wood. When the man was a suitable distance away, Mathias rose and began to hunt.

The man proved more adept than Mathias had anticipated, which made finding him that much more satisfying.

"Please," he whimpered as he backed away from Mathias. "My son. I have a family."

The man tripped and fell, landing on his behind. He crawled backward and reminded Mathias of a crab scurrying along the beach.

Mathias held out his hand. "Don't be afraid. You can go back to your boy and your family. I was just having a little fun." The man wanted to believe. Mathias took a step closer. "Let me help you up."

"Really?"

Mathias made his face serious. "Really. Your son awaits your return."

Relief washed over the man's face, and he reached up for Mathias's hand.

Mathias squeezed the man's hand so hard the bones crunched, then showed his fangs again. The man screamed.

Mathias yanked him up, intending to bring him in close as if they were lovers dancing. But he was amped up from the hunt and pulled too hard. The velocity with which Mathias jerked him up caused the man to fly over Mathias's head, only stopping as he collided with a tree. Mathias realized he was still holding the man's shattered hand in his own and when he looked down, he saw the entire arm had separated at the shoulder. He cursed his stupidity and dropped the appendage in disgust.

He growled at the smell of the fresh blood and turned. The man, curled up on the ground not moving, was either passed out from shock or dead from the impact with the tree. Blood spurted from his shoulder.

"What a waste," Mathias chided himself for his carelessness. He knelt beside the man and shook him. The man opened his eyes, but they were vacant. He'd be dead soon enough.

Mathias grabbed the man by his hair and lifted him. All he wanted was to feed. As he sank his fangs into the jugular, he lost himself to the sensuality of the blood spurting into his mouth. A shiver of pleasure washed through him, igniting each nerve in his body, and he drained the man—too fast. He felt like a newly made vampire who didn't know limits, pleasantly drugged.

He dropped the body. It hit the soft earth with a light thud. The leftovers would be a feast for the scavengers.

He trudged back through the woods, aroused at the thought of the sleeping boy. He spoke to the wilderness. "I am Mathias. Fear me, as I am the fodder for your worst nightmares." His fangs pulsed, and he picked up a trot. The cool breeze played with his long black hair as he closed in on the boy. The hunt had stirred his passions, and he let out an involuntary moan at the prospect of what was waiting for him ahead.

The boy still slept, though no longer a sound slumber. He seemed agitated, and Mathias wondered if his father's spirit was infiltrating the boy's dreams, trying to warn him of the danger approaching. Again, Mathias was patient, waiting for the boy to sense him on his own. He almost drooled in anticipation, imagining the look of fright on the boy's face when he saw Mathias's fangs. Would the boy wonder about the life he'd never have? The woman he'd never marry, the children they'd never bear; or would he simply succumb to the inevitable darkness that his death would bring? Sometimes, in the moments before death stole his prey, Mathias would sense their last thoughts. Their regrets or loved ones. He wondered what Alma's last thoughts had been. He'd know soon enough.

The boy roused, looking confused. "Who are you? Where's Fa...?"

Before he could finish the sentence, Mathias bore his fangs. The boy screamed; a sound so sweet Mathias let out an orgasmic groan as he sank his teeth into the pale, young skin.

CHAPTER 27

Mathias arrived at Stoney Ridge just as the sun peeked over the mountains to the east of the great plantation. Bound by the unseen laws of nature, Mathias couldn't enter the home of a human uninvited. He knocked on the massive oak door. An agitated and sickly Seth answered. Mathias wasn't sure if it was relief or fear on the halfling's face.

"Mathias? Please come in." He had a tremor in his hands as he shut the door and gestured down the hallway. Whether fear or side effect, Seth was a mess.

Seth shuffled down the hall, his back slightly hunched. Portraits of men that looked much like Seth lined the walls. One was on horseback, one in front of a fireplace with a hound at his feet, and one was just a floating bust, all in gaudy, gilded frames.

Like a dog not wanting to get too far ahead of his master, Seth turned several times in the short distance to the sitting room to see if Mathias was still behind him. He ushered Mathias into the small room and gestured toward the grand winged chair for his guest. The fireplace had the charred remains of a fire still clinging to life. Mathias sat with grace, crossed his legs, folded his hands in his lap, and waited for Seth to speak.

Seth picked at his face and stared at his hands as if he had no idea they were attached to his body. Then he looked at the great vampire. "I don't know where she is. She went out to hunt and never returned. Where did she go? What am I supposed to do? Where is she? Do you know? Please tell me what's going on." He dropped to his knees and sobbed. A thin line of spittle hung from his mouth. He was a far cry from the cocky young man Mathias had met at his own home, and he almost felt sorry for the halfling.

"She's dead."

Seth froze. "Dead? How's that possible?"

Mathias looked at his impeccably buffed fingernails. "Well, Seth, someone killed her. That's how it's possible. I'm here to find out who did it."

Seth looked confused. "Killed her?" He went on mumbling, but Mathias couldn't understand the nonsense coming from his mouth. Then his eyes widened. He picked harder at his face. "What's going to happen to me?"

"Breathe easy, Seth. I can finish the process." He rose from his chair and walked over to Seth. He ran his fingers through the halfling's hair and took a deep breath, trying to regain his patience. "I'm going to find out what happened to her. I'll be back."

Seth, still on his knees, looked up at Mathias. His blond hair was askew. Posture crooked. Mouth slightly ajar, bluish lips quivering. Mathias found his eyes most repulsive. Once deep with expression, they were now vacant. This was a part of the change, but he felt a twinge of irritation with the halfling that made him smile. In that moment, Seth's utter helplessness made Mathias want nothing more than to stay right there and watch him suffer and die his painful death, but he thought of Alma and reined in his desire. Perhaps he would make a fine vampire. He smiled and made his way out of the house. Seth's nonsensical words flowed out of the open window behind him.

Mathias walked a bit, his black cape billowing in the light breeze. When he was sufficiently out of range of Seth's rants, he stopped and breathed deeply, concentrating on Alma. He picked up her scent. It was more of an imprint she'd left behind, and it drew him to the spot of her death. He stood in the leaves and felt her inside of him.

He remembered the first day he saw her, when she was still human, when he knew he had to have her. It was a scorching summer afternoon in a small-town square in the agora of Athens. She was damp with sweat from the overbearing sun and humidity, drawing water from the well with a few other girls. He'd watched her for days. While she had a dazzling smile, teeth strikingly white against her tanned skin, he could see something sinister behind her green eyes.

The memory made him ache with grief. If he could produce tears, they would flow like the blood of his victims. She had completed him. He'd never realized to what extent until this moment when the full effect of her death hit him. He'd never known this kind of suffering. Mathias had witnessed the grief of humans, always mocking their weakness caused by emotion. But now he understood.

He felt their anguish, the utter helplessness that comes with death, and for a moment, understood their need for religion. It gave hope their loved ones were still out there somewhere, not really gone, but in a better place. How he wished he could believe that was true of Alma, that Jesse was right.

He knelt as if in worship and kissed the ground where she last stood, ready to find out what had happened to her. Still on his knees, he breathed deeply, her scent filling him and bringing a fresh wave of grief. If only he could bottle that smell and carry it with him forever.

He could see her now, dressed like a man in riding pants and boots, her honey hair flowing from underneath the wide-brimmed hat she wore to protect her from the sun. He smiled at the vision. In his mind, he followed her from the house to a small church on the property and saw Seth's dead father in a coffin. Alma's last meal. She walked to the church entrance, where a large Black man—a slave, but not a slave—was vomiting. Mathias felt Alma's desire for this man and saw her fangs grow as she told him to run.

Mathias followed her into the woods as she tracked the man. He saw what she saw and smelled what she smelled.

Then he knew.

She'd smelled the witches and waited. There were more than one, so she was cautious about approaching them. The slave had asked them for protection, mercy from the thing that chased him. Alma thought she could bargain with them for the man.

Mathias yelled, "Alma! Run! Run away from here! Leave him, there are plenty of others." His cries fell on deaf, dead ears.

He heard the witch crunching through the leaves before seeing her. She came into view, and his first thought was the same as Alma's. This witch was lovely. She had a menace about her. It was a shame she was a witch. Her gait was easy. Arms swinging at her side, it was as if she was coming to negotiate. He felt Alma relax as she said, "Give him to me, witch. He's mine. A runaway slave. You've no right to him."

When the witch was right in front of Alma, her demeanor changed. She hit her with a spell, rendering Alma immobile, then spat in Alma's face. Mathias knew what was next, and as the witch pulled a stake seemingly from nowhere, he leaped from the ground at her arm, trying to stop her, screaming as loud as he could.

"Stop!"

Then he landed with a thud in the leaves.

As real as this seemed, the witch was only an image, but he'd seen her pause, like she felt his presence. Her stake still hit its mark, and Alma lit up like a dying star.

Alma had been so stunned from this witch spitting in her face she hadn't had time to register the stake until the moment it pierced her heart. He felt her realization, bewilderment, and sheer anger at what had happened. Somehow, the witch could read Alma's thoughts, but Alma was unable to enter the witch's mind. Stoic to the end, Alma's last thought was full of venom. "He'll come for you."

And Mathias would.

Alma had expected a conversation with the witch but was met not only with destruction, but with disrespect. It was like the witch had a grudge or some axe to grind with Alma. Maybe she did. Coming out of his trance, he carried with him Alma's moment of death and her last thought, vowing his vengeance. It took him a minute to shake it off and, in that moment, his pain turned to rage. He let out a scream so intense animals took cover; birds were silenced and a tree or two split in half.

He made his way back to the house and found Seth still in the drawing room. He could smell the servants who'd recently scattered. Seth looked up, dazed and flustered, and Mathias was reminded again of Alma when she was in this state and how he nurtured and helped her get through the worst of the change. He'd held her for hours when she was at her worst. The thought of her doing the same for Seth now fueled his fury. She was *his* and no one else's.

With Alma gone, Mathias had no connection to this halfling. He imagined future conversations with a fully turned Seth about Alma and her savage beauty, how there could never be another lover as skilled as she was and how they both missed her so much. This image brought out the full force of his anger. This was a future that would *never* happen.

He walked up to the mumbling Seth, who grabbed Mathias by the cape. "Did you find her? Is she coming back? Help me."

Mathias brushed Seth's hands away. "Calm down, Seth. I told you I could take care of you."

Seth didn't relax. He still picked at his face, eyes still empty. Mathias held out his arms as if to wrap Seth in an embrace. Seth took a step forward.

Mathias put his hands on Seth's cheeks. "What a waste."

He twisted so hard Seth's head came right off. His body paused for a moment before it slumped at Mathias's feet.

He looked down at the face resting between his hands in disgust. Vacant eyes stared up at Mathias, the drool drying on its chin. Blood dripped from the stump of the neck onto the headless body below.

He couldn't get the vision of the witch thrusting that stake into Alma's heart out of his head. Raw devastation wrapped around his heart. He took a deep breath to pull himself together, but the smell of the tainted blood floated through the air like poison gas, and he gagged.

His frustration reached a crescendo, and he hurled Seth's head at the wall where it exploded like a melon. He would find that witch. Killing her would be his greatest pleasure. But now he needed to hunt.

He picked up the scent of a fleeing servant, and his fangs started to pulse.

MORGANA – TO HUNT OR NOT TO HUNT

CHAPTER 28

Morgana spent that spring helping Agatha with her baby and building their school. The witches had also befriended Fala, a neighboring witch from the Choctaw nation, whose tribe lived north of Morgana and Agatha. She visited often and helped with the magical aspects of constructing the school.

Trees budded, warmth and the smell of honeysuckle filling the air.

Fala visited Morgana to infuse the school's walls with magic for learning. "I've heard of a witch that killed an evil creature north of here. A monster woven into our legends that feeds on the blood of humans, one I never believed existed. What do you know about this?"

Morgana paused mid-spell and turned to face Fala. She hadn't thought about vampires since they'd created the barrier around their town. She dropped her hand, letting the spell dissipate. "Vampires. They exist, and I've killed many."

Fala nodded. "Put that spell back together, and let's finish this wall."

The witches spun their spells and tossed them at the interior wall. The spell would induce minds to open and be free to learn without prejudice.

"My mother taught me this spell before she lost her powers," Morgana said. "It was handed down by her mother and all the mothers before her."

Fala smiled. "Like a recipe."

"Exactly. A recipe for learning. I have some cooking recipes she taught me, too. I'll make perogies for you some day. Let's go outside. I need a break."

They went out and walked to the lake.

"Want to sit for a bit?" Morgana asked.

Fala didn't answer. She just sat on the grass, and Morgana followed suit. They remained in silence. Cicadas hummed, squirrels scurried around, and the songs of birds filled the air. Morgana sighed. "Why did you ask about the vampires?"

Fala shrugged. "I guess, if they really exist and you know how to kill them, I'd like you to teach me."

"Have there been sightings or attacks on your village?"

"Perhaps. We've lost men on hunts. We chalk it up to animal attacks, but sometimes we've found their bodies shriveled and grossly decomposed."

"That's a telltale sign of a vampire's work." She gave an involuntary shudder as she remembered her last kill. She'd hoped they were through with vampires. "Agatha and I created a spell around the perimeter of our land to keep them out. They can't come into your home without an invitation. We made our town—or what we anticipate our town to become—like a home. We can do it for you as well. Have to wait for the next eclipse. Agatha will know when that is."

"Interesting. Why is it they need an invitation?"

"I don't know. Maybe it's God or the universe's way of giving them boundaries. Maybe it's because a home is our own sacred space that creates its own kind of boundary."

"So, we're safe in our own homes. That's refreshing. Our legend says sunlight will kill them. Is that true?"

"I don't think so. I know they're creatures of the night, but Alma, the one I killed north of here, that was at dusk. She was an old vampire. So maybe that has something to do with it. Pausing before driving a stake in their hearts to question them about their powers wasn't exactly a priority."

Fala laughed. "Fair enough."

Morgana lay on the grass and stared up at the blue sky, clouds painted across it like cotton. A flock of birds rustled from the trees, their swarm-like flight pattern a patch of speckled dirt splattered across the pristine clouds.

"You know I have a special gift to aid hunting," Fala said.

Morgana sat up. "What do you mean, hunting? If we fortify your village, you'll be safe. If you know how to kill them, you'll be safe. They are vicious creatures, and it's best to stay away from them, not seek them out."

"If they're out there killing humans, and we know about them, aren't we obligated to hunt them?"

"These aren't bears or wolves, or some animal."

"No, but they're a threat to my people."

"A witch's blood is poison to a vampire. They're not interested in us unless they can manipulate us for something they want. I've witnessed firsthand what happens if you don't do as they want. It's not pretty. In my experience, staying away is best."

CHAPTER 29

That evening after Fala had left, Morgana shared their conversation with Agatha.

"I agree with Fala," Agatha said. "Despite the danger, we have an obligation. But the bigger issue is the barrier for her village. The next eclipse is in two months. I think we'll have to enhance our spell to accommodate the larger area and include three more witches."

Morgana nodded. "We should get started on the spell. Two months will go by like that." She snapped her fingers.

Over the next couple of months, they prepared the updated spell and were ready to go a few days before the eclipse.

Fala came for Morgana, Agatha, and baby Stetson. James hitched the wagon for them, and they headed north onto the well-worn path that cut through the tall grass. Fala's village was only about an hour's ride.

Fala rode beside them on her horse. "Morgana, would you like to marry again? I have some wonderful available men in my village." Her voice was teasing.

Morgana laughed. "Thanks, Fala. I had a husband and a child. I think I told you. Lost them both to a vampire."

"Yes, you did."

"That vampire, Cassius, was my first kill. Revenge, justice, whatever you want to call it, feels good, but it never brings them back. The thought of going through a loss like that again is unbearable, but I've considered it. My hesitation is because the potential for pain exceeds the happiness a relationship would bring. I want to protect myself, my heart. And a relationship takes so much energy. I want to put my energy into my craft and teaching, not a partner."

"Isn't our suffering a part of our life?" Agatha asked. "I know you don't want to hear this, Morgana. But I wouldn't be a good friend if I didn't say it. I believe you're missing out on an important part of life if you turn your back on love."

"But I've had that love. I had a wonderful man and a beautiful child, and they were taken from me. No woman should go through what you went through in Salem. I know you understand pain. I've been through that too, more than once. But there's nothing to compare to a loved one's violent demise. I wouldn't wish it on my worst enemy. So, yes, Agatha, suffering is a part of life, but I also think it's our nature to protect ourselves from it. Just as I wouldn't welcome a sword to my belly, why nurture a love that, when lost, cuts as deep as the sword? I've had my share. I never want to experience that pain again."

Agatha was silent for a moment. "You're right, I can't imagine Stetson or James being taken from me. I only know the good we have together now. I know eventually it will be taken away, but my focus is on enjoying the time I have with them now, not in the future when they're gone. And who knows, maybe I'll die first, unlikely, I know, but stranger things have happened."

Morgana smiled. "Fala, please chime in with your opinion. We've known you all these months and don't know if you have a family."

"No. No man or children. I chose my craft over family. As you said, Morgana, a relationship takes a lot of energy, and it wasn't where I wanted to focus. Like you, a witch in my village, Nita—you'll meet her—lost her husband and suffered greatly. I decided I wasn't strong enough to get through the trauma Nita experienced. I didn't want that kind of distraction in my life."

"Wise decision."

CHAPTER 30

When they arrived at Fala's village, Morgana was wide-eyed, like a child. A large group of people greeted them, and Morgana quickly realized witches were revered here, not persecuted.

Morgana and Agatha got out of their wagon, and someone took the horse and wagon and walked away. Fala introduced them to everyone as they made their way to her little chukka, a round structure made of wood and clay with a roof of thatched palmettos. They had to hunch down to go single file through the entrance, which wound around the hut.

"This is like a maze," Agatha said.

"Agatha, you can rest in here and feed your baby," Fala said. "Then I'll show you around."

There was a loud *coo,* and Morgana jumped out of her skin.

Fala laughed. "That's just my pigeon, Coo." It hopped on the ground and flew up to her outstretched arm. She pulled some corn out of her pocket and fed the bird.

Agatha went to the bird, stroked its head, and spoke to it. The pigeon closed its eyes and stretched its head out, leaning into Agatha's touch.

Agatha looked up, eyes wide. "*That's* your gift?"

Morgana looked at Agatha and then Fala, who had a puzzled look on her face.

Agatha continued to caress Coo. "My gift is to communicate with animals. That's amazing."

"What are you talking about?" Morgana asked.

"My gift is to inhabit the body of a bird," Fala said. She reached out and petted Coo's head. "She likes you. I use her as my avian chariot."

Morgana's mouth hung open. She'd never heard of this gift before. "Can you go into any bird?"

"Yes, but I prefer this girl. We've developed a kind of symbiosis."

"What a fabulous gift," Agatha said. "She's so vibrant and full of personality. Shall we go meet the others? I can walk and feed this baby at the same time."

Fala led them to another hut where the other two witches waited for them. Agatha lit up in their presence. Nita and Kinta didn't speak English very well, so Morgana acted as a conduit. If she touched both Agatha and one of the other witches, they could use Morgana's telepathy to communicate. Morgana's telepathy was such that language wasn't a barrier; she could communicate with anyone that way.

Kinta was still in her teens. Her mother, Nita, was the other witch Fala had spoken of—her husband killed when Kinta was still a baby.

Morgana wondered about Nita's powers. She'd watched her own mother lose her powers and grow old, but Nita still looked young and healthy.

"Tell us about the magic behind this barrier," Nita said.

Morgana nodded to Agatha. "She's the brains behind it."

Agatha smiled. "I couldn't have done it alone. As I learned from Morgana, vampires cannot enter a home without an invitation. So, we gave our town the same attributes as a home.

"First, we'll put up basic protection wards around the perimeter. But we'll infuse the wards with the spirit of the three of you. This is the most important part. The perimeter must always have the spirit of a witch that lives within its borders. Otherwise, it becomes the same as an abandoned house and vampires can come and go as they please. Then we connect the wards with a protection spell. Your spirits will flow from the wards into the spell, giving it extra protection. Fala, you've already staked out the perimeter of the village. Can you show us?"

Fala pulled out a map she'd created by flying over the village. Morgana traced her finger around the perfect circle drawn around the village on the map.

Agatha traced a five-pointed star inside the circle, creating a pentagram. "The five points of the pentagram will be where we place the wards." She touched each of the five points and murmured an incantation. "These spots will be marked on the perimeter. There are five of us and five points."

Agatha pointed to the northernmost point on the circle. "This point is of the spirit. Going right around the pentagram, the next point is water, then fire, earth, and air. Then back to spirit. During the eclipse, we'll each stand on these spots and use the celestial energy to create the wards and bind them to the corresponding element. We'll incorporate our spirits into each one. This is the most difficult and most important part of the process, but if among us we possess each element, it might be easier. Morgana is fire, and I'm earth. I've created a spell to do this. We can go through it a little later."

"I'm air, Nita is water, and Kinta is also fire," Fala said.

"Perfect," Agatha said. "The spell doesn't require each witch to represent a different element. But because we do, this will make it even stronger. Kinta can take the point of spirit. It will be best to have an inhabitant of your village bind their spirit with spirit."

"Once the wards are complete, we'll pull from the energy of the eclipse and do a protection spell to connect the wards and create the barrier," Morgana said, tracing her hand around the circle. "Adding mine and Agatha's magic will strengthen it. Your space is much bigger than ours, so the more magic, the better."

"The combination of our spirits, the elements, the power from the sun and moon, and the spell will create a powerful barrier," Agatha said.

"Why do we need the eclipse?" Kinta asked.

"The size of the area we want to protect requires a boost to our spell. We could use this spell on a house with the magic of just one witch. But because the space we want to protect is so large, using just our elements won't be enough. We need the power from the moon and the sun to enhance our spell and make sure it covers the entire area and lasts for many hundreds of years."

CHAPTER 31

The eclipse would be at full force around three in the morning. Morgana loved that time of night; it was her witching hour. The vast emptiness of the sky had an eerie and undefinable power. The endless stars made her feel like a speck of dust in the universe. Her magic was at its strongest, the moon full and enormous like a perfectly ripened fruit waiting to be plucked from a tree. Its energy flowed in the surrounding air.

The Choctaw witches rode their horses—Agatha rode with Kinta, and Morgana with Fala—in silence to the village border Agatha had outlined. Agatha had Stetson wrapped in a papoose, snug against her breasts. They all carried torches.

The first point they reached was fire, and Fala dropped Morgana off. Morgana soaked in the dark, drawing on the energy from the moon. She stood on the charred spot on the ground Agatha had put there earlier to mark fire on the pentagram. She lit her torch, sat down, and waited for the others to signal they were in place. The circle around the points of the pentagram was infused with magic that carried her thoughts to the other witches, enabling her to be a conduit for translation. She would speak the incantation in English, pushing it telepathically along the magic circle. She hoped it worked the same as it did when she was sitting right next to Nita and Kinta.

Morgana was nervous, but she and Agatha had completed the spell in their town on their own, so she knew if something went wrong, they could fix it. They had gone over everything before they left. To be safe, Fala had done the verbal translation. Morgana had held hands with Nita and Kinta to impress the feelings of the spell upon them.

She heard Agatha in her head, *ready*.

A few minutes later, Fala checked in. *I'm in place. Nita and Kinta should be around shortly.*

With Fala's response, the circle lit up and pulsed a deep orange color that reminded Morgana of fall. It illuminated the entire area. For a moment, she saw Fala and Agatha as dots on the circle. It faded as quickly as it had appeared.

She touched the circle and thought, *Did you see that?* The circle pulsed a deep indigo.

Agatha popped into her head. *See what?* The circle glowed bright gold with Agatha's message. Morgana touched the band of energy and felt its power.

The circle is taking on our essences as we communicate. I'm indigo, Agatha is gold, and Fala is orange.

Agatha responded immediately. *Yes. I see it.*

Agatha's gold intertwined with Fala's orange as she responded. *I see it too.* As Fala's words came through, a beautiful earthy green strand and a pale blue strand intertwined with the other strands as Nita and Kinta took their places and responded they were ready.

Looks like it's working. The eclipse is about to start, Agatha said.

As the circle glowed like a magnificent rainbow, Morgana took a deep breath, clearing her mind for what was to come. Energy pulsed through her, infusing its power and giving strength that touched her deepest corners.

Agatha entered her head again. *Now!*

I call to the elements, earth, air, fire and water, accept our spirits, and join together as a force against evil and protect our home that is this town.

The circle was now a pulsing prism of color, ropes of energy woven together like silk on a loom. It wasn't so much transmitting the incantation as it *was* the incantation.

Morgana stayed seated and rested her hands on the band of energy. It wasn't solid, but it held the weight of her touch. She closed her eyes. The magic of the other witches flowed through her. Their five spirits became one. Liquid flowing through the river of their spell. Kinta's youthful spirit, the pain of Nita's loss, Agatha's love for her family, and Fala's sheer strength. She wondered what they felt of her.

The wind picked up. She opened her eyes and looked down at her arms. They were spread out but disappeared below the elbow, either blended with or eaten up by the flowing energy. She still felt disconnected from the flesh, blood, and bone that made up her body. She'd heard of out-of-body experiences but had never had one.

She looked up. The eclipse created an illusion of the moon as a black hole in the sky above, an emptiness wrapped in a glowing ring of fire.

Sparks of light rained down over them. The energy of the witches' spells fused together and rose to meet the light from above, creating a dome over the village that shone with their magic. It was the most beautiful thing she'd ever seen.

As quickly as it started, it was over. The wind stopped and the ring of fire vanished. The moon, full and beautiful, was back. Morgana's spirit re-entered her body and as she floated back down to the ground, the witches' strands faded. She looked at her hands and flexed her fingers, reassuring herself they were back to normal. A chill ran through her body, and she wrapped her arms around herself, glad to have them back, but missing the feelings brought on by what they just did.

Closing her eyes, she took a deep breath. In her mind, Morgana could see the other witches. Nita plopped down on the ground. Fala had tears in her eyes, while Kinta stared up at the sky, her mouth slightly ajar. Agatha opened her shirt to feed baby Stet, unfazed by what they'd just done. She wasn't sure if it was just her imagination, but suspected they now each carried a piece of one another, like a talisman. Morgana lay back on the dewy ground and gazed at the puffy clouds decorating the night sky.

CHAPTER 32

When they returned to the village, the horizon glowed orange and red as the sun signaled the start of a new day.

They went to Fala's hut, and Morgana sat on the floor next to the dwindling fire. A chill in the air, she touched the embers, and a flame jumped in response.

Kinta muttered something under her breath and fresh wood floated through the door and into the little fire pit.

Morgana smiled. "Thanks."

They all settled around the fire, and Agatha said, "I've never seen anything like it. Even when Morgana and I did this before, it was nowhere near as spectacular. We're powerful together. We can accomplish great things."

"That was some powerful magic," Fala said.

There was no place Morgana would rather be than right here with these women. Life had a funny way of leading you to the most unlikely of places, and it was always exactly where you should be.

Agatha got ready to feed her baby and pulled her breast out for Stetson. "We should go on the offensive with the bloodsuckers. Fala can find them, and Morgana and I can kill them."

Morgana stared at her friend, taking in the paradox of a loving mother and the flippant way she mentioned hunting vampires. Why did she and Fala want to hunt vampires? How could she get them to understand the danger involved and not disrupt the beautiful lives they were creating together?

"Morgana?"

She jumped at the sound of her name. "Sorry, what? Guess I'm more tired than I thought."

"What do you think?" Agatha stroked her baby's cheek and kissed his head as he continued to suckle at her bosom.

This conversation now? She couldn't think clearly after what they had just gone through. She came here to escape vampires and live a simple life, but it seemed the universe had other plans for her.

"I think I'm exhausted and need some rest."

CHAPTER 33

Morgana woke at midday with Stet between her and Agatha, both still sleeping. She tried to get up without waking them, but had to move Stet. He stretched his chubby arms and smacked his lips. His eyes fluttered, and she touched his nose. "Sleep." He smacked his lips once more and was asleep.

Morgana found Fala in her hut making something that smelled delicious. "Good morning, Fala."

Fala smiled. "How did you sleep?"

"Like a rock. What smells so good?"

"Banaha. It's made from corn. Try one."

Morgana took the mysterious food and watched Fala peel back the corn husk and eat the delicate cornmeal mixture inside.

Morgana wasn't sure, but was hungry and took a bite. It was delicious. "You must teach us how to cook."

Fala laughed. "I will. Eat. We have a gift for you, for your help."

Morgana took another bite when Agatha popped her head into the hut. "Smells so good. Fala, you must teach us how to cook."

Morgana and Fala laughed. "I just said the same thing. Try this, it's banaha, made from corn. Did I say that right?"

"Perfect." Fala handed one to Agatha and showed her how to eat it.

They finished their food and followed Fala out of her chukka and across the village to the area where the livestock was kept.

Agatha went to the horses grazing in a fenced-in pasture. Their wagon was hitched and ready. Morgana got in and Fala said, "Wait. Your gift."

A young boy came their way, leading two horses.

"Those horses are for us?" Agatha asked.

Fala nodded.

"You'll have to teach us how to ride."

"I will." Fala took the horses from the boy. "This black and white one is Talulah, and the gray one is Panola. Talulah means leaping water and Panola means cotton."

Agatha petted Talulah and told her how beautiful she was.

"How can we ever repay you, Fala?" Morgana asked.

"This is our gratitude. For what you've taught us."

Morgana stroked Panola's face. "She looks like cotton."

"I'm going to ride back with you and give you your first lessons. Who wants to go first?"

Morgana looked at Agatha. "Let me take baby Stet and you try your hand with little Miss Talulah."

Agatha unwrapped the cocoon where her son slept from her body before Morgana could finish her sentence.

Morgana took Stetson and wrapped him secure against her bosom while Fala showed Agatha how to mount Talulah; and they were off, riding alongside the wagon.

Agatha glanced over at Morgana. "This is amazing!"

"Fala, what happens to your body when you enter your pigeon?" Morgana asked.

"My body becomes lifeless. I don't leave it unless I'm sure it's safe or I might permanently become a part of the bird world."

"This is the first I've heard of this gift," Agatha said. "It's so special."

"It's like nothing else to be flying above the trees," Fala replied.

"What would happen if something ate Coo while you were in her?" Morgana asked.

"So very sad. It happened to me once, with a different Coo. I just went back into my body."

"There's something I wanted to ask you. Nita still looks young and healthy, but Kinta is nearly grown. How is it Nita kept her powers?"

"It's true giving birth to a daughter can deplete your powers, but there are ways to maintain them. It's like the opposite of a son when a witch chooses to give up her powers; with a daughter, some can choose to keep them, some naturally lose them. Usually when a witch chooses a family, in her heart, she's committing to that life. Nita lost her husband when Kinta was still a baby. It was a simple decision for her to keep her powers."

"That's big news," Morgana said. "It doesn't make me want to start another family, though."

"My behind is hurting," Agatha said. "You want a turn, Morgana?"

"I do." She stopped the wagon, and they switched Stet, who woke up hungry.

Fala helped Morgana mount Cotton, and they were off again.

"Morgana, why are you so hesitant to hunt these vampires?" Fala asked.

Morgana's stomach turned at the question. She thought for a minute before answering. "This isn't a game. These creatures are dangerous, ruthless killers. I've seen the atrocities they orchestrate firsthand." She turned to Agatha. "What you experienced was only a glimpse into the chaos vampires bring to the world."

Tears welled in Agatha's eyes, which brought tears to her own. With a hitch in her voice, she continued. "I've had enough loss in my life. I don't know if I can take any more. When I left Europe, I wanted to start over and forget about vampires. I thought by coming here I could escape and live my life in peace. But vampires roam the earth and manipulate humans to do their bidding.

"We're building a school. Agatha has a family. That's what is important. We built these barriers to keep us and our loved ones safe. We don't need to put ourselves back in harm's way."

They rode in silence for a while. Agatha wiped her tears away. "That's a selfish way of looking at it."

Agatha's words put Morgana on the defensive. "Self-preservation is never selfish. I don't believe putting my self-interest and yours above that of strangers is in any way selfish. Some would argue that this sacrificial altruism is the height of stupidity."

"Sacrificial altruism? Really, Morgana? That's rich. We're talking about peoples' lives. Maybe it's stupid, but I see it as our duty. If we know of an existing evil and don't do our part to rid the world of it, we're complicit in that evil. I couldn't possibly live with myself knowing people are dying because I was too much of a coward to stop it. What does our school, my family, our friendships mean if we have to live in fear outside of our boundaries? What's the purpose of our lives? I would rather die tomorrow making the world a better place than live for hundreds of years in fear and cowardice.

"You left a trail of dead vampires as you made your way here, right where you're supposed to be. You might not want to admit it, but you're good at it. Some might argue, you're a natural and you owe it to yourself to live in your gifts. I've seen your kills, remember? You sealed them into your body, a permanent reminder of the evil and your ability and dedication to its eradication. But now, you don't have to do it alone. We're here. You felt how strong we were together last night. You can't ignore that."

Agatha was right. Morgana thought of her Aurelian and wondered what he'd want her to do. Visions of their lives played through her mind, walking through Krakow hand in hand, her baby boy strapped to her chest, how the soft fuzz on his head felt against her lips when she kissed him. His sweet giggle when she pinched his chubby cheeks. Her loving husband and their precious baby Max, taken by the foul scum residing in the shadows of the world. Her life before vampires had been perfect. Though it was an illusion, she'd been cloaked in ignorance. She longed to be back there, unaware of the wickedness skulking beyond her grasp of reality.

These memories seeped through the cracks of the vault she'd created in her mind to keep them at bay. If she could eradicate them like a plague, her pain would cease. It wasn't fair to herself or her dead, but the alternative wasn't appealing either. How was she to honor them if she'd sealed off the remnants of their lives and refused to acknowledge their existence?

She'd never recovered from her loss. Instead of dealing with her pain, she started a new life in a new country to forget about vampires and the incessant ache in her gut.

But she hadn't forgotten vampires. She encased her vampire kills in her body forever. The things she'd come here to forget were more real than the memories of her husband and baby. This realization had always lurked in the dark corners of her consciousness—like a vampire hiding in the shadows—and she ignored it. A wave of nausea caused her to shudder and hold back a retch. Aurelian's voice in her head took her breath away. *Moja miłość, don't let our deaths be in vain.*

She stopped her horse and cried. How could she forget the two loves of her life and push them aside like trash and instead, pay homage to the actual garbage?

Fala brought her horse to a halt and hopped off. She went to Morgana and touched her leg. "Come down."

Morgana slid off of her horse and fell into Fala's arms. She tried to breathe between her sobs, her body shaking, going limp in Fala's embrace. Then Agatha wrapped her arms around the two of them, baby Stet in the middle of it all.

Morgana's sobs tapered off. "I'm so sorry. You're right, Agatha."

CHAPTER 34

Stetson was one and no longer breastfeeding. The trees were in bloom and the tips of the tulips showed themselves. The air had lost its icy edge as spring made its appearance.

Agatha and Morgana had spent the year learning to ride their horses and were now as comfortable on horseback as they were walking. Morgana taught them about vampires. She showed them her kills etched in her thigh as a tool for teaching. They practiced getting stun spells off as quickly as they could, and they made weapons. Morgana carried an axe dipped in silver, Agatha a bow and silver-tipped arrows. They made an arsenal of wooden stakes.

Nita and Kinta wouldn't join their posse. Nita had been hesitant about putting herself and her daughter in danger after having lost her husband.

Fala took to the skies at night and found a lone vampire. She'd followed it, found its hovel.

"I think we should take our time and track it," Morgana said. "That way we can understand its habits. It will help us plan our attack."

"Absolutely not," Agatha retorted. "We won't allow him to continue to kill so we can track him. When we find a vampire, we kill it before it can kill anyone else."

Morgana opened her mouth in protest, but Agatha held up her hand, almost thrusting it in Morgana's face. "This is not about the greater good. We're here to save lives by destroying evil. So, you can save the *sacrificial altruism* speech because we're beyond that now."

Morgana sighed. "I think my telepathy is rubbing off on you."

Agatha looked at Fala, who said, "No argument here."

"Good. Let's go kill this bastard."

"Fala, you should stay in Coo and show us the way," Morgana said. "Agatha, you'll be armed and act as a backup. I'll be the one to confront the bastard."

"I want to kill it," Agatha said.

Morgana thought for a minute. "I guess if we're able to stun it, you can kill it. But only if we can get a stun spell off, okay? You have no sense of how fast these creatures are, and they are more vicious than any animal you've ever encountered. He'll smell us well before he can see us, so he's going to be ready." Agatha nodded. "Say the words."

"I won't engage unless we can stun it."

"Okay. We go tonight."

Agatha and Morgana rode their horses, and Fala flew in Coo—leaving her body with James—leading the way. Agatha was a better witch than she could ever hope to be, but Morgana knew the dangers of hunting these creatures.

They rode in silence through the dark of night, the air crisp as the horizon shifted from black to a deep purple. Coo landed on Agatha's shoulder.

Morgana laughed. "How convenient you can talk to animals."

Agatha smiled. "He's coming. We've got to go on foot from here."

Morgana dismounted and watched Coo take flight.

Agatha touched Morgana's hand and thought, *Telepathy from now on.*

Morgana squeezed her friend's hand. They followed Coo into the darkness.

They saw the vampire in the distance. It had its back to them, watching something Morgana couldn't see. A slight breeze came toward the witches. Morgana hoped it took their scent away from the vampire to give them extra time. It had been a long time since she'd hunted and she was nervous, especially with Agatha there. But she was also excited. Since her epiphany the year before, she'd missed the thrill of the danger and satisfaction of the kill. Alma had been different. She hadn't sought her out. A bonus kill.

Her thoughts were interrupted by Agatha in her head. *I can send a stun spell from here.*

It was a long way, but Morgana knew if anyone could send a spell that distance, it was Agatha.

She nodded, and Agatha sent the spell. The vampire twitched, then froze, and the witches were upon it in seconds.

Morgana smiled at the fear and confusion in its eyes.

Agatha pulled a stake from her skirts and the realization came into the vampire's eyes. Its death would be quick but painful. Morgana put her finger on the thing's chest, right over its heart. "You can spike it anywhere, but the heart is the best."

Agatha raised her hand and spat in the thing's face. "This is for all the pain you've caused."

She plunged the stake into its heart.

Morgana pulled her friend back to avoid getting burned by the explosion that would come. She'd learned over the years the younger vampires went out with a small poof, not much excitement. But the older ones, as Alma had been, were quite a spectacle. If you stood too close, you would get burned. She had a few burns as reminders.

This was a young vampire. Its face melted and its heart lit up, but quickly went out like a candle in the wind.

It was gone.

"Well," Morgana said. "Not much of a show for your first kill. The older they are, the grander their exit. They've grown old by being savvy."

Agatha picked up the stake from the ground. "That was amazing. I can't wait to do it again."

"I've created a monster. Let's get home. But Agatha?"

"Yes?" Coo landed on her shoulder.

"I don't want you to think it'll always be like that. We got lucky. It's not usually so easy to get them with a stun spell."

"Thanks for ruining it."

Morgana laughed. "You still did great. I just don't want you to be surprised next time. We have to stay diligent and prepared."

Coo cooed and flew off toward home, and the other witches found their horses and followed.

CHAPTER 35

A few weeks after their first hunt, a horse wandered into Agatha and Morgana's hamlet, its rider slumped over the steed's neck. James ran over and pulled the rider down. Agatha went to the horse to soothe and hear its story.

"Morgana, help me," James yelled.

She rushed to help him lay the body on the ground. The rider was a woman, her face disfigured and bloody. There were holes where her eyes and ears should have been, her mouth devoid of teeth.

"Oh my God, she's a witch," Agatha said. "How do you catch a witch so off guard this can happen?"

"Threaten her family," Morgana said.

Agatha gasped. They saw something inside of the witch's bodice. James reached down to pull it out.

Morgana stopped him. "Don't touch it. It may be poison." Morgana performed a spell on the rag paper, cleansing it of impurities. Then she removed it and read. "Agatha, come here."

To the witches, Morgana and Agatha,

I know you are both responsible for the death of my beloved Alma, and you and yours will pay dearly.

If you're reading this, you've seen but a fraction of my capabilities. I've been around for a very long time, and I don't foresee my own demise, ever. Fortunately, I've learned how to be patient, such a virtue, wouldn't you agree?

In the meantime, I will continue to torture every witch I can and send her remains your way, a reminder of my intentions for you, quid pro quo if you will. If I cannot claim your dying breaths for my own pleasure, your children and your children's children will suffer in your stead.

I've been to your little town, and I know of the barrier to keep me and my kind out, nice touch, by the way. One day you'll slip up or your barrier will wear off. Until then, I'll make do and continue to kill your kind.

Warmest Regards,

Mathias

Agatha took her hand and squeezed it. "What are we going to do?"

"You kill him," James said. "Like you killed Alma."

Morgana flinched at the sound of his voice; she'd forgotten he was there. "The *he* Alma spoke of, remember? *He'll come for you*?"

Agatha nodded. "I remember."

Agatha went to James and took his arm. "As long as he's alive, we'll never be safe. Stetson, the little witch growing in my belly, you and me. We have to go after him."

Morgana looked at Agatha. Her eyes glowed like golden orbs. Agatha's fury radiating into her otherwise calm aura. Then she forced herself to look at the dead witch. She seemed to stare at her through those empty eyes, accusing, blaming, asking why she'd had to suffer for their crimes.

"We need to give her a proper burial," Agatha said. "James, please go watch Stetson. Morgana and I have work to do."

James started to protest.

"She's a witch, James. We have to be the ones to bury her."

He walked away, then paused and came back to kiss Agatha before returning to their house.

"My mother's gift was to speak with the dead," Agatha said. "She always said it was more of a curse than a gift. I think she was happy to lose her powers to me."

Morgana gave her friend a look. "What about you? What Fala told us changes things."

"I can't imagine not being a witch." She patted her belly. "How can I teach this little girl to be strong and a powerful witch if I don't have my powers?"

"That's my girl." She paused as Fala's voice popped into her head. "Fala's on her way."

"Good timing."

"She's found a vampire that needs killing."

"I want to get in as many kills as I can before this baby comes. I tried to cut my leg like you do after our hunt, but it hurt too much. Guess I'm just weak. So, I started a journal instead."

"That's a better way to keep records of what we're doing. If I die, my kills go with me. Maybe we should record them as well in your journals."

"Let's not speak of your death, okay? We need to focus on this dead witch."

The rite of the dead was a spell innate within all witches. Most witches had performed it on their mothers whose powers had given their daughters life and magic. While they lost their powers to their daughters and died natural deaths, their souls still belonged to the realm of the immortal.

They positioned themselves, Morgana at the head and Agatha at the feet of the dead witch. Moving in tandem, as if they were in a trance, they raised her off the ground and spun a cloud of mist around the body. Morgana chanted in Polish, Agatha in English.

We honor this witch and pray she is embraced by the eternal.

May her journey beyond the veil be guided by all of those who came before.

Earth, cradle her spirit; Air, guide her spirit; Water cleanse her spirit; and Fire, light her path to the realm of the immortal.

We release you with love, knowing you are a part of all that is, all that was and

All that is to come.

The wind picked up and swirled around the levitated body, bringing with it earth and water. A cyclone of dirt and water encased the body, becoming one with the mist. As the wind died down, Morgana and Agatha, drawing from their own elements, called on fire. They touched the witch and lit her up. The fire encased her body and burned dazzling and bright, like the setting sun.

They stayed with her until she was ash in the wind.

AGATHA – A DAUGHTER

CHAPTER 36

Agatha closed her journal and put it on the shelf lined with her many previous ones. In the early 1700s, the American South—the Mississippi and Louisiana Territories, in particular—was sparsely populated. Their town, they'd called it Vision, was far enough north in the Mississippi Territory not to be noticed by the French or the Spanish, who were busy fighting over the ports in the southern areas of the territories. This was fine with the Vision witches.

The population in the territories had grown as people discovered how well cotton and tobacco grew in the rich, black dirt. With the increase in people came the increase in vampires. Even with the growing population, the area remained wild, a perfect hunting ground for the bloodsuckers. Missing and dead were chalked up to animal attacks or raids by the Native Americans. Agatha knew this was nothing more than a ploy by the vampires to turn the white men against the indigenous, something at which they were quite adept.

After a kill, she felt sated, but never satisfied. The hunger always returned. She believed with all her heart their kills were removing evil from the world one creature at a time. But for every vampire they killed, it seemed ten more came to life.

She smiled at the thought of last night's kill, an older vampire named Samuel. His face froze in shock when she hit him with the stun spell. After pulling the stake from her belt, the understanding registered in his eyes. She'd misjudged his age and hadn't gotten herself far enough away as the shower of his disappearing existence rained down. Agatha had a few minor burns on her hands and arms. She'd never imagined she'd be described as a ruthless killer, but that's what she'd become.

She stepped out into the crisp fall air and walked over to Morgana's. It was Sunday, so there was no school. They'd constructed a small building as a place of prayer, open to all denominations. A preacher came on Sundays for the Christian students. Agatha believed in a higher power and even prayed sometimes, but organized religion had landed her in jail for consorting with the devil, which—in her opinion—made them hosts for evil and the ultimate hypocrites. She agreed to adding the "church" only because it was important to the parents of their students, but insisted it be open to all faiths.

Morgana marked her leg with last night's kill.

"How many do you have now?" Agatha asked.

Morgana looked up, smiled, and shrugged. "I've lost count but I'm running out of room on my legs. Where's Raven?"

"Still sleeping. I didn't want to wake her. I thought I'd go visit Fala and company today. Nita's working on a new herbal concoction. Want to come?"

"Sure. Let me finish up here and we can head out."

"I'll meet you at the barn."

Morgana nodded. "Okay."

Agatha walked over to the barn; they'd had to expand it over the years to accommodate the horses the girls brought with them. A couple of students were saddling up their horses. It was a beautiful day for a ride.

"Morning, girls. Have a nice ride."

"Good morning, Ms. Agatha."

She pulled a carrot out of her pocket and gave it to her current ride, a big bay mare she'd named Annabelle Lee. After getting Annabelle ready, she got Morgana's black gelding, Midnight Sky, and saddled him up.

Morgana came out just as Agatha was finishing. "Good timing. Thanks."

Agatha smiled at her friend. "Ready?"

They waved to the girls as they rode north. Their old path had become a road after many years of frequent travel.

Morgana stopped. "Agatha, look."

She turned around to a perfect view of the town. From their vantage point, they had a view of the lake. The school loomed in the background, surrounded by houses and a few stores. The barn had a giant fenced-in field behind it peppered with horses, a few goats, a cow, and Agatha's pig Matilda—Mattie for short—grazing and lazy in the early morning sun.

"It never gets old," Agatha said.

It had been twenty years since they had met in that Salem prison. The school and town now flourished. They'd killed many vampires, yet Mathias still eluded them.

This was the one thing Agatha felt she'd failed. Over their first decade in Vision, he'd claimed the lives of several more witches, but then he disappeared. Morgana and Fala believed he'd moved on from his loss of Alma. Or maybe had been killed. Agatha didn't agree. He was too ruthless and wouldn't be so quick to give up a grudge. She knew in her heart he wasn't dead. She believed they'd scared him into hiding. Maybe they'd gotten too close to him or killed too many of his kind. She let it go because the dead witches had stopped showing up.

Morgana broke the silence, startling Agatha. "I wonder if Humility Parsons is still grabbing the pastor's crotch?"

Agatha hoped there was a special place in hell for Humility. The mention of her name brought a rush of anger and sadness. Not only had she accused Agatha, but the bitch had also been responsible for the slaughter of her last pig, Moo. She had to laugh at the spell Morgana had cast on her all those years ago.

After their prison break, Morgana had gone off on her own to extract revenge on Humility. Agatha believed Humility had met a violent end, but when Morgana told her what she'd done, she had a hard time reconciling the punishment with the punisher. The hardened and often heartless Morgana had given Humility something much worse than death. She'd cast a kind of love spell on Humility, having her not only believe she loved her pastor, but every time she saw him, she would try to bed him.

"If she's still alive, I hope so," Agatha said. "What made you think of that old hussy?"

Morgana shrugged and nodded at the town. "When I look at all of this, I'm in awe of how far we've come from that prison. Look at everything we've accomplished. If it weren't for Humility, none of this would exist. Something beautiful always blooms from the rotten, wouldn't you say?"

Agatha smiled and thought about what she'd said. "I just wish I could have saved my Moo, and she could have grown old with us in our haven. I wonder if we'd have met some other way. It seems like this was our destiny."

Morgana grinned. "Ah, but is it your destiny to beat me in a horse race?" Then she darted away from Agatha.

Agatha urged Annabelle Lee to follow.

CHAPTER 37

Agatha's daughter, Raven, had been a toddler when she first drew in the dirt. With the help of their Choctaw friends, Agatha and Morgana fashioned paint with berries and greens. They made brushes out of hair from horses' tails. Raven spent hours sitting in the dirt painting and not always on the rag paper they had provided. She fancied rocks, sticks, and trees. She often presented her gifts to Agatha and Auntie Mo.

When she was five, Raven handed a sizeable rock to Morgana with a painting of the ocean on it.

"Auntie Mo, for you."

"Thank you, honey."

Raven motioned for Morgana to put it to her ear.

Morgana turned the rock over and, following the little witch's lead, put the rock to her ear and listened.

Agatha watched. "Do you hear anything?"

"I'm not sure, but there has to be some kind of magic in here. How would she know how to paint the ocean? She's never seen it."

Agatha shrugged and took the rock. Raven put her hands to her ears again.

Agatha mimicked her daughter and nearly jumped out of her skin with shock. "You can't hear that?" She handed the rock back to Morgana. "Put it to your ear and listen. It's like a conch shell."

Morgana put it to her ear. "I don't hear anything."

"Interesting."

Agatha put the rock to her ear and nodded for Morgana to come close. "Come next to me and see if you can hear it while I'm holding it."

"Wow. I can hear it loud and clear. This must be her gift."

Agatha nodded. "I wonder why you can't hear it on your own."

"Maybe you can hear it because you're her mother?"

A decade and a half later, Raven painted a mural of the town.

"Agatha, Auntie Mo, come see my mural. I think it's done."

Agatha and Morgana followed Raven to the Witchery.

"Why must you call me Agatha?" Agatha asked. "Is there something wrong with Mom, Mother, or Mommy?"

Her daughter shrugged. "I don't know. You're just Agatha. Come on."

Raven bubbled with excitement as she opened the door and led them to the painting. "Ta da! What do you think?"

Morgana's eyes went wide. "It's beautiful."

Agatha ran her hand over the painting and felt its magic pulse through her fingers. It was Raven's first painting that wasn't on a rock or some rag paper.

"Auntie Mo, can you feel it?" Raven asked.

"No, honey, what is it? What's the magic?"

"Agatha, you touch it. It seems to work for you."

Agatha touched the mural again and left her hand there. After a few seconds, her hand disappeared into the painting. She pulled it back. "Did you see that?"

Raven grinned from ear to ear. "Keep going."

"What do you mean, keep going?"

"Go *through* the painting."

Agatha put her hand back on the mural and watched her hand disappear. She stepped forward and her entire arm disappeared. She stepped again, putting a foot in the mural.

"Keep going!"

Agatha pushed forward, and the painting absorbed her whole body. She floated through the night sky. Thought she even saw some stars. Then she sat on hard ground. A wave of nausea gripped her guts, and she leaned over to vomit, barely missing her lap.

She wiped her mouth, spit out the remaining bile, and looked around. She sat in a field. A shimmer in the sun caught her eye, and she spotted the lake, the school, and the town in the distance. She was in Vision and wondered how that was possible.

Someone walked toward her, and she stood up. Not a good idea. She had terrible vertigo and sat back down. She waved. "Hello!"

The girl—she looked sixteen—ran toward her wearing a huge grin. "Agatha!"

Agatha was taken aback. "Yes?"

The girl hugged her. Agatha was so surprised she momentarily froze and didn't hug the girl back.

The girl pulled away. "I'm Lydia, your granddaughter."

"What?"

"You came through the mural, right?"

Agatha nodded, too stunned to speak.

"It takes you through time. My mom paints them."

Agatha thought she might throw up again. "What? Who is your mother?"

She didn't hear Lydia's answer. She felt like she was being sucked under water and the world around her became fuzzy. Agatha reached for the girl's hand but tumbled back through the night sky and back on the floor of the Witchery, wondering what the hell had just happened.

Morgana was on her knees next to Agatha. "Are you okay?"

Raven grinned at her mother, and Agatha vomited again.

"What did you do to me, child?"

"Where did you go?" Raven asked.

"I'm not sure. I was still in Vision, and I met my granddaughter, apparently your daughter, Lydia."

Raven's eyes grew as big as saucers. "I didn't believe it, but you did it. You traveled to a different time."

Morgana looked at Agatha and then at Raven. "*That's your gift?*"

Raven shrugged. "I guess so."

"Did no one hear me say I met Raven's daughter?" Agatha asked.

Raven stared at her. "Well, that's not possible. I'm never getting married."

Morgana caught Agatha's eye. "You don't have to be married to have a child."

"Fine. I'm not having children."

Agatha sighed. "I'm going to throw up again and then go lie down."

Morgana smiled. "Raven, let's give your mom some peace and you can tell me about the father of your child."

"Auntie Mo!"

Agatha paused outside of the Witchery to put a hand against the wall to steady herself. She dry heaved. Then she made her way home. What was more disturbing, time traveling or knowing Raven would have a child? She was a grown woman, but Agatha still saw her as her little girl. She wondered how far into the future she'd gone.

James was outside in the garden as she approached the house. She wasn't sure if she'd make it inside. "James, can you help me, please?"

He looked up and came to her. "What's wrong?"

"I'll tell you later. Can you just help me to bed?"

He scooped her up and carried her to their bedroom. She was nearly asleep as he laid her on the bed and kissed her forehead.

CHAPTER 38

Over the next few years, Agatha went back and forth through the mural in the Witchery at least once a month. She honed her ability to choose *when* she would land, as well as controlling how long she spent there. She fought the pull to return to her own time. But she was never able to spend more than an hour there. She loved seeing the town's progress and meeting the people inhabiting Vision over the years. And though she saw her daughter, Raven, and even Lydia, Raven had kept her promise to never marry. The subject of Lydia's father was off limits on her visits.

She asked Raven if she could paint other pictures that allowed her to travel to different times and places.

"Where would you like to go?" Raven asked.

"What if I wanted to go back to Salem?"

"Why would you want that?"

"I have my reasons."

They were in the mural room when Morgana walked in. "What are you two scheming?"

"Agatha wants me to make a painting so she can go back to Salem."

"What? Why would you go back there?"

"Look," Agatha said, "it's not like I'm going to get stuck there."

"But what if you see yourself?"

Agatha shrugged. "It's a chance I'm willing to take. Can you do it or not, Raven?"

"I can try."

CHAPTER 39

Her final painting of Salem was hazy and ill-defined, but Agatha saw the town in the contrast of soft hues and striking blacks and grays.

Agatha, Raven, and Morgana were in the mural room of the witchery as they looked over the painting. Morgana ran her fingers over the picture. "This brings back some not-so-great memories. Are you sure you want to do this?"

Agatha nodded and stepped into the painting.

A few minutes later, she returned with Moo.

"That's why you went back?" Morgana asked

Agatha hugged Moo. "Yep. Now she can live the life she was supposed to."

"What the hell?" Raven asked.

"This was your mom's pig when she was accused in Salem," Morgana explained. "They slaughtered it, and Agatha never got over it." She looked at Agatha. "Did you see anything else?"

"I saw James. I told him to repeat to me when he saw me next that Moo was alive and safe."

Morgana knelt down and scratched the pig between the ears. "Let's introduce her to Mattie."

CHAPTER 40

T he vampires developed a healthy reverence for the witches of Vision and stayed out of their reach. Their vampire hunts had become fewer and farther between. But Fala flew in the depths of night, checking for changes in their surrounding areas.

One day Fala came to Vision. "I think I've found him."

"Found who?" Agatha asked. She'd just finished a Basic Elements class and sat at the table in the main room at the Witchery with Morgana and Raven.

"Mathias."

"How would you know?" Morgana asked.

Fala shook her head. "How long have we been doing this? How long have we been looking for him? He's not close, probably several days or a week's ride. It seems he's got a plantation or farm and brings humans in to hunt on his property. Mostly slaves. One of my people escaped him."

"This is how you found him?" Agatha asked.

"Yes. I've been flying over there. It's a long flight, so I had to spread my trips out. I didn't want to mention it until I was sure."

"How did one of your people *escape*?" Morgana asked. "I've never heard of anyone escaping a vampire."

"Immanuel escaped," Agatha said.

"Good point. He had a lot of help. But I guess it's possible."

"When do we leave?" Raven asked.

"You're not going," Agatha said.

Raven rolled her eyes. "Try to stop me."

"What if it's a trap?"

"Come on, Agatha, stop being so paranoid." Raven looked at Morgana. "What do you think?"

"Let's get him. Not only is he a disgusting vampire that feeds on the blood of the humans he mercilessly hunts, but he's also a witch killer. We've been waiting for this moment for two decades. It's our time for payback."

"I don't like this one bit," Agatha said. "It's awfully convenient."

"Agatha, put your emotions aside for a minute. Think logically about this. It's a gift."

Agatha sighed. "I know. I just don't want Raven involved."

"Agatha, stop," Raven said. "I'm as skilled as both of you, maybe more. And the more witches, the better our chances."

Agatha agreed only because she couldn't stop Raven from coming. She was sick with angst as they made their plans.

"I'll keep flying over the area to make sure it's him and it's safe," Fala said. "Well, as safe as it can be, considering what you'll be doing."

Agatha didn't like it. Her punishment for having children? Incessant worry.

"Raven, can you paint something that will take us there?" Morgana asked.

"I don't know, I guess I can try."

"Neither of you can go through," Agatha said.

"You brought Moo through time," Morgana said. "Maybe you can take us through."

"Even if I could, there's no guarantee we won't get sucked back before we kill Mathias," Agatha replied.

"Maybe we could do a test run and check the place out before we actually go in for the kill."

"That's not a bad idea. It might make me feel a little better about going after him."

Raven stood up and left. "I'd better get to painting then."

Fala squeezed Agatha's hand. "Agatha, I know this is hard for you."

"Thank you, Fala."

"I'm going home. I'll come back in a couple of days to see how preparations are going."

Raven reappeared. "Fala, wait. I'm going to need you for this, since you're the only one who knows where we're going."

"I guess I'll be staying!" She walked away with Raven.

CHAPTER 41

The four witches gathered in the art room.

Raven had completed the painting in a week. "I think because this painting only takes us through space—not time—we won't get sucked back."

"If that's the case, how will we get home?" Agatha asked.

"We can figure that out later."

"This is a problem we didn't think of. We need an escape plan."

"Maybe I can paint one to take with us; one that will bring us back?"

"I like that idea, Raven," Morgana said. "If Agatha gets pulled back without us, we just go home on our own. Or she can just come back and get us. You're sure this won't send us through time?"

Raven nodded.

"Okay," Agatha said. "We know we'll have at least an hour before we get pulled back, *if* it's going to pull us back, but I probably won't be at my best if I have to fight the force."

"Raven," Morgana said. "Paint another one we can carry through with us. We can leave it behind and let the elements take care of it. Other than that, we don't have too much to prepare."

"I'll need another few days."

Agatha nodded. "We'll leave you to it. I still don't like this, but I'll push my motherly worry aside for the *greater good*." She gave Morgana a wry smile, trying to make light of her worry. "I'm going to talk to your father about this."

Raven rolled her eyes. "Agatha, don't. He's going to get all worked up and tell us to let bygones be bygones and stop hunting. You know how he is."

"Exactly why I want to prepare him. Just paint, okay?"

"Fine."

Morgana took Agatha's arm. "Let it go, come on."

"Happy painting, Raven," Fala said. "See you soon."

When they were outside, Agatha said, "I don't like this one bit."

"We know," Morgana said. "It does you no good to complain or worry. Focus on what you can influence, okay? Go deal with James and relax."

"Relax? That's funny, Morgana."

"I'll leave you two to your bickering," Fala said. "I'm going home, and I'll be back in a few days."

CHAPTER 42

"Let's go tonight," Raven said after finishing the second painting a few days later.

It was a near match to the one Raven had just painted to take them where they were going. Lots of swirls of green with vague lines of brown that could be trees. This one would bring them home.

Agatha touched it and felt the familiar pull, but it differed from going through the mural and time. "No, we'll wait until tomorrow so you can get some rest."

Raven opened her mouth to protest, and Morgana jumped in. "Listen to your mother. She's right. And we have to wait for Fala to get back."

Raven nodded, then headed off toward their home. Agatha and Morgana followed. It was late, and she was tired.

"See you in the morning?" Morgana said.

Agatha hugged her. "Yes."

"I know this is hard, and I can't say anything to make it better. Just know I'm here and I love you."

"Thanks, friend. I know."

She slipped into bed next to a snoring James. The heave of his chest, a comfort she knew, had a time limit. He aged well, but still grew older.

Agatha remained the same youthful witch she'd been when they'd met all those years ago. She'd chosen to keep her magic and her youth at the expense of watching the men she loved get older. Stetson had grown into a wonderful man and was married to a young lady called Emily. They were expecting their first child. Agatha was relieved Emily wasn't a witch.

Agatha's raw passion for the looming kill was dulled by fear for her daughter. She lay in bed, awake and agonizing. Raven had been hunting with them for almost ten years, but Agatha couldn't shake her apprehension. It was her duty as a mother to care for her children, but how could she reconcile protecting her daughter and putting her in danger at the same time? Even though she'd seen her daughter in the future and knew she was fine, it didn't stop her from worrying in the present.

When they hunted, Morgana wouldn't let Agatha pair with Raven. Morgana said her mind was split between the hunt and protecting her daughter. She stayed with Fala—who was always within her bird on the hunts. Agatha could communicate with Coo and with Morgana from great distances through her telepathy. It made sense and kept them safe.

Agatha never quite lost the niggling in her gut that prevented her from focusing one hundred percent on the vampire. Most of their kills had been against younger vampires. Occasionally they came across an older one more difficult to kill, but still they were no match for the witch posse. She knew this time would be different, and she couldn't afford to lose her focus going up against Mathias.

Finally, she slept, though her sleep was restless. She dreamed of the great vampire laughing at her. *You think you can kill* me? *What a lovely delusion. Remember her?*

The eyeless witch from all those years ago materialized in her mind, and with a groan, she forced herself to wake up and rolled over. The sun was up, and James was gone.

Voices carried from the kitchen. She got out of bed and padded downstairs. Fala, Morgana, and Raven sat at the table laughing and drinking tea.

"Morning, sunshine," Fala said, handing her a mug filled with hot deliciousness.

"Is it? I feel like I didn't sleep at all." Agatha let the cup warm her hands and breathed in the steamy aroma of citrus and chrysanthemum. She sat down. "What did I miss?"

"We need to bring supplies in case we have to stay for a while," Fala said.

"Why would we have to do that?"

"Since it's too far away for Coo to scout," Morgana said. "We'll need to get there first and then find him."

"Auntie Mo thinks he'll be waiting for us," Raven added.

"*Auntie Mo*, care to elaborate?"

Morgana grimaced. "I don't think it's a coincidence one of Fala's own escaped. I think he's setting us up."

Agatha had thought the same thing. "You're probably right. He's too smart not to create a situation like that. I dreamt of him last night as well. He was in my head."

"That's creepy," Raven said.

Agatha shivered at the memory of the dream. "It was more than creepy. It felt real."

"I think I've heard of this before," Fala said. "In our legends, vampires can manipulate people by getting in their heads. For us witches, things are different in the dream world, and we have to be careful. Dreams are more than just dreams."

Agatha nodded. "I've heard something like this before as well. When we dream, we're on another plane of existence. My mother told me as a child to be careful in my dreams. She also told me it was a way to see our deceased loved ones. We could literally meet in our dreams."

"Same," Morgana said. "My mother used to tell me stories of meeting her mother in her dreams. Sometimes I have an imprint of having seen my mum when I wake up. But I never really thought about it."

"I wonder if we share this realm with vampires," Fala said. "They're biological immortals like us."

CHAPTER 43

They gathered in the Witchery, in what they now called *The Art Room*. They'd constructed a magic space around the mural, and Raven kept her paintings in there. Best to keep the magic locked up.

Agatha donned her quiver filled with silver-tipped arrows—and a few stakes for good measure—and slung her bow across her back. She looked around the room.

Morgana slipped her silver dirk into a leather holster around her waist. She'd traded in her axe because she preferred to get up close and personal when she killed. Agatha saw the way her daughter looked at Morgana's arms where embers from dying vampires had left their mark and knew she was in awe of all the scars.

Raven had a similar belt to hold her tomahawk. A brave in Fala's tribe had made it for her. It had an oversized sharp blade made of silver. She put stakes into a satchel worn on her back.

"I hope this works." Agatha looked at the painting spread out on the floor in front of her.

Raven handed her the sister painting they'd take with them, and she tucked it in the quiver. She was nervous, but the familiar tingle of blood lust was taking over.

Fala entered Coo, and Agatha tucked the bird inside her bodice to keep it snug during their trip.

"Let's go kill us a vampire," Raven said.

Agatha put her arms around Morgana and Raven. "Hold tight. This probably won't be fun." She stepped into the painting.

They landed on hard ground, and Agatha braced herself for the nausea that came with time travel, but there was none. She felt fine and was still hanging on to Morgana and Raven. "Everyone okay?"

"That was great," Raven said.

"Morgana, you okay?"

"Yes, I think I am."

Coo squirmed against Agatha's breast. She loosened her bodice, and the bird hopped up to Agatha's shoulder.

Morgana used her telepathy and said, *Only minds from now on.*

Coo flew off to scout the area as they'd planned.

If the witches didn't get pulled back to Vision, they might be there a while searching for Mathias. If Agatha got pulled back without Morgana and Raven, she would come back through the painting to get them.

The trio sat on the ground. They knew Coo might be gone a while; the moon was still high. Vampires hunted during what Agatha and Morgana called the Witching Hour, starting around 3:00 a.m. and lasting until dawn.

Coo came back periodically to check in. The second time she returned, she reported a house and outbuildings hidden deep in the woods.

Mathias's lair? Morgana thought.

Maybe? Probably? Raven responded.

For another time. Agatha thought. *Stay focused.*

Slow and steady, the moon traveled through the night sky. *I guess we're not getting pulled back to Vision,* Raven thought.

Agatha jumped, startled by Raven's words.

Coo finally returned with news of a vampire in the woods heading toward a village north of them. She wasn't sure if it came from the compound or not.

Agatha called on any large predators in the area for backup—just in case.

The witches would triangulate toward the vampire. Morgana and Raven would flank as they had the weapons for an up-close kill. Agatha would bring up the rear. With her bow and arrow, she could fire from a distance. Coo flew where they could follow her, checking ahead to make sure the vampire hadn't changed direction. They had done this over years of hunting, and it never failed.

Agatha glided across the damp earth, silent as a ghost. Sleeping birds ruffled their feathers as they shifted positions. Bats darted in and out of the shadows. A hooting owl startled her.

Complacency meant death. The anticipation of the kill was part of her edge. Morgana and Raven felt it as well. There had been a time, in their early years in Vision, when Agatha had grappled with the feelings brought on by their kills. She didn't like the feeling of taking a life. Morgana always talked her down, reminding her they'd never hunted a human or even an animal. "Vampires are different," Morgana had said. "They hunt for sport and they're incapable of remorse. We're making the world a better and safer place by killing them."

Morgana spoke the truth. By destroying even one vampire, they'd saved countless human lives. So, she kept her edge and savored every pair of melting eyes and every heart bursting into flames.

A stick cracked, and she sniffed the air. Vampires moved without sound. Probably an animal she'd summoned. But she pulled an arrow from her quiver and continued forward, loaded bow at her side.

Another *crack* vibrated in her ears. Again, she sniffed the air. There was a light wind in her face, and she only picked up the scents of the woods. Life and decay blended as one.

Morgana, any sight of it?

I can smell it. We're close.

Agatha picked up her pace.

There was a *whoosh* behind her. She whipped around and let her arrow fly. A flash of something scaled a tree.

Morgana! There's one here too. I'll...

Before she could finish her thought, she was hit from behind and fell to the ground.

Agatha! Are you okay?

She rolled over. A vampire approached with a knife. She conjured a stun spell and shot it at the vampire. It plummeted to the ground.

The spell missed, but the vampire dropped the knife, which bounced out of reach.

Agatha rose and summoned the knife. As it flew in her direction, another vampire came out of nowhere and plucked the knife from the air five feet in front of her. It kept moving forward and disappeared into the trees.

The vampire on the ground scrambled to its feet.

Agatha kept her calm and pulled an arrow from her quiver, loaded, and aimed. The vampire rushed her. She didn't have time to conjure a spell. Had no idea where the second one had gone. Time to improvise. She didn't stand a chance in hand-to-hand combat, so yelled to the animals to come to her aid.

She let her arrow fly. It pierced the chest of the vampire, and it went up in an unimpressive puff of smoke. She spun around, looking for the other one. *Where did you go?*

Another *whoosh* and she turned again to see it flying toward her. Before she could react, it knocked her off her feet with its impact. One hand clenched her throat. It straddled her, pinning her down with its weight. It raised the knife above its head, ready to strike.

A bear roared behind the vampire. It paused for a split second and turned.

Agatha freed a hand and tried to conjure a spell. The bear swiped a massive paw at the vampire's head. It missed its mark because the vampire suddenly melted on top of her. Bits of burning vampire flesh rained down, singeing her bodice and chest. The vampire turned to smoke and dissipated into thin air. The knife dropped onto her bodice.

She sat up and looked at the bear. *What the hell just happened?*

The bear had no answer, and it plopped down on all fours and padded back into the depths of the forest. In her head, Agatha yelled after it, *Thank you!*

It went about its business. Agatha had learned over the years bears kept to themselves but would drop everything to help her.

She looked around and saw nothing except the giant bear disappearing into the dark. Something had killed the second vampire. But what? She retrieved her arrow and put it back in her quiver.

Coo fluttered in Agatha's face. *Hurry.*

Agatha followed the bird through the woods, running to keep up. *Morgana! Raven! Are you okay?*

No reply. She ran faster after Coo.

She came into a clearing, saw Morgana and Raven in the distance, and sprinted the rest of the way.

Raven lay in Morgana's arms, blood covering her throat and clothes.

"Oh my God!" She fell at Raven's side. "My baby, oh my baby." She ran her hand through Raven's hair and caressed her cheek. Raven's eyes fluttered.

Agatha gasped and looked at Morgana. "What happened?"

"It was *him* and one more."

Agatha started crying.

"It's okay, Momma," Raven said. "It looks worse than it is. I conjured fake blood for effect. He still cut me, though. Just a flesh wound."

Agatha's heart leapt. She sat next to her daughter and ran her hand through her hair.

"Don't get comfortable, we need to go," Morgana said. "Mathias is going to be out for our blood. I...cut his hand off."

"What?!"

Raven coughed and spat up blood. "I'm fine, let's go."

"We need to get away from here and back to the Witchery," Morgana said. "Then we can swap stories."

Agatha grinned. "You cut his hand off?"

Morgana smiled and nodded. "Where's the painting?"

Agatha pulled it out of her quiver and spread it out on the ground. Coo flew down and landed on Agatha's shoulder. When Agatha started to put the bird in her bodice, it fell open, exposing her singed breast.

Raven laughed. "What happened to you? Is this something I need to discuss with Dad?"

Agatha ignored her daughter and grimaced. Her skin was blistered. "Can you put Coo in your bodice, Morgana?"

Morgana nodded and took the bird.

Raven stood, and Agatha jumped to her side in an instant. "Put your arm around my shoulder."

"I'm fine, Mom."

Morgana took hold of Agatha's arm. "Ready?"

Agatha nodded and stepped into the painting. They tumbled through space. She prayed for the safety of her daughter, and they landed in the Witchery.

"Everyone okay?" Agatha asked.

Morgana nodded. "Let's get Raven fixed up. Agatha, you might want to cover yourself up." She pointed to Agatha's exposed breast.

Agatha laughed and tried to cover herself, but the bodice was too burned. "I think I have a shawl here somewhere." She closed her eyes and summoned it. Her wool shawl floated through the air and wrapped itself around her.

Morgana released Coo and Fala's body came to life. "That was insane."

They went to the potions room, where Fala and Agatha put an herbal remedy on Raven's neck and watched the wound seal itself up.

"Do you feel okay, Raven?" Agatha asked.

She nodded and touched her throat. "My first battle scar."

Agatha sighed. "Tell me everything. What happened?"

"I'll make some tea," Fala said. "Start talking."

Morgana smiled. "Yes, ma'am. We were following Coo, and Raven got to the vampire we were tracking first and engaged. She called for me, so I headed in her direction. Just as I was getting to her, she drove a stake into the thing's heart. Her tomahawk was still attached to her hip."

Raven interjected, "I like to feel the heat from their flaming deaths."

Agatha understood and thought, *Like mother, like daughter.*

Morgana continued. "One minute, the vampire is melting and the next, Mathias has her in a chokehold with a knife to her throat. I have no idea where he came from. I'm guessing it was some kind of trap."

Agatha shook her head in disbelief. "Is he dead? Or is it just his hand that burned?"

Morgana shrugged.

"If he were dead, the way his hand lit up, we would've seen him burning too," Raven said.

"He's going to be really pissed now," Morgana replied.

"Like a hornet."

Fala returned with steaming cups of tea. "Maybe, maybe not. He could be seriously injured."

Morgana shrugged. "The way his hand was burning, he might be. What happened with you?"

Agatha relayed her story of the vampire turning to dust seemingly out of nowhere. "Have you ever heard of anything like that happening?"

"I heard of this long ago in prison, back in Krakow. When you kill a vampire, it's children die with it."

Agatha was a bit surprised to hear this. "So, if we kill Mathias, all his children will die with him? It can't be that simple. But maybe there's truth to it."

MATHIAS – ESCAPE

CHAPTER 44

He felt the death of his newly created child and a small reverberation as his child's child disappeared in a puff of smoke.

A slight irritation, but they were going to meet their deaths at the hands of the witches. That was why he created them. Though he'd hoped they would've presented more of a challenge for his nemeses.

He waited as George—such a boring name for a vampire—went up in an unimpressive *poof*. In one motion, he pulled the knife from his pocket and stepped behind the witch who had just put George out of his misery.

Mathias slipped his arm around her waist and positioned the knife at her throat. "Don't move, love, or I'll cut your head clean off." He smiled as he felt the witch tense in his grasp. For good measure, he cut her enough to sting and bleed, but not enough to do serious damage.

It was difficult not to cut her head right off. But he needed that bitch, Morgana, to see that.

He yelled into the night. "Morgana, come see what I've got!" He laughed, deep and hearty. But was savvy enough to be careful with the two witches together.

He smelled her revolting witch scent before he heard her.

Then she appeared. "Mathias, what a pleasure. I've been waiting a long time for this day."

He laughed again. "I guess this is someone you care about." He moved the knife up and down her throat, coating it in the blood he'd drawn.

"Yes."

She was trying to be stoic but was rattled. This made him smile. "Daughter? Sister? Friend? So hard to tell with you witches. No matter. Here's your choice, a little *quid pro quo*. Come after me or save this waif."

He waited for his words to register. He thought he felt something transpire between the witches and reminded himself to be careful.

"Choose." He moved his knife across the witch's throat and realized something was wrong. Where was the blood? The knife should have sliced her carotid, showering the Morgana bitch. Instead, she tossed a tomahawk to Morgana. He dropped the witch and ran into the woods. She came after him, and he felt something unfamiliar. Fear?

The thought was enough to stop him in his tracks. He was Mathias, the greatest vampire of all time. Afraid of nothing. He shook off his fear as a wet dog shakes off water. He'd faced magic before and won. Every time.

Mathias spun around, his dark cape flowing wildly behind him. His fangs quivered. The tomahawk soared toward him. He put his hand up to grab it out of the air. Its trajectory altered away from his hand and straight for his face. It was probably infused with magic. If he turned and ran, it would end up in his head. He had to face it and teach these witches a lesson.

Mathias positioned himself in front of a tree. He knelt, intending for the tomahawk to go over his head and strike the tree behind him. He lowered his head and took a hold of his cape, flinging it around to shield his face and body. His cape had magic of its own. Impenetrable to silver. Beneath the cape, he kept his arm up and head bowed, forming a tent to shield himself from the blow he knew was coming.

But his hand was still exposed, and the tomahawk sliced through his unprotected wrist—the silver was acid on his skin. The weapon cut through his bone, then lodged in the tree. The cape dropped open, and his hand fell to the ground. He howled, shaking his very being. The ground below him quivered as his cry reverberated throughout the forest.

It was all he could do to get up and move. He had to get home before the poison of the silver made it to his heart. His severed hand writhed on the ground like it had a life of its own. He smelled the witch coming in his direction and ran.

CHAPTER 45

Mathias had always employed men with wives and children to run his lands for him. He paid them well for their loyalty and they knew betrayal meant a violent death for their families—while they watched—and a brutal end to their own lives would follow. Fear and money, Mathias found, were the best ways to ensure the allegiance of humans.

Jesse was waiting for him when he returned. "Master! What happened?"

Mathias slurred as if he was drunk. "Sa, sa, sil."

"Silver?"

Mathias nodded.

Jesse took Mathias by the arm and led him to the bowels of the home where his sarcophagus was stored. Jesse opened the lid and helped Mathias get in. A vampire's sarcophagus was a place of healing and rejuvenation. Mathias rarely needed his, but for a young vampire it was an important place of respite.

The sarcophagus would induce a paralysis so his body could focus on repairing the broken parts. When the lid was closed—as it should be for serious injuries—the vampire's body entered a hibernation state, no longer requiring nourishment. This was important for healing and also traveling long distances by boat, so all the human passengers didn't end up as meals.

His sarcophagus had been built for him by the famous Alexandrian alchemist, Mary the Jewess, shortly after the death of Jesus and after he'd turned Alma. It was big enough for the two of them. Constructed of sycamore, a hearty, long-lasting wood, it was stained red, which had a double meaning of vitality and energy, and more appropriately, evil and destruction. Decorated with ornate artwork, Mathias had depictions of himself and Alma in orgiastic scenes with dying humans in artistic stasis. He hated that he had to use the sarcophagus at all, but climbing into it alone was even worse. Even in his poisoned agony, he pined for his Alma.

The magic infused during the construction enabled the healing. As far as Mathias knew, alchemy, as it had been, was a long-forgotten art. He'd had his sarcophagus for over fifteen hundred years, and it was the same as the day it was made.

Jesse fetched the large magnet stored under the sarcophagus and put it directly on the stub where his hand used to be. This healing process had also been discovered by Mary the Jewess. Her experiments on vampires and their healing had been priceless to Mathias. Vampires didn't bleed as humans did. Instead, the stump was charred and ragged, the poison from the silver eating through his skin and bone. The sensation brought on by the magnet was excruciating, but it would draw out any silver left behind and neutralize the effects it had on Mathias's body. Mathias had been through the tedious process before, but nowhere near the extent of his current state.

Next was the poultice. Jesse prepared an herbal salve to stop the poison from advancing. With the healing properties of the magnet, it would prevent death and additional damage to the vampire's body. Jesse wrapped Mathias's arm, chest, and neck with the poultice.

Vampires were like salamanders and could regenerate body parts. If the tomahawk that removed Mathias's hand hadn't been silver, it would grow back as normal. But this was unfamiliar territory. A learning experience. A younger, lesser vampire would have turned to dust from exposure to the silver and trauma to the body.

Jesse started to close the lid of the sarcophagus.

Mathias stopped him. "No. It must remain open while you're treating me. It can't be closed until the poison is gone."

Jesse nodded. "Yes, sir. Sleep well, master."

His body responded to the soothing poultice. Safe in his sarcophagus, his fatigue lulled him into a deep slumber. In his delirium, he saw Alma. She took care of him, changing the poultice, keeping him nourished and alive.

Now and then he'd come into consciousness, and it wasn't Alma tending to him, but Jesse. All he had to do was close his eyes, and she would be back. He'd thought she was a dream. He reached out and touched her beautiful face and ran his fingers over her luscious, blood-red lips.

She leaned down and kissed him. "Mathias, you're awake."

"Awake? Is it really you, my love?"

"Remember how you cared for me when I was a halfling? You held me so tight and spoke your love to me nonstop."

He smiled at the memory. "Yes, my love. You're my greatest creation."

She kissed him again. "That was a terrible time, but because of you, the memory brings comfort. It's one of my favorites."

He thought about her words. Of all those he could claim as his children, she'd been the only one he nursed through the entire change. Such was his love for her.

She reminisced with him, reminding him of the many adventures they'd shared over their centuries together. "Remember our time in Portugal? How you helped me with the turning of Mangus? The fun we had together? Remember Mangus, he's a loyal friend."

He smiled at the memories, but didn't remember specifics about their time in Portugal. The feelings evoked by the nostalgia brought an intense longing for Alma. He touched her face, smooth and cold as a Greek statue. "I love you, Alma. Are you real? You feel so real, but I'm afraid when I'm better, you'll be gone."

"This is real, Mathias. It's part of the magic in the sarcophagus. It takes us to the dream realm, where we can be together. Our bond was too strong to be broken by a wooden stake. But I'll disappear when you're healed. Let's enjoy the time we have."

He woke. Jesse was there again, and confusion washed over him.

"I heard you talking in your sleep, master. Are you okay?"

All Mathias could do was nod. He wanted to slip back into his dream world so he could see Alma again. He closed his eyes and faded to black.

She was there again, lying next to him.

"My love," he said. "What is this place? Can't we say here forever?"

"Mathias." She stroked his cheek and kissed him. "There's a way for us to be together again and perhaps get your revenge as well."

"What do you mean? We're together now."

She kissed him again. "This place is temporary. It's not sustainable. I mean *really* together. We can live and hunt and regain the happiness those witches took from us."

"Tell me what to do."

"You must recover. Go to Portugal, to Mangus. It's too dangerous to stay here in your condition. The witches will find you, and this time they'll finish the job." He took in her words and knew she spoke the truth. "Have Jesse find the painting they left behind and keep it with you in your sarcophagus. It's at the spot where you had your battle." Alma made him repeat the directions she gave him so he could recite them to Jesse.

Mathias was having a hard time following Alma. All he wanted was for her to hold him. Thinking was too difficult. "Painting? What painting?"

"It's magic. It's our first move in a very long game."

"Game?"

"Oh, my love." She caressed his face and kissed him. "One step at a time. Once he secures the painting, we'll go over the next steps. Wake up now."

He woke to find Jesse checking his wound. He was delirious, unsure how much time had passed. Time seemed to stand still while he was with Alma.

"Jesse, I need you to do something for me."

"Anything, master."

"There is a painting in the woods the witches left behind. I need you to find it, bring it here, and put it in the sarcophagus with me." He repeated exactly what Alma had told him about where he could find the painting. "Now go get it. It's most important."

"Yes, master."

Mathias forced himself to stay awake until Jesse returned.

"Master, it was right where you said it would be."

"Let me see it."

He showed Mathias the canvas with the strange painting.

"Thank you, Jesse. Please put it next to me."

Jesse rolled it up and put it in the sarcophagus next to Mathias. He removed the magnet and checked the wound, then put it back in place.

"Jesse? How long have I been in here?"

"Only a few days, sir. You're healing quite well, but still have a long way to go. Drink this, sir." Mathias tried to sit up and take the glass from Jesse, but he was too weak. "Master, lie down. Open your mouth, and I'll pour it in."

Mathias did as he was told and felt a hunger as the blood flowed across his tongue and down his throat. He closed his eyes and savored it. His fangs quivered slightly, but sleep overtook him before he realized what was happening.

Alma was back, running her fingers through his hair. His reverie seemed more and more real.

"My love."

"You're going to be okay." She pulled herself closer to him and kissed his nose.

"If it means I'm going to lose you again, I don't want to be okay."

"Mathias, I need you to listen to me. Once you close the sarcophagus, your hibernation will begin, and I'll be gone. I think you'll be safe to keep it open until you reach Portugal, but no longer."

"What do you mean?"

"Once the poison is gone, you must rejuvenate your hand, your mind, and your strength."

"Why do you have to leave?"

She shrugged. "I don't understand the rules. I just know you can't hibernate in *this place*. If you don't hibernate, you won't heal, and our plan will fail. We have to be patient with this for the big reward. We don't have a future in this realm. We're not living, just existing." She smiled and kissed him again, biting his lip. "The gods have given us a second chance, Mathias."

"Alma. I can't bear to lose you again."

"I know, a small sacrifice now, so we can be together forever." She took his hand. "Jesse will help you with everything. He's a good servant."

"Tell me what to do."

Mathias concentrated on her instructions. When she finished, his sleep came easy. The feel of her body next to his was the greatest of comforts. If her plan worked, he wouldn't let her out of his sight again. She was all he needed.

When he woke next, she was gone, and Jesse was there. His confusion was lessened, and he didn't know if he'd been hallucinating Alma or not. He didn't care, and just wanted her there with him.

"What else can I do, master?"

Mathias laid out everything Alma had said. Once again, he wondered if she was a construct of his sickness. In the untouched depths of his mind, he couldn't know these things. His fingers brushed the painting rolled up next to him and he knew it was her.

"Jesse, you and your family will be long dead when I'm able to return. I will take care of your children and their children, but I need your word that your family will stay here and take care of my property."

"Of course, sir."

"What's most important is they understand who I am and what I'll do to them if I return, and things aren't as they should be. They must be as diligent and loyal as you've been."

"You have my word, master."

Mathias slept, and Alma returned.

"Tell me about this painting," he said.

"The witch, Raven, can create paintings allowing for travel through time and space. Only certain witches can pass through, but they can bring others with them."

Mathias touched her face and knew she wasn't a figment of his sick mind. He felt a stirring in his loins and his fangs quivered. "Alma."

She kissed him, and pulling her skirts up, straddled him. As he lay helpless beneath her, she guided him inside her. She gasped. "Mathias, I don't think this is a good idea. You're too weak."

He responded by thrusting himself into the depths of her body and cried out. She countered by shifting her hips back and forth until she, too, screamed in ecstasy and collapsed on top of him.

She bit his neck, her fangs still sharp. Mathias put his arms around her and squeezed her close. He would travel to the ends of the earth and fight whatever demon came before him to have his Alma back.

He fell into what he'd now dubbed reality number one, and Jesse was there. "Master. Are you okay?"

"Yes, Jesse. I'm just going to sleep."

Jesse looked around. "I heard you scream. I thought I heard a woman's voice and feared the witches were here."

"It was not the witches, Jesse. I think it was a ghost. I'm fine. I need to rest. Really, Jesse, it's okay."

Jesse returned upstairs, and Mathias was even more confused. He slept, and there she was, her index finger drawing on his cheek.

"My love."

He didn't care if she was a figment of his imagination. She was as real to him as the sarcophagus in which he lay. Mathias had three states of being. He was fully awake when Jesse was there tending to his wounds. He had a sleep state when he was truly asleep. And this state. Some alternate reality or just a dream. It was magic in the sarcophagus. He didn't care.

"Mathias, you must go soon. Have Jesse secure the ship. He's going to need a supply of blood if you wish to keep your sarcophagus open."

"Will you be with me on the ship?"

She nodded. "Have him send word to Mangus so it will be a smooth transition when you arrive. You must go soon."

He slept, deep and restful, knowing he could wake up with Alma's arm slung across his chest, her soft lips nuzzling the space just behind his earlobe. He felt his body healing. Her presence was his panacea. He had a long way to go, but knowing she'd be with him on the ship gave him something he'd lost the moment she died. Purpose.

Together they'd been an unstoppable force. Before she died, they'd worked on their business with slaves as an ongoing source of prey.

Mathias had fallen into a deep depression once he'd killed Seth. His plot for revenge failed because he wasn't his complete self. Grief clouded his head. Revenge was an emotional task that required clarity of mind. No wonder those witches had gotten the best of him.

He thought back on the witch trials, Alma's wonderful creation. They'd had such fun with that endeavor. She shared his passion for studying humanity so it could be exploited, traveling, learning, hunting, and loving. She was irresistible as his lover. No other woman could satisfy him beyond fulfilling a need. They were like drinking blood from a fancy goblet. Alma was the hunt.

"Mathias."

He started out of his trance. "Yes, love." He drew her close and kissed her.

"Be careful, my love. I don't want you to hurt yourself more."

"Alma, I want to experience every piece of you I can while you're here. I have plenty of time to heal once you leave me again."

She kissed him hard and mounted him again and together they exploded in mutual ecstasy.

He slept. He woke. Jesse changed his poultice.

"Master, you're awake."

"Yes. What is it, Jesse?"

"You sleep more and more. I've been worried you're turning for the worse, but your wound is healing."

"I'm fine, Jesse. My body is preparing for the time you close my sarcophagus, my hibernation."

Jesse nodded. "I hear you talking, master. You seem to be asleep when I come down to check. Sometimes I hear another voice. A woman."

Mathias nodded. "Ghosts are real in my sarcophagus. Not to worry, Jesse. How long before the ship is ready?"

"Soon, sir. Tomorrow or the next day."

"And you have sent the letter to Mangus? He knows I'm coming?"

"I've sent the letter, master. It probably hasn't arrived yet; it's only been a few days."

"Yes, yes. Okay. Thank you, Jesse."

"The magnct, sire."

"Yes, what about it?"

"It's loosening. The poison from the silver is diminishing. Perhaps it will fall off on its own before we leave."

"That would be most favorable, Jesse. Thank you for your devotion to saving me."

"Your hand, sir. Will it grow back?"

"I'm not sure. I've grown back many a finger and toe!" He laughed at the thought of some of his clumsier accidents over the millennia. "Never had a major accident with silver. So, I guess we'll find out, won't we?"

"Yes, master."

"Thank you, Jesse."

CHAPTER 46

They left in the moonlight of the early morning hours for the port of New Orleans, where Mathias's shipping company did most of its business. Mathias felt the rough road beneath him as the carriage made its way to the port. His sarcophagus was well insulated and conformed to his body so he would be comfortable in his long hibernation. It had only been two weeks since his battle with the witches, and he understood the urgency of his escape in a weakened state. He would be the only cargo on the ship for the month-long voyage to Portugal.

Jesse would travel with him and tend to his wounds. Mangus would greet them upon their arrival in Lisbon and take him to his home in the mountain village of Sintra. He could stay there as long as he needed to heal, and he would be safe.

Once he settled at Mangus's home, the lid to the sarcophagus would be closed, and Mathias would begin his healing hibernation—and lose his Alma again. He would make the most of his journey and the time he had left with her. His time with Alma made all his suffering worthwhile. He still dreamed of revenge, but if he could get Alma back, he might just forget about the Vision witches. He smiled at the thought. *Who are you kidding?*

Mathias was alone in the carriage and immediately closed his eyes and waited for Alma.

"Hello, lover." Her red lips moved across his ear as she spoke.

"Alma."

She stroked his cheek with a long nail. "Mathias."

He could get lost staring into the deep well of her eyes. Kissing her again was what he imagined heaven must be like, and time stood still when they made love. He was determined to make this fleeting time together the most meaningful they'd ever had.

"Can we stay in this place until it's time to close the sarcophagus?"

"You need nourishment, Mathias. You have to wake up sometime."

"What about you? Don't you need to feed?"

Alma shook her head. "I remember the satisfaction we got from hunting and how the blood was like a drug to us, our reward. But I don't have the urges. That's how I know this place can't be real. I'm bound to the sarcophagus." She smiled. "I'm glad it's a double."

They lay in the sarcophagus, the ground rumbling below them. He took her hand and wished for the moment to go on forever. He hadn't believed vampires had any kind of soul, but maybe he was wrong. Maybe her energy moved on to another plane of existence. And somehow, in his injured state, their two planes overlapped.

CHAPTER 47

They arrived in Portugal without incident, and Mangus was to meet them on the ship.

"It's time, my love," Alma said. Mathias felt his heart might burst at the thought of losing her again. He kissed her beautiful lips. "Remember our plan."

He touched the painting. "It all starts with this." He kissed her again. "Can Mangus see you?"

"I don't think so. Mathias, it's time. I feel it. I love you."

He touched her cheek and went to kiss her again.

But she was gone.

Just as his heart was breaking once again, Mangus barged in. "Mathias! Old friend. Seems you've gotten yourself in a bit of a pickle! Let me see that hand."

Mathias smiled at the sight of his old friend and lifted his arm. "Mangus. Thank you."

Mangus took his arm and looked at the stub where his hand once was. "Looks to be healing up."

"Any idea if it will grow back? This is outside my realm of expertise."

Mangus laughed. "No idea, mate. I was shocked to hear the great Mathias was dealt such a wound. I guess we'll find out when you come out of hibernation."

Mathias nodded. He wanted to be numb to losing Alma again. But this time, the loss came with a promise that gave him hope.

"Okay, Mangus, let's get on with it."

"See you in a century or three."

"Thank you, Mangus."

The lid to the sarcophagus closed, and Mathias drifted off into nothing.

AGATHA – THE DECISION

CHAPTER 48

Agatha couldn't help but think she'd overstayed her welcome on Earth. She'd raised her children. The natural progression of life was death.

It was different for Morgana and Raven, who had chosen their lives, solitary and childless, with no real attachments.

Well, there was Lydia. They'd grown quite close through Agatha's time travels, but she had yet to be born. Agatha still didn't know who her father was.

As she grew older and watched her children and grandchildren grow up, she felt out of place. She finally identified the nagging in her gut as a slap in the face by Mother Nature. *She* was strong and pure and unchanging. By staying alive, Agatha was defying Her laws, which

Morgana and Raven lived outside of. They could move on in time without repercussion or regret.

She believed Mathias was dead. He'd disappeared after Morgana cut his hand off, and she assumed the silver had killed him. Since then, vampire activity had slowed. Fala had searched for signs of Mathias for an entire year and found no evidence he lived.

The memory of that hunt still haunted her. Raven had been injured more than she let on. She'd dulled Mathias's knife some, but Mathias had inflicted a nasty wound. Just not a mortal one. He hadn't cut deep enough to sever her carotid, but even with a dulled knife he caused a significant loss of blood. Morgana had stopped the bleeding immediately, but Raven still had a nasty scar.

Raven wanted to keep the scar. It was her first proper battle wound, and she was proud of it. Agatha was just thankful her daughter was alive.

It was the witches' sixty-second year together. Agatha sat with Morgana by the lake watching the sunset. Agatha's latest pig, Luna, lay on her back between them. Agatha rubbed Luna's large, spotted belly.

She looked at Morgana, who stared at the sunset, leaning back on her arms. She hadn't changed since the first day they met all those years ago in prison. Her pale skin glowed in the fading sun. A faint smile touched her soft pink lips. The conversation would be the most difficult one of Agatha's life.

It was October. Trees shivered in their nakedness. Agatha loved this time of year. A sense of endings came with fall; a wrapping up of Mother Nature's earthly endeavors before she tucked everything away for winter. But with those endings also came a kiss of hope.

Agatha had lived many years. Many lives. Child. Wife. Prisoner. Parent. Vampire killer. The common thread that wove her lives together in the patchwork of her soul was *witch*—this part of her life about to end.

As she severed that thread, the rest of her parts would slowly die. She was relinquishing a piece of herself, to whom she had no idea but understood the importance of this transformation. Endings brought change. They also brought new beginnings.

She focused on the subtle vibrations of the earth as it too prepared for the shifting of the seasons, wishing she could absorb its infinite knowledge on how to proceed; anything to prolong her task at hand.

"This never gets old," Morgana said. "All the years we've been here, I never tire of this sunset."

"It's so beautiful."

They sat in a silence so uncomfortable for Agatha she thought Morgana had to feel it radiating off her.

She finally mustered her courage. "Morgana, there's something we need to talk about."

Morgana looked at Agatha, and she could tell her friend already knew what she was going to say.

Agatha reached across Luna's wide girth and took Morgana's hand. "James is in the ground ten years. Stetson is growing old, his sons now fathers."

"But what about us, and Raven?"

Agatha had been over this in her mind a million times, but still she paused, the lump in her throat trapping her words, the tears refusing to be dammed. She gave a little gasp as she tried to regroup. "She's as strong a witch as either of us. The two of you can carry on without me." *Carry on without me.* The words lingered in her mouth, as if she'd eaten something unpleasant.

"That's your response? Of course, we can carry on without you. That's not the point. I don't *want* to go on without you. Our years together have been perfect. We could go on like this forever. We're doing so much good in this terrible world. Why do you want to give that up? What we have is destiny. I've loved you for an eternity already. Our souls are woven together in a tapestry so intricate it can't be undone."

Luna gave a slight grunt and rolled onto her side as if she knew the importance of the conversation and didn't want to miss out on anything.

Agatha was silent for a long time. Tears slipped down her face, and although Morgana's words were as true as the sunset before them, so was what she had to do. "I have to do this. Everything you said is true for me as well. I couldn't be more blessed to have had a fraction of all of *this.*" She made a dramatic gesture with her hand to encompass everything around them. "This decision isn't driven by emotion, but what's in my heart, if that makes any sense. James was one thing, and maybe even Stetson, but I can't outlive my grandsons."

"What about the mysterious Lydia? Don't you want to see how that plays out?"

Agatha shrugged. "I've spent so much time with her already."

Morgana started to cry now too. Agatha got up and moved to her other side and put her arms around her shoulder. Morgana leaned into her. The slight jolts of her sobs were knives to Agatha's soul.

"Hey." She took Morgana's face in her hands and kissed the tears that dampened her cheeks. "I still have time. It's not like I'll be gone tomorrow. Look at us, we may as well still be eighteen. I have a lot of aging to do, so let's make the most of the time we have left. If our souls are tied together, then nothing, not even death, can keep us apart."

Their embrace held the depth of them, their time together, their accomplishments and setbacks and the raw passion between them. It was all palpable. They were an unstoppable force. Agatha knew it was selfish to leave Morgana behind. But she had to be true to herself. Without that, she'd never stay true to Morgana. As much as she never wanted to let go, it was her season to shed and prepare for the next phase of life. She pulled out of the embrace and kissed Morgana's tears away.

"I want to make the most of this time. I don't know how long it will take. I'll keep visiting you and Raven in the future for as long as I can."

Morgana shot her a look. "You know, there's a simpler way to accomplish that, right? Stay with us."

CHAPTER 49

Over a decade passed before Agatha aged enough to succumb to the darkness. Without using her powers, time caught up with her quickly. As she lay dying, she was vaguely aware of Morgana and Raven's presence.

But she was somewhere else, tethered to her body and the earthly things. The thin string connecting body and consciousness—torn and frayed as it was—held her back. The sadness in the room surrounded her, but she felt nothing in return, just a deep emptiness.

The essences of Morgana and Raven faded, and she saw little Moo. A tear formed in her earthly eyes. She reached for Moo, but the tether kept her away. *Why?* she wondered. She saw James and Stetson off in the distance, walking through a field toward the lake, as they had done so many times.

Was this some kind of mirage or was death just like life? How boring it would be. She'd been hoping for a new adventure, a fresh start, not more of the same. What if she'd made the wrong decision? What if this next phase of life was just an illusion? A trick of a tired mind. What if it was all a mistake, and she needed to stay behind to be with Morgana and Raven? What if she'd chosen the coward's way out and left behind a beautiful life for no reason at all?

Moo oinked at her, driving her gaze to the edge of the forest. She felt more present in this other place. She looked closer, she saw things were slightly off. The edges were softer, dreamlike. The colors had a sepia hue to them. She focused on what Moo was trying to tell her, and there, at the edge of the forest, stood someone familiar. Agatha couldn't quite place her. Then, as she felt her earthly shackles fall away, she realized it was Alma staring back at her, beckoning with a wicked smile.

"Welcome to the underworld of the immortals, dear Agatha. Welcome to your worst nightmare. Don't worry about me, love, I'll not be bothering you here. I'll be leaving this place soon enough. It's your family you have to worry about now. That family you chose to leave behind."

Agatha tried to spin a stun spell, but everything seemed sticky. Her thoughts were cloudy like she'd just woken up. Her hand wasn't fully there, flickering like a shadow at dusk.

Moo looked frantic, trying to tell Agatha something. She dropped her hand, giving up on the spell, and focused on Moo. She willed herself to get closer, but her feet were stuck. It was like time traveling, that viscous feeling, and she wondered if it was a similar journey to the underworld. If it was, could Raven paint a picture that would bring her here?

Alma laughed, the sound grating to Agatha's core. "Agatha! Aaaa-gaaathaaa! Welcome to hell."

Moo broke through Alma's screeching voice. *Go back!*

Agatha shot up in her bed and gasped, opening her eyes in horror, pointing at what she was seeing in the other place. Morgana was there, holding her hand. Agatha squeezed it and thought *I want to live!*

PART V

NOW

THOMAS –
THE BEST LAID PLANS

CHAPTER 50

After saying goodbye to Martha and her family, Thomas headed back to his condo to kill time and gloat over his success with Martha. Now and then, he'd come across a student with a brilliant understanding of philosophy that made teaching worthwhile. Martha had been one such student, but his plans for her had always been different. A damned shame for such a talent to go to waste.

He texted Martha. *Miss you already, love. Almost home?*

She responded immediately. *Miss you too, almost there.*

Thomas grabbed his keys and headed down to the garage. He took his spacious G-Wagon and drove to Martha's apartment to visit Gretchen. Her car wasn't anywhere to be seen. Had she already left for spring break? He went up to the apartment and let himself in. His nose was as sensitive as a dog's, and he could tell Gretchen hadn't been there in some time. "That's okay. I'll make do without her."

The apartment door remained ajar as he searched inside. An unfamiliar scent from outside tickled his nose. He waited in the kitchen with a view of the door.

"Hello? Martha? You here?" The person knocked on the door and nudged it open. "Gretchen? Anyone here?"

Could it be? Thomas thought and smiled. He stepped into view of the door. "You must be Jake." He held out his hand. "I'm Thomas."

CHAPTER 51

It was easy enough to get Jake in his car, telling him he'd take him to Martha. Either Martha hadn't told Jake about him, or he was so wound up he didn't put two and two together. He drove back to his garage, and when they alighted from the car, he hit Jake hard enough to knock him out.

But not hard enough to kill him. Thomas zip-tied Jake's hands and legs, gagged him in case he woke up, stuffed him in the back of his SUV, and headed for his hunting lodge—insurance for his upcoming endeavor.

He turned on the Rolling Stones' *Beggars Banquet* and smiled as the jungle sounds of "Sympathy for the Devil" filled the car. The Stones had an unusual understanding of humanity. Their music spoke to all walks of life. He'd been listening to them for nearly sixty years now—their music as relevant today as it was in 1964. He identified with "Sympathy for the Devil" and thought of himself as Lucifer, wreaking havoc on humanity just because he could.

CHAPTER 52

He stood with a doped-up, smelly Jake, a steady stream of morphine running through his veins, admiring the beautiful and naked Martha handcuffed to his bed.

Thomas grinned. It was even better than planned.

Martha had been hesitant about the handcuffs, but she'd do anything to please him. For all her bravado, she was just another insecure girl driven by low self-esteem and a desire for people to like her.

Getting her in bed the first time had also been much easier than he expected. He'd done his homework and knew about Jake, as well as her penchant for older professors. He'd expected some resistance, but she'd moved on him like a hungry lioness devouring her prey. And just like that, she was his.

He'd used the promise of sex as his weapon of innocent manipulation, making her think the handcuffs were a natural progression in their sex life. He smiled at the thought of it.

He'd kidnapped Jake for a specific purpose, but the look on Martha's face when he showed her this *surprise* was a most satisfying bonus.

Like an afterthought, she whispered, "Jake." She turned her head and vomited all over his bed. She looked at Thomas. "Why is he here?"

"Collateral."

Thomas read the confusion on her face and smirked. He pushed Jake down into an oversized armchair. "Be a good boy and stay."

He strode over to Martha, struggling against the handcuffs. Her olive skin and blonde hair against his dark maroon bedding looked good enough to eat. A pity that was out of the question.

He straddled her and put his index finger to her lips. "Shh. No more questions. I want you to prove you love me." Thomas leaned in to kiss her, just to see how she'd respond. He wasn't surprised when she kissed him back. He wondered if she'd let him fuck her in front of Jake. Not like she could stop him. She tugged against the handcuffs and squirmed beneath him. He ran his fingers over her soft belly and across her perfect breasts. "What's wrong, love?"

She gasped as his fingers circled her nipples, eventually relaxing beneath him. She couldn't resist his touch. Too easy. He kissed her again. "Do you love me?"

Thomas looked at the massive mirror positioned on the wall above the bed. It gave him a perfect view of Jake. He was so high Thomas feared he might not register what was going on. But he saw a flicker of confusion, then fear, in his eyes.

She whispered, "I love you."

"Louder. I want him to hear you say it."

"I love you."

"That's my girl. Now I want you to prove it."

Thomas smiled as he bent down and bit one of Martha's erect nipples hard enough for her to let out a little scream. He kissed his way down her belly to the softness between her legs, knowing exactly how to make her shiver with pleasure. Just as he felt her about to climax, he stopped. He looked up at her and waited for her to beg. "Prove your love for me, Martha."

He saw the conflict in her eyes, so he touched her with fingers like feathers.

She moaned. "Don't stop."

"What was that, love?" He continued teasing her.

"Please."

"Please what? Say it." He heard the venom in his voice. "What do you want me to do, love?"

She writhed in the silk, looked up at him. "Fuck me."

"What was that, love? He didn't hear you." He put his face between her legs again and stopped as he felt her respond.

"Fuck me." This time there was venom in *her* voice and a gleam of a tear in her eye.

He looked in the mirror to see if Jake had registered what was happening. Then he pulled his pants down and taunted her with what she wanted until she thrashed under him.

"Please, Thomas."

When he entered her, she let out a moan that reminded him of a wounded animal. Quick to climax, she let out another low, guttural sound.

He looked in the mirror again to see Jake's reaction. Then he made her cum again and lost himself for a moment as he let go inside of her.

"Thank you, love. That really meant a lot to me." He dismounted her. "Aww, don't cry, love. Now I know you really love me."

He pulled his pants up and walked over to Jake. "Does she scream like that for you, Jake?"

He didn't respond.

"Thomas, stop, let me go now."

He walked back across the room to her. "Not yet." He ran a finger across her breasts. "Darling, you look so like your mother when you orgasm. She was a screamer, too. Did you know that? Like mother, like daughter."

He smiled and ran his finger across her forehead. "Her brow used to furrow, just like this, when she was deep in thought." He touched the scar under Martha's eye. "She wasn't flawed with scars, either. Did I ever mention how unattractive I've always found yours? It's a symbol of all your weaknesses, letting your little sister best you and all."

He saw her brain trying to catch up with his words and waited on the edge of the bed for the moment to come. If he had to pick the best looks of his victims, it was when they realized he was a ruthless sociopath, Martha would be at the top of his list. He was so pleased with himself he laughed out loud. She still didn't know *what* he was—not yet, at least—which made the look on her face even better.

He tweaked one of her nipples, hard, and brought her back to reality.

She cried.

"Humans and their emotions."

She tugged on the handcuffs, looking over at Jake. "Let me go, Thomas, please? You've had your fun."

"Thomas is such a nice boy's name, a name you can trust, isn't it, dear? Thomass don't cuff their *girlfriends* to the bedpost and fuck them in front of their exes, now do they? Thomass are sweet, church-going guys who open doors for their women and say please and thank you every time they cum. They make you breakfast and coffee and take you out to dinner. Pretend your scars are beautiful and give you a certain depth. They certainly haven't shared a bed with their partner's mother." He paused and caressed her cheek; it was damp with fresh tears.

"What are you saying, Thomas? Let me go, please." A twinge of panic in her voice.

"Do you think I'm a nice boy, love?" She didn't respond, just looked at him through hurt and teary eyes. He leaned down and kissed her. "Do you think I can be trusted? What's wrong, dear—can't spare a kiss for me? Are you upset with me, love? Your Jake will be just fine, as long as you do exactly as I say. Wait, is it Jake you're confused about? Or is it your mother? Didn't I tell you? It must have slipped my mind. She was my student at Tulane all those years ago, just like you. She wasn't as easy to fool as you were, but a lot more fun to fuck. And she was much better at her craft than you. That's why we didn't work out. She almost got me, but in the end, it was I who got her. Killing your kind is such a sweet pleasure."

Martha's eyes widened, and she struggled against her restraints.

"Ah, there's my scared girl. Have you figured it out yet? My name?"

He made his fangs quiver and bore them to her, to enjoy the full effect. Her beautiful olive skin turned an awful shade of ash, and he smiled.

"Ah, there we are, love. You're poison to me, but your boyfriend over there, he'll make a fine snack."

He watched her panic-stricken face as she registered his words and started to retch. "Oh, dear love, pull yourself up. We can't have you choking on your own vomit just as the fun is about to begin." He grabbed her by her hair, already streaked with vomit, and yanked her up just as she vomited all over her naked self.

When she finished puking, he let go of her hair, took her Apple watch from her wrist, and pocketed it. Then he took her phone from her purse and held it in front of her face to unlock it, watching as her eyes widened.

Motion fluttered across the mirror. Jake had gotten up, sneaking behind him. His pathetic attempt to save his girl made Thomas laugh. Martha shook her head, and Thomas turned just as Jake was upon him.

Thomas hit Jake so hard, he lifted off the floor and slammed into the wall with such force he crumbled like a rag doll. "Fool. You humans. Always trying to be brave, and where does it get you?" He walked over to Jake on the floor. "Don't be a hero, dumb boy. I'll knock your head clear off your body and smash it like a melon."

"Jake, stop," Martha said. "Just do what he says."

"That's good advice. Listen to your girlfriend." He turned to Martha. "Can you guess my name yet, love?"

He was getting amped up and knew in this state it would be too easy to accidentally kill Jake. That might ruin his plans, so he put Jake back in the room he'd come from. It was soundproof and where he kept his prey until it was time to hunt. Then he sent a text from Martha's phone.

He walked over to Martha and caressed her stomach, just to see the sheer disgust and horror on her face. Leaning down, he whispered in her ear. "Mathias, my dear girl. I'm Mathias, and I'm going to kill you and your entire family." Anger flooded her eyes. "Oh, poor little love. You can't use your magic here. It's a protected space. Nice try though."

He left her and wandered to the front of his house to his security room, where he had his grounds monitored constantly.

He said to the technician, "I don't know where they'll come from, but they'll be here soon. Call me as soon as you see them." He grabbed a radio off the desk.

"You got it, boss," replied Sergio, one of Jesse's loyal descendants.

He went to his kitchen, pulled a pint of blood from the refrigerator, and guzzled it straight from the bag. Thomas needed his strength and there was no time for hunting tonight.

He took a second bag for good measure and returned to his bedroom to admire his work and taunt Martha more. After three hundred years, his vengeance had come full circle. His smile disappeared as he stepped into his room and blinked hard, thinking his imagination had gotten the best of him.

But no, the handcuffs dangled from his bed posts, devoid of their prisoner, one of them still swaying.

His walkie-talkie crackled. "They're here, boss. There are three of them."

RAVEN – THE DREAM

CHAPTER 53

The dawn light peeked through Raven's shutters. She was awake but reluctant to give up the comfort of her bed. The house creaked and groaned, a sign of its age. She got up to pee, but when she saw it was only four o'clock, she crawled back into her cocoon of blankets, hugging her dog close and falling back to sleep.

It was bad-dream sleep. In the woods, she picked up a weird scent—both familiar and foreign. Pleasant like peonies in the spring. But beneath the honeyed smell, an undertow of something unpleasant, perhaps something long dead. She followed it like a bloodhound deeper into the woods until she was completely lost. All that mattered was getting to the source of the smell. Focused on tracking the scent, she didn't see the woman and ran right into her. Raven backed away, shocked by the strange woman's beauty.

She reached out and touched Raven's cheek. "Aw, poor little Rae Rae."

Raven jumped back, recoiling at the touch of the icy hand. The smell and the woman were one, each the essence of the other. She tried to turn away and run. But the woman grabbed her ponytail and yanked her back, turning her so they were face to face. The smell was so strong she could taste it like rancid peanut butter in her mouth. She started to retch, and the woman grabbed her by the neck and lifted her off the ground. She hissed in Raven's face, squeezing her throat tighter.

"I'm coming for you." She bore fangs like Raven had only seen in pictures.

Raven woke up before she could scream and sat up gasping for air. "Just a dream, a terrible dream."

She might never sleep again with dreams like that. Raven dragged herself out of bed and went to scrub her face clean, hoping to wash the memory down the drain with her dead skin cells.

Ranjit popped in and she nearly jumped out of her skin. "Jeez, are you trying to scrub your face off?"

"Maybe." She smiled at him in the mirror. "I'll meet you downstairs."

He nodded and was gone.

Raven couldn't shake the dream. Had it been an actual vampire? Whatever it was, she'd like nothing more than to watch its heart explode and eyes melt. She dressed and went downstairs. Ranjit munched on a bagel.

Raven pulled out some berries from the fridge, found the granola in the pantry, threw it all in a bowl, added some oat milk, and sat down next to Ranjit.

He brushed her long hair back behind her shoulder. "What happened to your neck? Did you have a hot date last night you forgot to tell me about?"

"What are you talking about?"

He touched her neck just under her ear. "You've got one on each side. Looks like hickeys."

The chill ran up her arms like a light breeze. "I can assure you it's not that. I need a mirror." She wasn't supposed to use magic to enable laziness, but now and then, it was just easier. The mirror from her bathroom flew into her hand, and she inspected the marks on her neck. She put the mirror down and resumed eating her breakfast.

"Hello, do you care to elaborate?"

She put her spoon down. "Give me a minute, okay? Just finish your bagel."

Ranjit took a bite of his bagel. "Never a dull moment with you, eh?"

After they finished eating, Raven said, "Let's go for a walk by the lake?"

They headed out the back doors and Raven stopped. "Looks like a storm is coming."

Flashes of light blinked through the black clouds every few seconds.

"Looks like a big one," Ranjit said.

"We can watch from the den. Come on."

They returned inside and settled on a sofa facing the window, sitting in silence for a bit. She was relieved Ranjit wasn't grilling her with questions about her neck.

Thunder rumbled in the background and the lightning flashes became more frequent.

"I had a dream," Raven said. "A terrible dream. There was this smell. I followed it into the woods and got lost, but I didn't care. I was determined to find the source, and I bumped right into it."

"It? How do you bump into a smell?"

"The smell was a woman. Young and beautiful like no one I've ever seen. She wasn't the source of the smell; she *was* the smell. Does that make sense?"

Ranjit nodded.

"Then she grabbed me by the neck. She was so strong, she lifted me off the ground. Then she just squeezed, choking me. I forced myself to wake up, but just before I did, she hissed at me like a cat. She had fangs and said, *I'm coming for you.* Obviously, she was a vampire. Thank God I woke up."

Ranjit moved her hair again and ran a finger over a bruise. "That's pretty messed up."

The rain spattered a few heavy drops.

"We need to tell someone," Ranjit said.

"What?"

"Your dream. You need to tell Nanny or Ms. Tengos. She called you Rae Rae. Only your dad calls you that, right? What if he's in some kind of danger?"

"Yeah. Probably Ms. Tengos? Nanny's gone anyway."

Ranjit stood up. "Maybe she'll know what the smell is. Let's see if we can catch her now."

They went out the front door, and Raven tried to conjure the protective bubble—she'd been practicing and wanted to see if she could do it.

"Maybe I should get an umbrella," Ranjit said. "I don't want to get drenched again."

"Hey! I've been practicing."

"Fine, I guess I won't melt."

Daisy Mae trotted along beside them as they made their way to the Witchery. Raven's creation wasn't perfect, but it was better than the last time she'd tried with Ranjit, and they stayed mostly dry.

The Witchery was beautiful in the storm. Witches had been studying their craft for hundreds of years within its walls. It was probably as alive as she was.

Ms. Tengos refused to change the old building, including AC, but it was never unbearable, even during the humid Alabama summers. The energy of this space was perfect for teaching and learning. The residual essence and magic of the witches who came before them lingered in its walls. Ms. Tengos and Nanny didn't want to chance ruining that vibe with modern updates.

Raven felt it every time she walked in, like ghosts had settled in and made themselves at home. It was a sacred space. Even Ranjit noticed it the first time she brought him.

She texted Nanny saying she'd be at the school and then Ms. Tengos; she didn't like surprises.

Raven used magic to unlock the door and headed into the lair. Ms. Tengos sat at the giant chem table eating soup and reading a book. She looked up. "Have you read these *Outlander* books? Brilliant writing. And what a great story. You can borrow mine if you'd like."

Raven laughed. "I think I'm the one who told you about those books."

"Unlikely. What do you want?"

"I need you to put the book away and focus on what I'm about to tell you."

Ms. Tengos scoffed, but she closed the book. "Fine. But know this: if I don't like what you have to say, I may conjure Jamie Fraser into existence, and you'll never see me again."

Raven sat down at the table across from Ms. Tengos. Daisy Mae lay at her feet as Raven told her about her nightmare.

When she'd finished, Ranjit said, "Show her your neck."

Raven pulled her hair back and twisted so Ms. Tengos could get a look at both sides.

"If this happens again, you run," Ms. Tengos said. "Do everything you can to wake up. Our dreams can be outside of time and space as we know it. It can be quite dangerous. It's something we know little about. Fala has spoken of Dream Walkers. They protect humans when they sleep, but witches are on their own."

"What do you mean? Should I use magic then?"

"Wait, back up. *Dream Walkers*?" Ranjit said. "I swear there's something new every day. Please explain."

Ms. Tengos sighed. "Raven, I think it's best if you can wake yourself up. Or just run. Since it is technically a dream, you should be able to conjure a stake, or an axe, and kill it. Maybe bring a weapon with you when you go to sleep each night." She looked at Ranjit. "According to Fala, Dream Walkers are a part of the spirit world. They protect humans from the evil that lurks on the outskirts of our minds, often exposing itself in our dreams. Dream Walkers keep the evil contained in dreams, preventing crossover to the physical world."

"What do you mean?" Ranjit asked. "Like Pennywise or Freddy Krueger?"

The mention of Pennywise gave Raven goosebumps, and she remembered the red balloons her sister had taunted her with. "Pennywise is not real. What the hell? What about us? Why don't they protect us when we sleep?"

"Dreams are on another plane of existence," Ms. Tengos said. "Witches can exist on that plane and use their powers. I guess vampires can as well. She can't come into Vision, so she went into your head instead. Interesting approach. This is why I don't like you to leave Vision."

Raven rolled her eyes. "We all know how I feel about that. Sounds like I can't go to sleep now either."

"No. This is the first time you've had this happen. It can't be easy for them to do, or they'd try to kill us all as we sleep. Next time, kill it. I don't know if it works, but those marks on your neck are very real. I'll speak to Fala about it and see what she has to say."

Their phones vibrated on the table. They picked them up and viewed the texts.

Nanny burst into the room. "We've got to go."

"What's going on?" Ranjit asked.

"He's got Martha," Raven said.

"Who?"

"Mathias."

"You mean *the Mathias?* The vampire of all vampires? How did he get Martha, and why?"

"It was her boyfriend, Thomas," Nanny said.

"I knew it," Raven said. "That guy was super creepy."

"What does the text say?" Ranjit asked.

Raven read from her phone. "*Ah, patience, such a virtue. I suggest you use one of your magic paintings to get to my hunting lodge, NOW. Looking forward to it. M.* He sent it from Martha's phone."

"Let's go." Nanny started toward the art room.

Ms. Tengos stood up. "You stay. I'll go. It's me he wants anyway."

"No, you have to stay."

Ms. Tengos glared at Nanny. "You will stay. Understand? One of us has to stay alive, for the wards."

Nanny huffed but acquiesced. She unlocked the secret room, and they all went in.

"Won't we get pulled back if we go through a painting?" Ranjit asked.

Raven had been wondering the same thing.

"Only with time travel," Nanny said. "With space travel, it's not a problem."

"Ms. Tengos, how can you go through?" Raven asked

"You can take me through."

"Let's do this," Ranjit said.

Raven looked at him like he was crazy. "You're not going."

"What? Of course, I am."

"No. You're not."

"Enough," Ms. Tengos said. "We have to go now."

Nanny pulled out a picture. "This is a generic travelling picture and will get you there. Concentrate on Martha and getting to where she is. Be careful."

"Wait," Raven said. "There's something I need to do first."

Nanny and Ms. Tengos protested.

Raven held up her hand. "It's important. Just give me a minute."

CHAPTER 54

Raven was ready and looked at Nanny. "Take care of Daisy Mae. Promise?"

"Of course." She hugged Raven. "Be careful."

Raven put her hand on the painting and thought about Martha. She felt Ms. Tengos's hand on her shoulder and let the painting do the work.

They landed on the other side, crouched as if ready to pounce. She'd been practicing going through the mural and the picture Nanny painted to see her mother. She concentrated on herself, getting centered and focused. This was nowhere near as shocking as when she and Ranjit went back in time. Ms. Tengos was getting to her feet, and to her horror, next to Ms. Tengos was Ranjit.

"What the hell, Ranjit?! I told you to stay."

"Hush. He's here now, nothing you can do," Ms. Tengos said. "Let's get our bearings."

They were in the middle of a forest. Raven heard a whizzing noise and looked up. "There's a camera in the trees."

"Well, he knows we're here," Ms. Tengos said. "He's probably got magic blocked, so beware."

"How can he do that?" Ranjit asked.

"Just be careful. If he does, we can still use our gifts."

Raven crossed her arms and glared at Ms. Tengos. "I'm furious with you. How could you not tell me? I saw you. I saw you three hundred years ago. You should have told me. What does that make Nanny? Agatha's daughter?"

"Hush, child. We will talk about this later. But for the record, she's still your grandmother."

"Told you what?" Ranjit asked.

"Later, Ranjit," Raven said. "We need to focus on killing a vampire."

Raven conjured a simple wind spell, the colors vibrant in her hand. She released it and spun up some leaves in a wind funnel.

Raven touched Ms. Tengos on the arm. *I have my powers. See if you can conjure.*

Ms. Tengos spun up the same wind spell. The colors came together in her hand, but they lacked the energy to give them life and vibrance. They were muted and dull.

"Maybe I can." Raven made a show of trying to conjure and not being able to. "Well, this sucks. Fucking Martha."

"Watch your language."

Raven rolled her eyes. "Let's get this over with."

"Can I have a weapon or something?" Ranjit asked.

Ms. Tengos pulled a dirk out of her backpack and handed it to Ranjit.

Raven stared at it. "Wow. That's some weapon." The wooden handle was well-worn and shiny from the sweat and oil of the witch's hand.

"From my private collection."

Ranjit stared at the knife like he was hypnotized.

"Snap out of it, Ranjit," Ms. Tengos said. "Aim for the heart."

He looked up. "Got it. Heart."

"Let's go."

Raven had grabbed the old axe she sometimes practiced with and held it by her side. The slight bump of it against her leg as she walked was comforting. She'd made it invisible before they went through the painting. She touched Ms. Tengo's arm. *Can you see the axe?*

Yes.

They easily found their way through the woods to the house. They'd been deposited about a half mile away and passed several more cameras on the way. As they neared the clearing where the house stood, they came across a garage.

Ranjit found a window and looked inside. He jumped back. "I think that's Rosie James in there."

"What the hell?" Raven replied.

"He was using her for something," Ms. Tengos said. "Probably to steal a painting. That's why we kept seeing her in the art room."

"There's someone else in there," Ranjit said.

Ms. Tengos looked in the window. "It's probably her mother. Mathias uses family to make witches compliant. Ranjit, this is a job for you."

"What?"

"Go in and free them. Then get out of here. Martha's car is probably around here somewhere. The keys will be in it. Head home and stay with Nanny. We'll take care of the rest."

MARTHA – MEA POTENTIA

CHAPTER 55

Martha lay on the bed, still nauseous.

The Chipotle she'd thrown up made a home in the creases of her naked body. She thought she must be in a dream when Mathias pulled Jake from the bowels of some room she hadn't noticed. She tugged on the handcuffs. All too real. They held her in her nightmare-like stasis, rubbing her wrists raw. She struggled to hold herself up, breathing becoming difficult. She was vaguely aware of Mathias walking out of the room.

Martha needed to pull herself together. She didn't know how to understand the many conflicting emotions going through her head and took a deep breath to pull herself up. She wiggled her butt onto a pillow and pressed her back against the headboard. Her arms were still at an awkward angle, but she could breathe, and the pressure was off her wrists. Bits of vomit dislodged from her body and fell onto the bed.

She wanted to crawl into a dark corner and cry. She'd gotten herself captured by *Mathias*. Her whole family was in danger now. Pathetic. Her chest heaved with a sob.

Then she heard Gretchen's voice in her head. *You're Martha Fucking Beaumont, you can do anything.* She certainly didn't feel that way, but she took a breath and thought about her options. Ms. Tengos taught them Morgana and Agatha had used their gifts in prison, even with no powers.

"My gift."

Martha's gift had revealed itself shortly after the slapping incident with Raven. She often wondered how their lives would have been different if it had come before the slap. After being humiliated by her three-year-old sister, she told no one when she finally discovered her gift.

Ms. Tengos and even Nanny, to a degree, judged her for her lack of witchiness compared to Raven. Of course, she turned away from their craft. It didn't matter that Martha excelled at Vision history and had a deep understanding of her ancestors. Ms. Tengos wanted practical magic and was so concerned with vampires and protecting the town, she didn't have time for witches like Martha who couldn't help in her quest. As a result, she'd had a lot more freedom than they gave Raven.

Nanny was more compassionate since their mother died. As their grandmother, she had an interest in the well-being of both Beaumont girls, no matter how good or bad they were at magic. But she was also entrenched in vampire slaying. Now that Martha had met Mathias, she couldn't blame them, and it made her wish she'd bucked up and tried harder with her magic.

So, she'd kept her gift a secret. When she was young, she used it just to prove to herself that she could. It was fun to listen to conversations or sneak in the movies as she had the night before. As she grew into her teens, it became her escape from the world. She'd read Plato's *Republic* in junior high school, and they spent a week discussing *The Ring of Gyges*.

Gyges was a poor shepherd who fell into a ravine and found a dead man wearing a beautiful ring. Gyges took the ring and eventually realized when he turned it one way, he turned invisible and when he turned it back, he became visible again. He used his power to seduce the queen. Together they killed the king and Gyges became ruler of the land. The lesson being, without fear of being caught, people will resort to acting in their own selfish interest.

Martha never lost her fear of getting caught while invisible and had no aspirations for power. If she revealed her gift, she'd become an object for Nanny and Ms. Tengos to use in their alternate world of vampires. She enjoyed her freedom, and their ignorance was her bliss. So, she'd kept it to herself.

She went over all the things Mathias had said, any of which could break her spirit on its own. Together they should have crushed her soul. For whatever reason she was becoming energized by the churn of emotions. *I'm Martha Fucking Beaumont* passed through her mind. She opened herself to her emotions. Pathetic had its turn, and she pushed it away along with her tears. Mathias had kidnapped Jake, and she let a swirl of anger flash in her gut.

Of all the awful things Mathias said, the one that stuck was his plans to kill her family. She needed to see the text he sent from her phone. As much as she hated her sister, she didn't wish her dead. And what of her father? Hopefully he was safe in Atlanta. And had Mathias really had an affair with and killed her mother, or was he just trying to tear Martha down even further?

She closed her eyes and let her emotions churn like butter, evolving into thick and viscous rage. It pushed away her fear, pain, and humiliation. It consumed her. Then she was free.

She got out of bed, brushed the remaining vomit off, and strode into Jake's prison. Unlike Gyges, Martha not only turned invisible, she became the ether, a ghost. She could walk through solid things, like walls.

Jake sensed her presence and backed away. She thought about making herself visible but was afraid of possible cameras in the room.

He looked so pathetic, his legs were splayed out in front of him, his hands tied behind his back. His face glistened with sweat and was too pale. This was all her doing. She touched his cheek. "Jake, it's me. I'm so sorry."

He flinched, pulling his head away from her touch. and hissed drunkenly. "Get away from me."

She took a step back, surprised at the anger in his voice. "I'll be back for you."

Before he could respond, she walked back through the door and into the bedroom. Mathias stood in the doorway, supremely confused. She beamed and wanted to go after him, but knew it would be futile. Plus, she didn't want him to know she hadn't run away, and certainly didn't want him to know she was invisible.

She heard someone on Mathias's radio. Three of them, who? She waited for him to leave and grabbed her phone. He'd texted Nanny, Ms. Tengos, and Raven. Would they all have come for her? She thought about sending another text, letting them know she was okay, but if they were here, what was the point?

She wandered out of the room and glanced around. A long hallway led to the living space and entrance. That much she remembered. She followed it to the living room and heard an unfamiliar voice. Following the sound of the stranger, she came to what looked like a command center. The door was open, and Mathias was looking over the stranger's shoulder at a bank of monitors.

There they were, standing beside a small structure she'd not seen on her way in. There was no audio, but she saw Raven and Ms. Tengos talking to... Ranjit? What the hell was he doing here?

Raven and Ms. Tengos left him and headed toward the house.

"What kind of host would I be if I didn't greet my guests?" Mathias asked.

Martha stepped aside, not wanting to find out what would happen if he passed through her. She looked back at Ranjit. He was opening the door. How? No way it was unlocked. Then Mathias came into view, gesticulating a greeting. Raven tried to conjure a spell, but Ms. Tengos grabbed her arm, stopping her.

Martha gasped out loud. The security guard turned around, saw nothing, and went back to the screens. Raven still had her powers. She must have unlocked the door for Ranjit.

Mathias ushered them toward the house. She slipped out of the security area and into the giant common room just as Mathias escorted Raven and Ms. Tengos inside.

"Please, have a seat so we can work this out in a civilized manner," Mathias said.

"Where's Martha?" Raven demanded.

"We have other business to discuss first."

Martha went to Ms. Tengos, put her hand on her should and sent a mental message to her. *I'm here, invisible. He has Jake.*

Ms. Tengos gave the slightest nod. Before she could respond, Raven sent what Martha assumed was a stun spell to Mathias. She caught him off guard, but he hadn't lived for thousands of years by being fooled by witches' trickery. He moved so fast, Martha barely saw him escape down the hall. He was going to get Jake.

Raven started after him, but Ms. Tengos grabbed her arm. Martha heard her in her head. *No, he has Jake.* Raven's face dropped.

Mathias came back down the hall with Jake in tow, just as someone else came through the front door.

Ranjit, escorted by the most beautiful woman Martha had ever seen. Raven gasped when they entered

"Aww, little Rae Rae," the woman said. "So nice to see you again." She looked at Mathias and held up a silver dirk.

"Whatever did you plan to do with that?" Mathias asked.

Ranjit's brown skin turned pale, and Martha thought he was crying.

Shit.

Raven had her powers, and Martha had the advantage of being invisible. But that wasn't enough to take out the vampires without getting Jake and Ranjit killed. Especially after seeing how fast Mathias moved. And how many more were there?

Mathias held Jake by his long hair and dropped him in the middle of the room. "Looks like we're having a party."

"Where's Martha?" Ms. Tengos asked.

Something flashed in his face. "She's safe."

"We want to see her, now," Raven demanded.

"You don't give the orders here, little lady."

He strolled over to the wall and touched an oil painting. A mass of greens and purples, no structure to it at all, a sea of color.

"Do you recognize this? Thanks to your friend out there, I learned all sorts about these magic paintings. I even took several trips with young Rosie. She couldn't get me where or when I wanted to go. Such a shame about her father. He made a lovely snack. Families are such a beautiful way to manipulate you witches. And here I have three of yours."

Ms. Tengos's face dropped. "Where's Martha? How do we know you have her?"

"She's safe." He nodded at the vampire holding Ranjit. She bore her fangs and got dangerously close to Ranjit's neck.

Raven's face turned a dark crimson, and Raven raised her hand to cast a spell. Ms. Tengos grabbed her. "Control yourself."

The beautiful vampire laughed. "Aww, Rae Rae, did I upset you?"

Martha saw the axe in Raven's hand. She wondered why the vampires hadn't taken it from her and realized she'd made it invisible.

Martha needed to get her sister's attention. She was like a loose cannon right now. Although Martha didn't know who the woman vampire was, she and Raven had obviously met before.

Martha spun a spell, hoping something would show so her sister could see it and get her focus off Ranjit. If Raven did anything to that vampire, Jake was dead.

It worked. Raven did a double take as she looked where Martha was standing. She hoped Mathias hadn't seen it.

Raven looked back at the woman vampire. "I can't wait to watch your eyes melt and your heart explode." Her hand pulsed on the axe handle. *Please don't do anything stupid.*

To her relief, Raven loosened her grip and leaned the axe against Ms. Tengos. She walked over to the painting and touched it. Her hand disappeared into it, and she looked at Mathias. "Are you coming?"

Mathias—still holding on to Jake—touched Raven's shoulder. Raven looked at Ms. Tengos. "You joining this train or what?"

"No," Mathias said. "She stays." He looked at his beautiful vampire. "I don't come back, they die."

She bore her fangs, hissed like a cat, and nodded.

He looked at Raven. "Take us to the time—"

Raven cut him off. "I know where we're going, asshole. And I'll have all my powers."

A flicker of doubt touched Mathias's face. "And I have your boyfriends, Martha, and Morgana. Shut up and let's go."

Morgana? What was he talking about? Martha touched Raven's other shoulder, and her sister gave the slightest flinch.

Then Martha was being ripped apart from the inside out as they tumbled through time and crashed into the rough ground.

RAVEN – THEN AND NOW

CHAPTER 56

They tumbled across the rough ground of 1692 in what was northern Alabama in Raven's time. Raven was exhausted, like she'd carried three people across time and space. But she jumped up ready to stun Mathias. He still held on to Jake, who looked terrible.

Raven worried he might not make it back home. "You know if Jake dies, so do you. I suggest you be a little more careful with him."

"Shut up and move, witch."

She needed to get her bearings and find Morgana and Agatha.

Martha was somewhere as well. How had she made herself invisible?

"Go on, girl, find your witches," Mathias said.

"Hey, asshole, I got us here. You figure it out." She hoped she'd gotten them to the right time and place.

"I see why your sister hates you."

Raven grinned. She smelled the air for water, picked up the stream, and knew they were close. Mathias would also pick up the scent of the witches. She listened for the familiar voice in her head.

"You know it's three of us against you and your Alma."

"Shut up, witch. Have you forgotten about this one?" He gave Jake a shake. "And don't forget about your boyfriend."

Raven laughed. "You really think Ms. Tengos won't turn that bitch to dust before we get back?" She hoped she was under his skin.

"Quiet. Let's go, get in front of me."

She obliged and wondered again where Martha was, looking around and hoping she'd made it through okay. "What's so special about this Alma, anyway?"

"Nothing you could ever understand. Though I believe you humans call it a soulmate. She completes me."

Raven was hit with a sudden wave of nausea and realized the vampire was in her head. She fought it and inside her head, he said, *Calm down, witch.*

She saw Mathias and Alma like a movie. There was something familiar about Alma. She had a strong resemblance to the vampire holding Ranjit and Ms. Tengos, and the vampire in her dreams. She felt his passion when he first saw her. He cared for her as she transitioned from human to vampire. Pure love. Raven didn't expect it. They traveled the world through the centuries, love never fading, holding hands, kissing. Their love encased them like an orb outside of time and space—*eternal* came to her mind.

He left her mind. "Yes, eternal. You understand now?"

Raven was shocked silent. Was there something romantic about his effort to save the love of his life? She looked at Jake, who could barely walk, and realized Mathias had left out all the killing and evil the two of them had done. That's how they completed each other. She wished she had her axe to cut the vampire's head off.

Then she heard it. Immanuel running through the woods yelling for help. Mathias stopped and sniffed the air. "Alma." She heard him say, almost under his breath.

In her head she yelled, *MORGANA! Where are you?*

We're here. Look left for your weapon.

She scanned the trees, spotting the silver dirk's wooden handle sticking out of a vast oak tree. It was invisible to Mathias, but she had to be careful as his senses were like nothing she'd ever seen. She used caution while summoning the dirk, tucked it in the front of her jeans, and walked on.

Before leaving for Mathias's hunting lodge, Raven had asked if she could have a moment to herself with a specific goal in mind. She had used a painting to warn Morgana and Agatha of what was coming and enlisted their help. She had also wanted to practice and confirm she could get to the correct place and time. Morgana had hidden the dirk in the tree for her, and they came heavily armed as well.

Raven had learned in her Vision history that by killing the parent vampire, its children would also expire. A tidbit she'd shared with them. They'd planned to focus their energy on killing Mathias, even if it meant Alma escaped. She was a child and would turn to dust upon Mathias's death—hopefully.

Mathias stepped in front of her like she was an afterthought. She raised her hand to send a stun spell. Then Alma darted through the woods. They locked eyes.

"Do it and you'll watch your human die as I drain him dry," Alma said.

Raven nearly forgot her spell. Alma *was* the woman from her dream, the woman in her time holding Ranjit and Ms. Tengos. How did she get here?

Mathias turned around and glared at Raven, then turned back to Alma.

"Alma." He took her hand.

"Mathias, what are you doing here? What's going on? Why have you brought this witch?"

"I'll explain later. You need to go back to Stoney Ridge."

"I'm hunting."

Raven heard the rustling of leaves. Morgana dashing through the woods.

"Mathias, what's going on?" Alma asked.

"These witches mean to kill you. Leave the slave and go back to Seth."

Mathias dropped Jake and reached for Alma's hand. Suddenly, Morgana surfaced and fired a stun spell at the vampires. The vampires escaped, and the spell hit an old oak tree. Alma lunged at Morgana, who drew her stake and plunged it into the air where Alma had stood mere seconds before. She'd flipped aside and dodged destruction by inches. The vampires' speed amazed Raven again. Morgana held her stake, facing Alma, who had only her speed and strength to defend herself.

"Alma, leave her," Mathias said.

Alma, never taking her eyes from Morgana, hissed. "Not before I kill this witch."

Agatha's sudden appearance caused a momentary lull in the chaos. Raven assessed the scene. Jake, a lump on the ground. Agatha hovering behind Morgana, one hand poised with a stun spell, the other carrying a stake. Her sister was somewhere. Raven took her shot.

She pulled the dirk from her waist and lunged toward Mathias, striking at his back. She stabbed air and tumbled forward, landing on her face, tasting a mouthful of leaves. How did he move so quickly?

She rose and felt a boot press down on her neck. She couldn't breathe.

"You little bitch," Mathias said. "You'll pay for that."

The weight lifted and she jumped up, summoned the dirk, and prepared to pounce. Mathias was nowhere. She peered around and caught Agatha's eye.

"I missed," Agatha said. "He's got the boy again."

Raven turned and saw Mathias against a giant tree, bearing his fangs. "Jake's death is on you, little witch."

She wondered where Martha was and stole a glance at Morgana, still engaged with Alma.

Mathias made a show of Jake and licked his neck. Raven shot her protective bubble spell at Jake, praying it would work better on Jake than it had for her and Ranjit in the rainstorm.

Mathias looked up at Raven. "You watching?" He went to bite Jake's throat, his fangs like nails on a chalkboard as they squealed against whatever material Raven had conjured around Jake.

She sighed with relief as Agatha sent another stun spell at Mathias. He dropped Jake and jumped straight up the tree.

A light breeze tugged at Raven, and she knew time was about to run out. She concentrated to pause time and yelled, "Martha!"

They had to kill Mathias before they got sucked back. She needed to get Martha and Jake so they didn't get left behind.

Mathias jumped down from the tree and rushed Agatha, poised again with spell and stake. She fired the spell. Mathias avoided it and hit her hand holding the stake so hard the bones crunched. He pushed her, and she flew, landing with a thud. *He's too fast for a spell and too strong to fight.* Now she understood Nanny and Ms. Tengos's fear of these vampires.

Raven headed for Mathias, wanting nothing more than to kill him. "Thomas, Mathias, whatever your name is. Let's go." She twirled the dirk in her fingers.

It was invisible to him, and he laughed at her stupidity. "Go back to your dolls, little girl."

"Screw you, asshole." She charged him.

He stuck his hand out to tell her to stop and looked poised to jump again.

She was slowed by the sucking, which grew stronger. "Oh, shit."

A spell floated next to Mathias, an indigo thread pulsing, needing to be released.

He hesitated when he saw Raven struggling. He grinned and headed back toward Jake, Martha's spell following close behind.

The sucking became stronger. Raven resisted, but knew if she could move toward Mathias, he was too fast to kill. She had to trust Martha, who was right behind him.

Martha's stun spell hit Mathias in the back, and he froze mid-step. She smirked at the shock and horror in his eyes as Martha made herself visible.

"Martha!" Raven yelled, tossing the dirk to her sister, who was, for some reason, naked.

Martha plucked it out of the air. "This is for my mother, you asshole." She plunged the dirk into his heart. Mathias lit up from the inside. His arms flailed dangerously close to Martha.

"Martha, get out of the way!" Raven shouted. The stun spell wore off. Martha turned and dove to the ground, but not before Mathias's left arm swatted her across the back.

He was burning, and Raven saw the welt of a handprint on Martha's back. He reached down and grabbed her by the hair. Mathias jerked Martha up. His burning hand seared through Martha's hair, and she fell back to the ground.

"Martha!" Raven screamed. "Get away from him." His insides glowed. If his heart exploded, it would be like fireworks at close range. He stood, but lost his bearings, turning away from Martha and running into a tree, leaving a singed imprint of himself on the aged bark.

Why is this taking so long? Raven felt the pull growing stronger and panicked. "Martha! Come to me, hurry."

Agatha looked up from nursing her broken arm; Alma and Morgana paused in their silent battle.

Mathias's eyes melted and ran down what remained of his once handsome face. He lit up from within like a supernova. Vibrant reds, yellows, and purples. It reminded Raven of a sunset. She wondered how such evil could be so beautiful. Maybe the beauty of his death was in response to the ugliness of his life.

Then his heart exploded. After a brief rain of ash and fire, he turned to dust. Just like that, he was gone.

Alma screamed, but before any of the witches could react, she dashed into the woods and instantly disappeared. Morgana ran after her.

"Let her go, she's dust," Agatha shouted. "Go help Martha."

The sucking grew stronger. "Martha!" Martha appeared unconscious and, for all she knew, Jake was dead.

"Agatha, Morgana! Help!"

She used her magic to pull Jake toward her. It took all of her strength, but he flew into her arms, his dead weight knocking her over. She grabbed his arm and held on.

She tried to use her magic to pull Martha toward her, but was too weak.

Morgana rushed to Martha and sent her through the air to Raven. She landed on the ground in front of Raven. Raven tried to grab her sister, but she was out of reach.

She felt herself slow down, sticking her hand out. "Martha! Wake up!"

Morgana gave Martha one last push, and, in a panic, Raven stretched her arm out, grasped a clump of Martha's hair, and succumbed to the sucking.

CHAPTER 57

Raven lay on the ground of the hunting lodge, exhausted. Her sister lay next to her, still unconscious. She tried to push herself up and collapsed again. The room was in complete disarray, and she remembered the other Alma. Her whole body ached.

Then someone stood over her. "Don't move, witch."

A man's voice.

What the hell? She was confident Ms. Tengos had killed Alma's doppelgänger and wasn't expecting anyone else. Stupid.

"Where's Mathias?" the man asked. A gun cocked. She took a deep breath, still recovering from her time-traveling excursion, and rolled over, looking into the barrel of a pistol. She pushed herself up on her elbows and saw Ms. Tengos and Ranjit on the couch, zip-tied and gagged. Then she heard Ms. Tengos in her head. *He's human. He thinks your powers don't work.*

"Hey, asshole, we need a doctor," Raven said. "Why don't you put the gun down and call 911?"

"Don't talk to me like that, little bitch. Where's Mathias?" He kicked her in the gut, and she gasped. She closed her eyes and breathed in slow and deep. Adrenaline returned, erasing the fatigue and weakness, and she jumped to her feet.

"You are one rude motherfucker. Mathias is dust."

He laughed. "Impossible."

Raven worried he was going to pull the trigger. She spun her spell so fast he didn't have time to register what was happening.

The gun flew from his hand into hers. She had no idea how to use a gun, but guessed that didn't matter as long as she pointed it at him.

"How, how did you do that?" he stammered. "There's no magic here."

"I'm basic, bitch." She froze him with a stun spell.

She untied Ranjit and Ms. Tengos. "Martha and Jake are both really hurt. They need help."

Ms. Tengos went to them. "Martha is breathing okay, but I can barely feel Jake's pulse. Raven, you're going to have to do it."

"Do what?"

"Put the life back in his body. Ranjit, see if you can find some ice or a first aid kit."

Martha moved and her eyes fluttered. Raven raced to her. "Martha! Are you okay?"

She nodded. "Jake."

"Raven, let's tend to Jake," Ms. Tengos said.

Raven had never done anything like this before.

Ms. Tengos touched her arm. "I'll guide you through. If I had to guess, Mathias or that vixen bit him, to poison him and keep him compliant. She tried to bite Ranjit. We have an antidote back at the Witchery, but I don't want to take him through another painting. We need to act now."

"It was scary, but we got her," Ranjit said. "Didn't we, Ms. T?"

"Ranjit, go!"

"Okay, okay."

Raven knelt beside Jake. "Tell me what to do."

"This is an important spell for this kind of circumstance," Ms. Tengos said. "I want you to think about conjuring a storm. But stop just before you release."

Raven formed the spell and let it sit in her hand. "Okay, now what?"

"This will be like an adrenaline shot to energize his heart and blood flow. Focus on the energy of the storm and let your spell get stronger, but keep it contained. Do you feel the power?"

Raven nodded. Martha moved to Jake's side and took his hand. Her tears fell on Jake's chest.

"When you don't think you can contain it any longer, I want you to put your hands on Jake's chest and send that power into his body. Are you ready?"

"Yes, I can't hold it much longer."

"Do it now," Ms. Tengos said.

Raven set her hands over Jake's heart and pushed the energy from the spell into his body. The light spreading through his chest reminded her of the dying Mathias.

It took a minute, but Jake's body jerked beneath her hands. She sighed and sat back on her haunches.

Martha gasped. "Jake, Jake! Are you okay?"

Jake's eyes fluttered open. He looked up at them and his eyes widened. He jerked his hand away from Martha, and he tried to back away.

Martha, still crying, grabbed for his hand again.

Ms. Tengos caressed her arm. "Martha, stop. Let him be. Ranjit, take Martha to find her clothes." She looked at Raven. "Send a calming spell to him." Raven did as she was told, and Jake sighed, his body relaxing. "Go to your sister. I'll deal with Jake."

Raven found them in a somewhat disturbing bedroom. Martha was still crying and putting on her clothes. Raven considered hitting Martha with a calming spell but thought better of it. "Martha. Are you okay?"

"No. Fuck, Raven. Jake almost died because of me. I was having an affair with Mathias. I'm not okay." She sat down on the bed and put her head in her hands.

Raven looked at Ranjit standing in the doorway with a first aid kit. "Leave that and go check on the others, please."

He shuffled out.

Raven sat next to Martha, putting her arm around her sister's shoulder. She and Martha hated each other, and affection was completely unfamiliar.

To her surprise, Martha leaned into her. Her body hitched as she sobbed. Raven put her other arm around Martha and hugged her tight. She cried as well when Martha put her arms around her.

They sat like that until Ms. Tengos came in with a painting in hand. "Girls. Let's go. You need to go through the painting to get home. I'm going to drive Jake and Ranjit back to Vision."

"What about Rosie and her mom?" Raven asked.

"They used this painting to get home. The stun spell will wear off Mathias's human at some point. So, we need to go."

Raven stood and helped Martha up. "Let's go, Martha. Hold on tight, okay?"

Martha nodded and took Raven's hand, and they stepped through together.

CHAPTER 58

When they were all back in Vision, Ranjit told the story of Alma's twin. She was an actual descendant of Alma's family. Mathias had gone back to Greece to find her people and found Allegra.

"I taunted her," Ranjit said. "Asked her what Mathias was going to do with her after he saves his beloved Alma? Told her she'd be abandoned like an unwanted dog."

"I was talking to him in his head the whole time," Ms. Tengos said. "Instructing him what to say. Do you think he listened to me? No."

Ranjit laughed. "Whatever Ms. T. We made a great team."

"He almost got us both killed."

"You'd have had her, Ms. T. If she hadn't turned to dust first, you'd have taken her head right off."

"All I can say is, it's a good thing you killed Mathias when you did, or Ranjit would've been a nice snack for Allegra."

"No way. We could've taken her. You had the axe. I know you would have gotten her before she got me."

"Even though it was invisible to her, she knew I had something. She grabbed Ranjit's arm and twisted it behind him with one hand and grabbed his hair with the other and made to bite his neck. I threw the axe at her, but she turned to dust, and it went into the wall. Ranjit is lucky it didn't hit him."

"It was crazy! One minute I felt her teeth on my neck and the next she was gone. Don't worry, she didn't break the skin. She said something disturbing, though."

"Ranjit was being his obnoxious self and said something about Allegra and Alma turning to dust when they killed Mathias. She laughed her evil laugh and said, 'We're too old to turn to dust.'"

"But she did, right?" Raven asked. "Allegra turned to dust. Maybe she said that to taunt you. Alma took off into the woods and disappeared. How would we know if she's still alive?"

Ms. Tengos shrugged. "All our data suggests she's gone. If she's not, she'll come after us, just as Mathias did. They could both be alive in the other timeline. This time travel thing is a mess. We may have caused even more problems. The wards are even more important now. The eclipse is in a few days."

"I want in."

"Me too," Martha said.

"Look at this!" Ms. Tengos said. "You two sisters working together."

"What about Jake?"

"On our way home, we stopped as soon as I got my powers back and I erased Jake's memory. When we got to Vision, I gave him the antidote to the vampire poison. He recovered almost immediately. I drove him to Birmingham and got him a flight back to Indianapolis."

"Maybe I should go visit him."

Raven glanced at her sister. She looked a mess. Her hair was singed and different lengths and she had bruises around her wrists. But she wasn't in a mental institution, so that was a good start.

"No, Martha," Nanny said. "Let it be."

Martha nodded and wiped a tear from her cheek.

"What about Rosie?" Raven asked. "What was going on with her?"

"Poor child," Ms. Tengos said. "Mathias had a painting that was left behind in his showdown with the witches, when he lost his hand three hundred years ago."

"Brachydactyly," Martha whispered.

"Yep. His hand was still regrowing. He kidnapped Rosie's parents and used Rosie to get what he wanted. He'd kept that painting and tried to get her to take him through to Vision to execute his plan. The wards stopped him from getting in. Every time they tried to go through, the painting would let her in, but not Mathias."

"Why didn't he just have Rosie take him back to Alma?" Raven asked.

"He tried. When she couldn't get him into Vision, she told him she could time travel. He had her steal a time traveling painting. She tried to take him back in time and could never get him to the right place or time. The day she saw you and Ranjit come out of the mural, she realized you had the gift as well and told Mathias. That was when he switched his tactics."

"How did he know she could go through the paintings in the first place?" Ranjit asked.

Nanny shrugged. "We haven't figured that out yet."

Martha smiled. "Ms. Tengos, you have an uncanny resemblance to Morgana, but she had no children, did she?"

Raven laughed. "Busted."

"Why don't you just own it? Let everyone know you're the baddest of bad-ass witches?"

"What do you think would happen if the government found out about a couple of 300-year-old witches living in the quaint little town of Vision, Alabama?" Ms. Tengos asked. "For now, let's just keep it among ourselves, okay? I'd like to keep my privacy."

Raven nodded. "That's fair." She looked at Nanny. "Your turn to fess up."

"I knew it," Ranjit said. "You and Raven are sisters."

Nanny laughed. "Not exactly. I'm still a grandmother, but Agatha was my mother."

"She's also Raven," Ms. Tengos said.

"Cool," Ranjit said. "I've always known you as Nanny. It never occurred to me you had an actual name."

"And here I thought I came from a long line of Ravens and really it was just you all along," Raven said. "Wait, how old was our mother?"

Nanny shrugged. "Old. Our age old."

"What the hell? What else are you keeping from us? Agatha? Where is she?"

Nanny and Ms. Tengos exchanged a look. "That's a story for another day. Let's get some rest."

Martha said, "One more thing, who was Lydia's father, our grandfather? You've always been so secretive about it."

Nanny smiled and Raven thought her eyes turned a little glassy, "I was quite young when I got pregnant. He was a lovely Choctaw man from Fala's tribe. He was killed before Lydia was born, before we could get married. A young unmarried pregnant girl in the 1700s wasn't a good look. But I didn't care." She looked at Ms. Tengos, "I was lucky to have an understanding family."

Ms. Tengos said, "She always was a wild one. Even more so than the two of you."

CHAPTER 59

The next morning, Raven sat in the kitchen, munching on a bagel, when Martha came down.

Martha poured herself some coffee. "That looks yummy."

There was still half a bagel on her plate, slathered with cream cheese and hot pepper jelly. Raven passed the plate to her sister. "It is yummy."

Martha took the plate. "Thanks."

"Have you heard from Jake?"

Martha took a bite and shook her head, eyes filling with tears. "I really fucked that up. I've texted and called, I'm sure he's blocked me. Doubt I'll ever hear from him again. Even with Nanny's spell. I wouldn't talk to me again either."

"I'm sorry. But I have something that might cheer you up."

"Do I want to know?" Martha raised her eyebrows. She'd cut her hair to even it out after Mathias burned it off. Raven marveled at how much Martha resembled their mother, Lydia, even without her long hair.

Raven shrugged. "I have an extra ticket for Eras in Atlanta."

Martha coughed and Raven worried she'd choke. "Why aren't you taking Ranjit?"

"He has his own tickets and is taking his new boyfriend. That's the price you have to pay, driving us all to Atlanta."

"You're not messing with me, are you? You really got tickets?"

Raven sipped her coffee and nodded. She shifted to face her sister. The morning light was coming through a window in the front of the house. A strip of golden light shone on Martha's blonde hair, giving it the effect of a halo. Raven reached out and touched a singed lock and said, "You can cut this into a cute bob, get bangs, and be in between the *1989* and *Reputation* eras.

Martha touched her hair and lifted her eyes to Raven. "Thanks. The In-between era sounds good for me. What about you?"

"I think I'm *1989*. I have such great memories of that from when we were kids. I think I was nine when it came out. It was my first real experience with her."

"Gretchen is going to be so jealous." Martha took another bite of bagel.

"Hurry up and finish that. I have something to show you."

Martha put the bagel back down, "I'm feeling a little woozy, I don't think I can finish this."

"Okay, side effects of time travel?"

Martha nodded and sipped her coffee. "What do you have to show me?"

"In my room."

They went up to her room. "Sit."

"Okay." Martha sat on the bed and Raven went into her closet.

She got the picture of their mother and held it facing her so Martha wouldn't see what it was when she came out. She stepped out of the closet, "Close your eyes."

"What? Why? Just show me."

The top of the painting was at Raven's collar bone and almost as wide and very heavy. She had it resting on her toes and stepped forward, shifting the painting with her forward motion.

"What are you doing?" Martha asked. "You're a witch, right? Can't you just use magic?"

Raven felt the heat in her cheeks and smiled. "Fair point." She freed one hand and spun a spell. The picture levitated, then turned toward Martha.

Martha gasped. "Mom."

"Take my hand. We've got questions."

Martha's eyes widened. "Really? It's magic too? Oh, so many questions!"

Martha took her sister's hand and together they went through the painting.

EPILOGUE – MARTHA & RAVEN

It was April twenty-eighth, the day before the concert, and the foursome had just rolled into Atlanta in Nanny's Bronco.

Ranjit had sprung for hotel rooms for him and Stephen. Raven and Martha dropped them off and went to their dad's condo.

"Do you want to text dad and tell him we're here?" Raven asked.

"Okay. I'll see when he'll be home or if he wants to meet us for dinner somewhere."

"Sounds good."

Raven went into the spare room. "Hey sis, we're sharing a bed, unless you want to sleep on the sofa."

Martha came to the door, still typing. "I'm the oldest. I get the bed." Her phone dinged. "He'll meet us for dinner. Says he'll make a reservation and send us the address. At least Nanny and Ms. Tengos told him about Mathias. Hopefully that won't be a topic of conversation."

"Amen, sister."

***

They met their dad and settled at a table, ordering a round of drinks.

The atmosphere was uncomfortable and stiff, and their dad's awkward small talk didn't help.

"How was your drive?" he asked, tapping his fingers on the white tablecloth.

"Fine, uneventful," Martha said.

"Too bad Ranjit couldn't make it."

"He's out with his new boyfriend," Raven said.

"How exciting for him."

Raven caught her sister's eye, and Martha gave the slightest shrug.

The server came back with the drinks, and their dad took a long gulp, finishing half his Manhattan.

"I'll come back shortly to get your orders," the server said. "Unless you want an appetizer or something in the meantime."

"We need a minute, thanks," their father said. "But you can bring me another one of these." He held up his drink.

The server nodded politely and slipped away.

"What's going on?" Martha asked. "Why are you acting so weird?" She took a long sip of her own drink. Raven sat in paralyzed silence, wondering what was happening.

"Girls, I've taken your advice. I started dating and I've met someone special."

Raven looked at her sister and wished she was old enough to drink.

"Advice?" Martha said. "I don't remember suggesting you start dating."

"Sure, you did. Anyway, I've met someone, and I want you to meet her. She lives in New Orleans, but she spends a lot of time in Atlanta as well. Do you think you can stay an extra day and have dinner with us Sunday night?"

"I have to get back to New Orleans and take Raven and her posse back to Vision. Maybe another time?"

Raven stayed silent; she didn't want to meet this woman, but she didn't want to hurt her dad's feelings either.

"Maybe you can bring her to Vision for a weekend, or we could all meet up in New Orleans?"

"Not a bad idea, Martha. I'd still like you to meet her before you leave. Do you think you could at least come with us for brunch or something before you hit the road?"

Raven looked at Martha, trying to gauge her sister's feelings. "Up to you, Martha. You have a lot of driving ahead of you."

"Okay, Dad. Are you okay with Ranjit and Stephen being there?"

"Sure, the more the merrier!"

***

"That was epic!" Raven said as they exited Mercedes-Benz Stadium.

Martha nodded. "The set list was perfection."

"Except she forgot a song," Ranjit said.

Stephen laughed and pointed at Ranjit. "He's the one upset about it. How does she do that?"

"What?" Martha asked. "Sing and dance for four hours and have multiple wardrobe changes without missing a beat?"

Raven chuckled. "Yes. I'm hoarse just from singing along."

They got to the car and Raven looked around the parking lot at the sea of Swifties all leaving at the same time. It was a sight to behold, thousands of joyous people with their clever costumes still singing and smiling and dancing.

Raven thought Martha won the night. She'd cut her hair into a bob and gotten bangs. She wore a red tube top and a long, flowing hot pink skirt, the front open, exposing her long legs. She'd found a choker at a thrift shop that completed Taylor's 2016 Grammy outfit. Raven wore high-waisted faded blue jeans with a white tank top to represent *1989*. Ranjit went all-out *Lover* and wore a button-down tie-dyed in pastels with purple shorts, while Stephen wore a white T-shirt with "Hey Stephen" on the front and the *Fearless* album cover on the back, dark jeans and cowboy boots.

"We may not make it home in time for brunch tomorrow."

"I completely forgot," Martha said. "I must have blocked it out. Ranjit, Stephen, would you like to go to brunch with our father and his new girlfriend while Raven and I sleep in?"

They got in the car "Excuse me, what?" Ranjit said. "Did you say girlfriend?"

"Yep. We tried to get out of it, but no luck."

"That's a hard pass. I'll be getting us a late checkout."

Martha laughed. "On that note, let's serenade Stephen."

Raven took Martha's phone, found "Hey Stephen," hit play, and turned the volume up.

***

The next morning, Martha, Raven, and their dad rode together to Cultivate Food and Coffee.

Their dad rode shotgun. "Thanks for doing this, girls. I'm really nervous."

"No problem, Dad," Martha said. "We support your dating life."

Raven caught Martha's eye in the rearview mirror and rolled her eyes.

They arrived at the restaurant and dropped off their dad so he could get a table while they parked.

As they walked to the restaurant, Martha said, "Thanks for taking me to the show last night. I really needed it. After all that's happened. Taylor is way better than therapy. But don't tell my therapist I said so."

Raven smiled and slung her friendship-bracelet-laden arm around Martha's shoulder. "Anytime, sis. It was so fun."

They got to the door. "You ready?"

"No, I'm not. So, let's get this over with."

As soon as they walked in, Raven spotted her dad waving from a table in the back. His girlfriend sat with her back to them.

They made their way to the table and their dad stood. "Girls, I want you to meet Alma. Alma, these are my girls, Martha and Raven."

Alma stood and turned to face the girls. She extended her hand. "Aww, Rae Rae, what a pleasure it is to see you! And Martha, lovely as your pictures. How is your boyfriend? Jake, is it? Such a shame he couldn't make it."

WHEEL OF FATE AND FURY

I f you enjoyed this first book in the Wheel of Blood and Magic series, don't miss out on the next book in the series, Wheel of Fate and Fury.

Blood binds. Time fractures. Love destroys.

Raven and Martha are sisters cursed by blood and haunted by choices they cannot escape. Raven, a witch who bends time through enchanted paintings, carries the burden of holding their fractured family together. Martha, fragile but fierce, still grieves the vampire she was forced to kill—the same man she loved.

But Mathias' shadow has not faded. Seducer, monster, martyr—his ghost lingers between timelines, while Alma, his ruthless vampire mate, will tear the realms apart to claim him again.

When rifts between worlds open and demons spill through, the sisters must choose uneasy alliances with ancient witches, blood-hungry vampires, and powers that defy fate itself. To survive, they must decide if Mathias is worth saving... or if he must be destroyed all over again.

Perfect for fans of Jay Kristoff's* Empire of the Vampire *and* Holly Black's **Book of Night,** *this dark fantasy brims with twisted love, haunting magic, and the kind of danger you can't turn away from.

Order your copy today!

https://mybook.to/WheelOfFateAndFury

AUTHOR'S NOTE

I 'm so grateful to everyone who made this book possible. Natasha and Andre of M4L Publishing saw something in Wheel of Blood and Magic, took me under their wing and guided me across the finish line. They've helped me realize a dream, and for that, there are no words big enough to hold my gratitude. My editor, Melissa Prideaux, has been an absolute joy to work with and an expert at uncovering the heart of what I was trying to say, even when my words refused to make sense.

When this book was in its infancy, Carolyn Macullough of Gotham Writer's Workshop guided me in my writing and storytelling and helped me with the framework that turned WOBAM into the book it is today. I'm indebted to Ashley Hower for the marketing wisdom she has so patiently tried to impart. One day I'll be a wiz, one day. Cristina Calandra is my photographer extraordinaire. Thank you for your keen eye and always keeping me on brand.

And to all of my friends and family who've supported and cheered me on throughout this process, Sam and Derek Davis, Hilly Walrod, Alisha, Khaleesi and Hunter, Bryce Baird, Mona Lisa Da Silva, Donna Myer, Ryan Wertenberger, Duke Bund, Magdalena Harnage, Andi McAlister, and Denise Smith, I humbly thank you all.

FREE SHORT STORIES

We hope you enjoyed Wheel of Blood and Magic from Grace Pevear.

Here at M4L Publishing, we aim to provide readers with fresh voices across the thriller, horror, and sci-fi genres. Be sure to join our newsletter to stay up to date with all upcoming and new releases (and deals!).

As a thank you for joining our list, we will send you a 4-book bundle of short stories to enjoy!

Just head over to the M4L website and sign up today!

www.m4lpublishing.com

ENJOY THIS BOOK?

We hope you enjoyed this release from M4L Publishing.

Reviews are the most helpful tool in getting new readers for any book of minutes. We don't have the financial backing of a New York publishing house and can't afford to blast our books on billboards or bus stops.

(Not yet!)

That said, your honest review can go a long way in helping us reach new readers. If you've enjoyed this book, we'd be forever grateful if you could spend a couple minutes leaving it a review (it can be as short as you like) on the Amazon page. You can jump right to the page by clicking below:

https://mybook.to/WheelOfBloodAndMagic

Thank you so much!

ABOUT THE AUTHOR

When she's not writing, Grace Pevear is either lost in the world of whatever book she's reading, binge-watching every TV show ever made, running until she questions her life choices, or hopping on a plane to explore some new corner of the world. If she could jump into a magic painting and travel through time, she'd head straight for ancient Greece to wander the Agora with Aspasia and Socrates, unraveling the mysteries of life, the universe, and everything. Grace lives in sunny Scottsdale, AZ, with her mischievous cat, Squeak, and her dog, Scottie, the undisputed queen of naps, treats, and everything that makes Grace's days brighter.

WHEEL OF BLOOD AND MAGIC

Sweethaven *RJ Clark*

Timber Beast *A.K. Hughey*

Alice *Audrey Brice*

Wish *Courtney Konstantin*

Quixote *Stephen Wertzbaugher*

Arturius *A.K. Hughey*

Steamboat *Courtney Konstantin*

Strangled *Stephen Wertzbaugher*

Dethroning Oz *Audrey Brice*

Scorned *Z.S. Diamanti*

Followed Away *Andre Gonzalez*

Followed East *Andre Gonzalez*

Followed Home *Andre Gonzalez*

A Poisoned Mind *Andre Gonzalez*

Snowball: A Christmas Horror Story *Andre Gonzalez*

www.ingramcontent.com/pod-product-compliance
Lightning Source LLC
Chambersburg PA
CBHW051137300726
48978CB00011B/309